THE SOUND OF
SILENCE

George Dalton
Oct 2016

2 Samuel 22:11

GEORGE DALTON

THE SOUND OF SILENCE

TATE PUBLISHING
AND ENTERPRISES, LLC

Published by Tate Publishing & Enterprises, LLC
127 E. Trade Center Terrace | Mustang, Oklahoma 73064 USA
1.888.361.9473 | www.tatepublishing.com

Tate Publishing is committed to excellence in the publishing industry. The company reflects the philosophy established by the founders, based on Psalm 68:11,
"The Lord gave the word and great was the company of those who published it."

Published in the United States of America

ISBN: 978-1-68270-185-0
1. Fiction / General
2. Fiction / Crime
16.03.17

In memory of my best friend Greg Standerfer

CONTENTS

1

CORRUPTION IN HIGH PLACES

The young engineer rushed into the CEO's plush paneled office. "Sir, I have discovered a flaw in the engine parts we're shipping out."

"Johnson, what're you talking about?" the CEO said, looking up from his monitor.

"Sir, the nitride coating on the parts we're shipping out is too thin. Those parts could fail in flight. If they fail, the whole aircraft engine'll fail," he said, gripping a printed report in his hands.

"Johnson, listen to me carefully. Fix the problem from here on, but keep quiet about the ones already shipped. If this gets out, the stockholders are not going to like it. Our stock is already in the tank, so this could ruin us. Don't say anything. Just fix the problem for everything we ship out after today."

"But what about the ones we've already shipped?" Johnson asked.

"Johnson, this company takes care of team players. You are a team player, aren't you?"

"Yes, sir."

"Okay, just fix the problem, but don't tell anyone about this conversation. Then I want you to run these same tests every few days and document that every part going out after today is tested. I'll call production and tell them to do whatever you tell them to do."

Walking slowly back to the elevator that would take him back to his desk, Johnson was sick. He thought, *People could be killed if these airplane engines fail.*

If I say anything, I'll lose my job. With Juanita being pregnant, I can't lose my job and my insurance. He shivered and said, "I guess I'm not going to say anything. I am going to have a record of this." So he sent a detailed account of the conversation to his wife's e-mail account.

In the e-mail, he wrote,

> My name is Harold Johnson. I am an engineer for the ACE Foundry. In running routine test on aircraft engine parts that my company is shipping out, I found that the nitride coating is too thin. I tried to talk to the production manager about the parts being too thin. He informed me that orders to reduce the amount of coating came from the

executive office saying it was done to save a million dollars a month in production cost. I then went into the executive office of Mr. Horace Thorn, the CEO, and informed him of the problem. He told me, "Fix the problem on all parts going out after today, but say nothing about the parts already shipped."

I am very concerned that an aircraft engine could fail and lives could be lost because of this.

2

DANCING ON THE WIND

Jim Colburn loved to fly. There was something magical about climbing up where the eagles flew. It was always fun being up here. All of life's problems just took on a different perspective when viewed from above. The grass that needed mowing did not look bad from here.

There was something magical about rolling a control wheel to the left or right and having an airplane that weighed more than the family sedan pirouette left and right. Dancing on the wind.

Jim keyed the mic button on the control yoke.

"Center control, this is seven one Mike-Mike with a request."

"Say request, seven one Mike-Mike."

"Mike-Mike requesting five thousand and an aerobatic box."

"Mike-Mike, stand by."

Jim preformed a couple of lazy circles around a red barn far below.

"Mike-Mike, are you ready to copy?"

"Mike-Mike is ready."

"Fly two seven zero for five minutes, aerobatic box assigned three thousand to five thousand, fifteen south of Wells."

"Mike-Mike is cleared to perform aerobatic maneuvers, fifteen miles south of Wells at all altitudes between three thousand and five thousand feet."

"Read back is correct. Report Wells in sight. Box is assigned until fifteen after the hour. Report back on one one eight point seven when leaving the box."

"All right, big girl, they just gave you and me permission to wring your tail feathers out for the next half hour. Airplane, are you ready to have some fun?"

I know it's crazy for a grown man to talk to a machine, but airplanes have personalities, and some are temperamental.

As Jim made his first loop in the sky, he thought, *There is only one thing in this world I love more than flying, and that is my wife and family. After I sold the company, I bought this flight school just so I could spend all day around airplanes. Thank you, God, for letting me be a pilot. There are millions of earthbound guys who wish they could do what I'm doing right now. Thank you for letting me be one of the few who get to see the sights only a pilot sees.*

The thrill of a takeoff, the calm and serenity of flight on a cool fall day.

God, thank you for the incredible beauty of a sunrise at ten thousand feet. The wonderful peace of a landing at sunset. Father, thank you for my beautiful wife, my children and their mates, and my wonderful grandchildren. Thank you for letting me be me. There is not one man on the whole earth I would trade places with. In Jesus's name, I thank you. Amen.

Jim spun the control yoke to the right and stomped on the right rudder. He felt the thrill of the airplane whipping into a tight banking turn to the right, then pushing the yoke forward until the nose of the airplane dropped down. He dived toward the cotton fields below.

Down, down, down, he flew. Then at the last moment, he stomped on the left rudder, leveled the wings, snatched the control wheel all the way back to this stomach, and rocketed skyward.

Running a flight school was a business; being a pilot was a love affair.

3

DAVID'S FIRST SOLO

One of the things Jim was most proud of was the fact two of his grandchildren were taking flying lessons—his grandson David and his granddaughter Ann. They were both doing very well according to the instructors. He was disappointed when he couldn't get either of his daughters to take flying lessons. They were more like their mother. Todd was a pilot, and now Rene's kids were both learning to be pilots.

The sun was shining, the sky was blue, only a few clouds in the distance. September 28 was a day never to be forgotten.

David woke up early that morning to drive out to an airport thirty miles away from his house to do something he had always done. David, at this time, had been taking private pilot lessons for six months.

David pulled up to the airport, got out of his car, and walked inside to the little classroom where he and his instructor always met for a briefing before the flight.

The instructor said, "David, we are going to be flying to an airport not far from here to do some touch-and-gos. Then we will go onto something else."

David did the normal preflight checklist, making sure that the airplane was in the right condition to fly. After this checklist was complete, David and his instructor flew out to an airport not too far away to do some touch-and-gos.

The instructor picked up his flight bag and said, "David, make this next approach a full stop, opposed to a touch-and-go."

David wasn't completely sure why his instructor had him do this, but of course, David did what his instructor asked. After David landed, he taxied off the runway to the taxiway and parked in the parking lot right in from of the control tower.

David's instructor looked at David and said, "I'm getting out. You go ahead and take the plane up yourself."

When David heard his instructor say this, he was overwhelmed with excitement.

Once David's instructor left and walked into the control tower, David started up the engine and called the tower to request to taxi to the runway. "Denton Tower, this is Cessna two five zero five four, requesting permission to taxi to runway one seven."

"Cessna two five zero five four, permission granted, taxi to one seven."

David taxied to the runway to do his before-takeoff checklist. After completing his checklist, David was ready to take off. Before calling the tower, he said a quick prayer, "God, I know I can do this, but please be with me."

"Denton Tower, this is Cessna two five zero five four, ready for takeoff at one seven."

"Cessna two five zero five four cleared for takeoff at one seven."

David taxied to the middle of the runway.

Rene stood holding her breath. "She had never been afraid to fly in one of her dad's airplanes. Since she had lost her mother in a crash, the idea of David being up there all by himself was terrifying.

"Don't let Ann see how scared you are." Then she said a quick prayer. "Oh God, please watch over my little boy. I know he thinks he is a big man, but, Lord, he is still my little boy."

David pushed the throttle in and felt the vibration as the airplane began to build up speed. David was surprised how fast the plane lifted off without his instructor being right there beside him. At this time, David felt like he was on top of the world, flying a plane by himself with no one in the plane to tell him what to do or how to do it. The fear David once had about flying alone left him. All he could feel was excitement as adrenalin raced through his veins.

"Is he banking too much when he turns?" someone in the crowd said.

"No, I think he's about right."

"He better watch his turn to final. That is when most crashes happen," another Monday-morning quarterback said.

"There he is. He's right on the glide path to land," Ann said.

All the café crowd watched as the little trainer gently touched down for his first solo landing. David added full power, and the little airplane leaped back in the air to go around again. As the little airplane banked left, Rene realized the hangars prevented her from seeing it at all times.

When she lost sight of David's airplane behind the hangars, her heart started to pound. She tasted a bitter bile in her throat. *Where is he?* Then she saw him again when he turned on the base leg back to the airport.

After two touch-and-gos, David made his third approach a full stop. On the third landing, David's tires bounced a little, but he was okay. He turned off the runway and taxied back to that same parking lot in front of the control tower. His instructor and his family met him at the plane, congratulating him on his first solo. Grandpa was there with his camera.

Rene unclenched her fist and started to breathe normally again.

4

TRIP TO ALABAMA

A few weeks later, the morning was crisp and cool. A gentle breeze was blowing out of the south. It looked like a perfect day for a quick trip to Rockford, Alabama.

Allie's hobby was genealogy since her family had arrived from England in the 1500s. The family arrived in South Carolina and migrated westward, settling in an area that is now known as Coosa County, Alabama. Allie had wanted to go to the courthouse there to see what family records she could find.

Jim smiled when he remembered he always looked up all of the outlaws who had been hanged when they went to a southern courthouse. He teased Allie. He expected to find most of her ancestors in those journals.

While he was preflighting the Bonanza, Allie was in the café chatting with Christie.

Jim climbed into the pilot's seat and busied himself with entering all of the data into the flight director. Jim loved the aroma of an airplane, the new leather, the smell of new paint, the smell of aluminum—all mingled together to create a unique aroma that was in an airplane.

Just as he finished entering the radio frequencies needed to allow the pilot to communicate with departure control, he looked out the airplane's window as Allie breezed out of the café and tossed her overnight bag into the back of the Bonanza. A person entering the airplane would step up on the walk strip of the wing to enter the cabin.

"Okay, Captain, all passengers are on board and ready for departure," Allie said, closing and locking the door.

"If you spill that coke in my airplane, you better have a parachute with you because I'm going to toss you out."

"You just keep the shiny side up. Don't worry about my coke. If you're real nice, I might give you a sip every now and then."

Jim shifted his scan back to the instrument panel, then to the area in front of and around the airplane. It was the result of years of habit, but he never started that big powerful prop spinning without first making sure no one was about to walk into it. Then he opened the small window on his side and yelled, "Clear," telling everyone within the sound of his voice to stand clear of the prop area. The big Bonanza engine caught and started running smoothly on the first turn of the prop. He had seen guys sit there and grind their starter until the battery ran almost down before the engine actually started, but Ralph was a great mechanic and took a lot of pride in the fact all of their engines were so fine-tuned they always started immediately.

Half of the café crowd was on the ramp, waving good-bye to the Bonanza as Jim taxied out for the two-hour flight to Alabama.

The flight was going beautifully. Jim was at nine thousand feet. The air was crystal clear and smooth as velvet, with only a whisper of a cloud occasionally. Allie was doing her normal copilot duties. She was sleeping.

Then he had to smile as he thought, *I love her. I remember the first time I actually noticed her. It was in a history class our junior year in high school. Allie was a cheerleader, and her best friend, Francis, had just come into the class, which was being held in a portable building the school had brought in because the new wing was not finished in time for school to start. I had transferred in from another school over the summer. This particular day, it was a little warm. The two girls were seated against the wall away from the windows.* He smiled as he remembered. *I found out later that Allie had turned to Francis and said, "Want to have some fun with that cute new guy over there by the window?" Allie spoke up. "Excuse me. Could you open that window please?"*

Jim smiled as he remembered. *I stood up and opened the window. I no more than sat down when Francis spoke up and* said, *"Excuse me, can you close that window. It is too drafty in here."* Jim chuckled to himself as he remembered standing up, closing the window...

All at once, the whole airplane shuddered, and the engine catastrophically destroyed its self. Oil started to coat the windshield. Jim reached down and turned off all fuel tanks. He secured the airplane, then keyed his mic. "Mayday! Mayday! Bonanza seventeen miles west of the Macomb VOR has catastrophic engine failure. We are going down."

"Bonanza calling Memphis center, say N number and souls on board."

All airplanes registered in the United States have a tail number beginning with *N*.

"November four four niner niner Delta Charley, we have three hours fuel and two souls on board. Do you see an airport close to me anywhere?"

"Niner niner Delta Charley, ident (which meant to press a button on the transponder that causes your particular airplane to flash on his screen so the controller would know exactly which of those dots was his airplane)."

Jim reached over and pressed the identification button.

"Niner niner Delta Charley, the closest airfield we show is nineteen miles northeast of you. Turn to a heading of zero two five degrees."

By now the airplane was violently shaking like it was tearing itself apart.

Allie woke up and asked, "What's happening?"

"We have a blown engine. Hang on."

He was trying to keep the airspeed at the recommended 105-knot speed the pilot's handbook called for to give him the maximum gliding distance with the engine dead. It was getting harder to see out the windshield because of all the oil. For some reason, the prop control wasn't working, so he couldn't feather the prop. He was descending at a fast rate. There was no way he could keep the Bonanza flying for nineteen more miles.

"Niner niner Delta Charley can't feather the prop. We'll never make the airfield. I am going to try for that road down there."

"Good luck, niner niner Delta Charley. I'm notifying the sheriff's department in that area. They'll have emergency crews on the way."

It was a pilot's worst nightmare, a dead engine in a high-performance airplane, a windshield coated with oil, the oil now wrapping around to cover the side windows. Jim looked at the solid mass of forest below them. The only possible place to land this airplane was on a tiny road running through the trees. Jim was straining his eyes, trying to see the road, but it was like looking through a glass of dirty water—everything was distorted.

Carl and Billy Joe were on their way to town in Billy Joe's Dodge Ram pickup. When they topped the hill on FM

4329, they could not believe their eyes. About a quarter of a mile in front of them was an airplane coming right at them. Billy Joe slammed on the brakes, skidding sideways down the road for fifty feet. Then everything seemed to happen in slow motion: first, the left wing of the plane struck one of the pine trees on the side of the road. Then the wing sheared off, the plane jerked around, the right wing slammed into the ground, and it sheared off. Then the body of the plane was tumbling toward them—rolling over and over stopping about one hundred yards in front of the truck.

Fire was everywhere. The wings sheared off and exploded in flames, but because the body of the plane had rolled beyond where the wings came off, it was not on fire yet.

Both guys leaped out of the truck. The first thing Carl did was grabbed his cell phone and call 911.

"This is 911. State you emergency," the operator said.

In his excitement, he yelled, "This is Carl McQuestin. We're out here on FM four three two nine, and a plane just crashed right in front of us,"

"Where on FM four three two nine are you?"

"We're just past Joey Thornton's place. You better send a fire truck and an ambulance right away. This is a bad-en."

Billy Joe yelled, "Tell 'em mile marker thirty-nine."

They both ran to the crumpled airplane. Billy Joe said, "Carl, I see two people in there. Oh man, I see blood everywhere."

"Look out, Billy Joe! That fire has set the grass on fire beside of the road. It's coming toward the body of the airplane."

"We can't help them. Grab those old quilts out of my truck, and let's see if we can keep the fire off 'em until somebody gets here."

The flames were racing toward the crippled airplane with the people still inside. Billy Joe yelled, "You take the right side. I'll take the left." The guys started beating the fire frantically with the old quilts. They would get it out in one area, only to have it reignite in another.

As they were fighting the grass fire, a state highway patrol raced over the hill from the opposite direction, with red and blue lights flashing. The officer blocked off the road from the west, then ran to the crumpled airplane. At that same instant, a fire engine arrived from the east, followed by a deputy sheriff's car.

Two exhausted young men were thrilled to see that fire truck. All Billy Joe and Carl could do was watch as two of the firemen pulled a hose line off the truck and started spraying water on the fire, while all of the other firemen and the policemen worked on getting the people out of the crumpled airplane.

"Billy Joe, do you think those people in the airplane are dead?"

"I don't know. This is worse than that truck wreck out on the interstate that time." They watched as one fireman ran back to the fire truck and returned with the Jaws of, life, a machine that looked like a giant pair of scissors. The rescuers used it to cut the airplane apart like it was made of paper.

The "Jaws of Life" worked like a superstrong pair of scissors. It was designed to cut victims out of steel car bodies. It made short work of cutting through the airplane's aluminum body. By now, two ambulances had arrived from Macomb. Carl and Billy Joe were still in a state of shock as they watched the paramedics strap a man to a rigid backboard and then load him into the first ambulance. Then they saw them gently lift a woman's body out of the wreckage and place her on a gurney. A sheriff's deputy walked over to Carl and Billy Bob. "Are you the guys that called in the accident?"

Carl said, "Yes, sir, I was the one who called 911."

The deputy pulled a notepad out of his pocket and said, "I need for you boys to tell me exactly what you saw."

Billy Joe spoke up. "We was going to town, and when we came over that there hill, we seen this airplane comin' right at us—like he was landing on the road. Then all at once, he hit one of them pine trees with his left wing. Then all hell broke loose. The left wing down yonder broke off. Then the right wing broke off, and they both exploded. Then the main part, with the people in it, came tumbling right at us. So I slammed on the brakes. I thought we was goin' to run into it. Then the grass started to catch fire, and since we didn't have any water or anything, we grabbed them two old quilts and started beating out the fire so the people wouldn't catch fire too."

The *Times Sentinel* reporter took Billy Bob and Carl's picture, and the next morning there they were, on the front page of the paper, showing the wreckage in the background.

5

THE ENGINEER'S DILEMMA

Harold Johnson was watching the news when they showed the crash in Mississippi, and they played the tape of Jim telling the controllers that his engine had failed and that oil was all over his windshield. Harold had a sick feeling in the pit of his stomach. *There is only one way that engine would blow oil all over the windshield. Something from inside the engine had to crash through the outside of the engine, allowing the oil to escape.*

Juanita walked to the top of the stairs and called down, "Honey, are you going to stay down there all night? Come on to bed."

"Be there in a minute, baby," Harold called back. He was terrified. What if that airplane engine failed because some of the parts came from his company?

Harold sat down on the chair at the end of the bed. He looked over at his beautiful young wife, with her rounded belly that carried their first baby. A touch of sadness washed over him. He had grown up in the ghetto and worked hard waiting tables to put himself through the university so that his wife and baby could have a better life. He had taken his socks off and sat there with his head down, twisting a sock around his hand.

Juanita looked at him and said, "Baby, what's the matter? You have been moping around like your dog died or something. What is it?"

"Do you ever read your e-mails?"

"No. The only thing I use my computer for is to look up something. Why?"

"I have something to show you." He picked up his laptop and laid it in the bed beside her. Finding the e-mail he had sent to her, he opened the file.

Pushing the laptop over next to where she sat propped up in the bed, she looked down and read, My name is Harold Johnson. I am an engineer for the ACE Foundry. In running routine test on aircraft engine parts, my company is shipping out, I found that the nitride coating is too thin. I tried to talk to the production manager about the parts being too thin. He informed me that he was told to reduce the nitride coating to save one million dollars a month in production cost. I then went into the executive office of Mr. Horace Thorn, the CEO, and informed him of the problem. He told me "fix the problem on all parts going out after today but say nothing about the parts already shipped."

I am very concerned that an aircraft engine could fail and lives could be lost as a result of this greed on the part of our company.

She read it slowly. Then she read it again. Looking up, she said, "Harold, what are you going to do?"

"I don't know. If I tell anybody, I'll get fired."

"Harold, can airplanes really crash if you don't?"

"One may already have. Tonight on the news, there was a story about an airplane that crashed in Mississippi."

"How do you know that was because of a faulty part made by your company?"

"I don't know, but there are very few things that would cause an airplane to spray the oil out of the motor and onto the windshield. The pilot reported just before he crashed that his windshield was coated with oil. That tells me that something inside the engine failed and broke through the side of the engine. That would cause all of the oil to spray out through the broken hole, and the wind would blow it back onto the windshield."

"Oh my God, Harold, does that mean you could go to jail?" Juanita bit her lower lip and then said,

"No, honey, I'm not worried about that. What I'm worried about is what I can do with this information. If I could save people's lives and don't, what does that make me?"

"But if you do say something and you get fired, we won't have any insurance to pay for this baby," Juanita said. "Maybe you should go talk to our pastor."

"I wonder if I should go talk to a lawyer. After all, I'm the only black engineer working there. What if they try to blame it on me?"

6

COMING HOME—ALONE

When Jim first became aware of anything, he was confused. Where was he? What was happening? Then he saw a lady in what appeared to be a nurses uniform? Everything was so scrambled. There was tremendous pain.

Allie came and sat beside him and said, "Jim, you're okay now. I'll always love you." She leaned down and kissed him gently.

Then he saw the nurse take a needle and inject something into the tube attached to his arm. He went back to sleep.

The phone rang at the flight school, and a strong male voice said, "I would like to speak to a member of the Colburn family."

The instructor who answered the phone said, "There's no one here that is a member of the Colburn family. Maybe the chief instructor could help you."

"This is John Samuels. Can I help you?"

"Sir, this is Sergeant Boyd from the Mississippi Highway Patrol. Do you know Jim Colburn?"

"Yes, he owns this flight school. Why are you calling?"

"Sir, I hate to inform you that he was involved in a crash near Macomb at eleven hundred hours this morning."

"He had his wife with him. Are they all right?"

"No, sir, the pilot is in the trauma center at Macomb right now, but a helicopter is on its way to transport him to the trauma center in Jackson."

"What about Allie, his wife?"

"Sir, I am sorry the female passenger died in the crash."

"Officer, is there a number the family can call for more information?"

"Yes, they can call the Macomb County Sheriff's Office, or they can call the Jackson Memorial Hospital in about an hour to check on the survivor."

"Yes, sir." Then reaching over, John pulled a legal pad toward him and said, "Can I get your name and a number where I can call you back if I need to?"

"My name is Sergeant Boyd with the Mississippi State Patrol. My number is 800- HIGHWAY/extension 6422."

John thought, *Pull yourself together. I can't even think straight. Allie is dead, and Jim is in critical condition. My God, what happened? Jim is a superb pilot, and the Bonanza was a cream puff airplane.*

"Officer, can you tell me what happened?"

"Sir, I don't know any more than I just told you. Can you handle notifying the next of kin?"

After he hung up, John walked back to Ralph's office, tears streaming down his rugged face.

"Man, what's wrong?" Ralph said when he looked up when he saw John walk in.

"Ralph, the Bonanza crashed near Macomb, Mississippi." John wearily lowered himself into the chair in front of Ralph's desk.

"What happened? Are they all right?"

"No, the state police just called. Jim's in critical condition, and Allie is gone."

"You've got to be kidding. John, I'm sorry that was a dumb thing to say. What happened?"

"I don't know. All I know is the state police just called and told me they had crashed and Jim was being airlifted to the trauma center in Jackson. Allie did not survive the crash." After a long pause, John said, "My mind is in a fog. I don't even know what to do next."

"Why don't you call JR and let him tell the rest of the family? In the meantime, I'll call Derrick and get him headed this way."

"Yeah, they are going to want to go there as quickly as possible so he can take them in the King Aire." The news spread to the café, then to the whole airport.

John picked up the phone and dialed JR's number. "JR, I've got some really bad news. Your dad's Bonanza crashed in Mississippi just a while ago."

"Are they okay?"

John's voice broke as tears streamed down his face. In a squeaky voice, he said, "No, your dad is being airlifted to Jackson." His voice broke again. "I'm so sorry. Your mom is gone."

It took JR a few seconds to realize what he meant by "Your mom is gone."

"Call Derrick, and tell him he should come to the airport and get the King Aire ready to fly the family to Jackson."

"Ralph is calling him now. Is there anything else I can do?"

"I don't know. I'll see you out at the hangar in a few minutes."

––––––––––––

Derrick had the King Aire pulled out and gassed up when the family got to the airport. As soon as Derrick saw JR, he said, "I'm so sorry. I'm ready to go when you are, and I will stay as long as you need me."

JR asked, "How many can you carry in the King Aire?"

"The problem with the King Aire is it only has nine seats."

"John, are the kids good enough pilots to fly one of the smaller airplanes that far?"

"Absolutely. In fact, Ann and David have both flown trips that are farther than from here to Jackson."

"Can you line them out in two of the smaller airplanes and let them fly the other kids over?"

"JR that is not a problem. I'll get the two larger Cessnas ready so when they get here, they can just go. If Ann and David don't feel like they are ready, I'll send two of the flight instructors."

Ann and David walked through the door together. Ann obviously had been crying. David looked like he was about to cry. John asked, "Are you two able to fly the two 172s over to Jackson?"

David turned and looked at Ann. "Yes," they both said.

"Both of you, listen to me. When you get in that airplane, you are the pilot in command. You cannot let your emotions interfere with your ability to fly the plane. Your life and the life of your passengers are depending on you. Tell me now if you don't feel you can do it."

Ann answered first, "John, it is hard. We loved our grandmother so much, but you have trained us well. Yes, when I get in the plane, I can do it. I am a pilot."

"Yeah, me too."

"Okay, both of you go check the enroute weather than file a flight plan. Ann, you take three three one one niner Delta. David, you take five three three eight zero Charlie."

Ann took off first with her were her two sisters. David took the other Cessna with JR's three kids.

Ann called the Fort Worth departure controllers soon after takeoff. "Fort Worth Departure Control, this is Cessna

November three three one one niner Delta a flight of two off Millport for Jackson."

"Three three one one niner Delta, you are radar contact five north of Millport. I understand you are a bereavement flight of two Cessna 172s."

"That's affirmative," Ann answered.

"What is the tail number on the other airplane?"

"Five three three niner zero Charlie."

"One one niner Delta, only you are to make the radio calls."

"All radio calls to be by one one niner Delta," Ann replied.

"Read back is correct. Stand by for clearance."

Ann just clicked her mic button, signaling that she had heard and understood.

The controller called back. "One one niner Delta cleared as filed. Climb and maintain seven thousand. Fly heading zero seven zero."

"Cleared as filed. Climb and maintain seven thousand, heading zero seven zero."

"Read back is correct. Switch your radio to departure on channel one three three point zero eight. Have a good flight."

"Switching to one three three point zero eight. Good day."

As soon as they we leveled off and on course, Ann called David on the backup radio. "How did he know we were a bereavement flight?"

"I told them when I called in the flight plan. I figured it wouldn't hurt, and if we messed up in any way, it might keep us out of trouble."

Jim and Allie's youngest son, Todd, and his wife, Kay, took their airplane and headed west from Atlanta. They would arrive last.

A lot of prayers were silently prayed as the planes winged their way to a rendezvous that none of them could yet grasp. All they knew was their beloved grandma was gone, and Grandpa might be too by the time they landed. It was inconceivable. Not Grandma and Grandpa, he was a superpilot.

One by one, the airplanes landed at Jackson, first the King Aire, followed by the two airplanes from Texas, then the airplane bringing Todd and Kay.

The next thing Jim knew after the crash was he opened his eyes and his two sons were by his bed. He was vaguely aware they were there; then he drifted back to sleep. On the third day, he woke and both his daughters were there. This time he was more awake. He asked them about their mom. They didn't have to say a word; he knew by the look on their faces. Then the nurse gave him another shot, and he was asleep again. After six days in intensive care, he was moved to a step-down unit. By now he was awake as much as he was asleep. Slowly the story started to unfold. He had lost his engine. The windshield got covered with oil while trying to land on a narrow road. With a blacked-out windshield, the left wing had clipped a pine tree. The plane had crashed, and Allie—his precious Allie—was gone.

His family could only come in for twenty minutes every two hours, and there were enough tears shed to flood the Mississippi River. Somehow they got through the first ten days. The thing that hurt him the most was the fact that he was still in intensive care when they had a funeral for Allie, and he couldn't even attend. They buried his precious Allie, and he couldn't even say good-bye.

JR, being an attorney, handled everything; and on the day of the funeral, Jim spent the day crying and reading his Bible. He seemed drawn to the book of Job. He also kept asking God, "Why didn't you take me too? God, this pain is more than I can bear." Then a thought came to him, *You must bear up for the rest of the family. They are hurting too.*

Back at the hangar, John and Ralph had learned from the accident investigators that the engine had destroyed itself and blown oil all over the windshield, completely blocking the pilot's view. John said, "There was nothing he could have done."

"Yeah, I know, but what I don't understand is why. Airplane engines don't just blow up in flight. That engine was running great. We just checked it six weeks ago, when we did the annual inspection. Do you think someone could have sabotaged it?"

"Why would anybody want to?"

"I am going to keep digging through these logbooks. Something is just not right," Ralph said.

Finally, after fourteen days in the hospital, Jim was released. He was wearing a steel cage that held his entire upper back and shoulders immobile. Doctor Phillips said, "Jim, I'm amazed to see you going home. The day you were admitted here, you had a fractured skull, internal bleeding in your brain, both shoulders fractured, nine ribs and another three vertebrae in your spine broken. I wasn't giving you much chance to survive, but by some miracle, you are going home. I'm sorry about your wife." Reaching down, he patted Jim's shoulder gently and said, "You take care now."

As he was being wheeled out in the wheelchair, all the doctors who had been involved in his care and all the nurses who were on duty that day were there. Jim held up his hand for the nurse to stop the wheelchair. With tears in his eyes, he said, "I don't know how to thank all of you. You're wonderful." Two of the nurses reached down and gently hugged him; then JR wheeled him out to the rental car. Todd had pulled up to the front door.

When he got to the Jackson Airport, Derrick had the King-Air all clean and shining, sitting on the ramp right in front of the door. Jim looked at both Derrick and David, who had on black slacks with creases so sharp that they could cut. Jim said, "You guys look good in those starched white shirts with the gold bars on your shoulders." Jim could walk carefully; he just couldn't use either of his arms because of the broken shoulder blades.

Todd and JR both said, "Dad, don't try to hold on to the handrail. One of us will be on each side of you as you walk up into the airplane, okay?"

As he started up cautiously, he said, "JR kept repeating, 'Easy does it. Easy does it, Dad. Don't get in a hurry.'"

When he was in his seat, Jim said, "I can't even buckle my seat belt. That is pathetic." Then tears came unchecked as David closed the door on the airplane. Todd hooked him up to the portable oxygen bottle the hospital had sent with them.

"Dad, Todd and I have arranged for a nurse to be with you around the clock, and they have installed a hospital bed in the den next to your pool table. If you don't like it there, we can have them move it. It's just there. It was the easiest place to put it without moving a lot of furniture. You'll have an oxygen generator so you'll never run out of oxygen." That turned out to be a wise choice of places to put the hospital bed.

The delivery company had placed the oxygen generator under the pool table and ran the tube up to his pillow. Jim was in so much pain by the time they got him home and into bed. The nurse gave him a shot, and he was instantly asleep. For the next two weeks, he slept more than he was awake.

When he did wake up, he was in a tremendous amount of pain and confusion. He would wake up and expect to see Allie. Instead he would see a nurse. For a moment, he would think he was still in the hospital. Slowly the days turned into weeks, and the big strong Texan hardly recognized himself in the mirror—he had lost so much weight. After being home for a few weeks, if you wanted to call this cold empty house a home. He was able to take a shower by himself. It was painful, but it was a victory.

Jim had no use of his hands or arms, which made just trying to get out of the hospital bed impossible. Then one afternoon, he had a young nurse, named Brenda, for the first time. Brenda watched him struggle to sit up without using his arms or shoulders for a few moments, then walked over and said, "Jim, I want you to swing your legs over and hook your feet under the pool table, then use your thigh muscles to leverage yourself into a sitting position." He did and was surprised how much easier it was to just drop his feet to the floor, and he could stand up. Jim said, "Thank God for the pool table."

When JR dropped by later, Jim said, "Watch this." He swung his feet under the pool table and popped right up.

"Hey, Dad, that's pretty good. That makes it a lot easier, doesn't it?"

"Yeah, and with the leather cover still on the pool table, it makes a great place to set stuff." He had the nurses keep the fireplace going all of the time for some reason—watching the fire was soothing.

Jim had lost all desire to do anything except sit and think about Allie. He just couldn't imagine going on without her. She had always been his soul mate, his right arm, his wife.

The only thing that gave him any cheer was when one of the grandkids cane over, which they often did. David kept saying, "Grandpa, let me take you out to the airport. Everybody out there is dying to see you."

All Jim would say was, "No, David, not yet."

All he wanted was Allie back.

Four weeks after he was released from the hospital, the National Transportation Safety Board investigator came to record his statement about the accident. The investigator asked, "Sir, can you tell me what happened?"

"No, all I know is I killed my wife." Then he broke down and cried. The nurse came in and gave him a sedative and a glass of water.

The investigator was very patient. He told Jim, "Mr. Colburn, the crankshaft in your engine broke in two. That destroyed the engine. There was nothing you or any other pilot could have done to prevent it from happening. Once it did happen, then there was nothing you could have done to prevent the crash. A catastrophic engine failure in that area, with no safe landing area, with oil all over the windshield, there was nothing any pilot could have done to prevent the crash that followed."

Jim stared at him for a moment and then said, "Sir, I wish to God that right now you were telling that to Allie instead of me."

The inspector kindly said, "Sir, I understand, but we need to get on record all you can remember, so please walk me through all you remember. I know it's painful, but you know it's important."

Jim just nodded his head.

Two hours later, the investigator turned off his recorder and put it into his briefcase. Then he said, "Mr. Colburn, so you'll know there will be no finding of any error on the part of the pilot."

Jim nodded his head. The nurse showed the investigator out and then helped Jim back to bed and gave him a morphine shot. Within minutes, he was asleep.

The days and nights were a jumble of pain and pain pills (they had stopped the shots) and utter despair at the thought of never seeing Allie again. The nurses were kind. They came, did their twelve-hour shift, and left. Another one came on and did his/her shift and left. His minister popped in almost every day. Jim and Lyle had always been close, and it helped to talk with him. Ann and David came by almost every day, and that helped. He just could not grasp how he was going to live without Allie. She had always been there, and now she wasn't.

JR and Todd called their dad every day. He wasn't supporting the family they were trying valiantly to hold him together. They had lost their mom, and they didn't want to lose their dad too.

7

KEEPING THE FLIGHT SCHOOL GOING

John, Ralph, and Shirley Smith were doing a good job of keeping the business going.

One morning, Shirley walked into John's office and said, "It's breaking my heart to see Jim like he is every time I go by his house. Today I went by to give him the sales report from last week, he doesn't even look at it."

"I know. Here is a guy who used to be on top of every little detail."

"John, if we could get him back to work, it would help take his mind off losing Allie."

"I know. Jim and Allie did have a special thing going."

"John, he sees me every week. Why don't you go talk to him?"

"I'll do that. The new trainer airplanes he ordered before the accident are in. I'll go talk to him about them."

To Jim's surprise one day, he looked out the back door and flowers were starting to bloom—it was spring. Then tears started to fall like rain. These were the bulbs that Allie had planted last fall. Jim slipped on a sweater and walked out in the backyard. All at once he had a plan. Jim waited until David came later that day. "Hey, buddy, would you do me a favor?"

"Sure, Grandpa. What do you need me to do?"

"See that area between the Crape Myrtle and the Live Oak tree? Could you get a shovel and spade up that ground for me? I want to plant a garden." Jim pointed across the backyard.

"Well, I suppose you can't do much shoveling in that brace. I guess I could do it," he said with that impish grin on his face. "Grandpa, we could call that guy with the tractor that plows gardens for people."

"Sure for a space not much bigger than a postage stamp. I don't think so. I can't move my arms, but there is nothing wrong with my legs. I can still kick your butt, if you give me any more lip."

They were both laughing.

"Well, you must be feeling better, and you sound more like your old grouchy self. You sit down right there in the lawn chair and supervise. I'll be right back."

Jim had very limited used of his arms because his shoulders had been so badly crushed. The nurse had been taking him to therapy three times a week. He was getting some movement back in his arms and shoulders.

Jim and David had no way of knowing that they had started a project that would eventually save his sanity.

"Okay, after we have the ground dug up, then what are we going to do with it?"

"I want to plant a vegetable garden."

"What are you going to do? Park your truck down at the farmers' market and sell produce?"

"Yeah, that sounds like a good idea. I'll set up a vegetable stand out in the front yard." Jim was actually laughing.

"Well, I have to be back at school next Monday. We only get one week for spring break. We better get started if we're going to get a crop in before I've got to go back."

"David, take me up to the store and let's pick out some seeds."

"That sounds like a plan. Let's go."

Looking at the big display of seeds, David asked, "What do you want to plant?"

"How about some beans, tomatoes, and corn to start."

When they were finished, they had bought corn, beans, tomatoes, peppers, cantaloupe, and watermelons.

"We have to buy some marigolds."

"Why? Grandpa, this is supposed to be a vegetable garden."

"Always plant marigolds near your vegetable garden because they attracted the bugs away from your vegetables."

David did all of the heavy stuff, the digging and grubbing out weeds. "Okay, Grandpa, I have the rows laid out. Do you want to actually drop in the seeds?"

"Yeah, I can do that."

After about three hours, Jim was exhausted. "Hey, David, let's quit for today. My string is about played out."

David helped him back into his hospital bed and asked the nurse to give him something. She brought Jim a hydrocodone pill, and within minutes, he was asleep.

The next day when David got there, Jim was sitting in a deck chair out on the patio, waiting for him.

"How are you feeling, Grandpa? We didn't work you too hard yesterday, did we?"

"You know this sunlight feels good on your skin. Nope, you didn't work me too hard. Today, I would like to make the hills for the cantaloupe and watermelons. What do you think?"

"Sounds good to me. Then when I get home in May, we can sit out here and eat watermelon on your back porch. How many hills do you want?"

The next week, David had to go back to school, but Jim had his garden in. Every day, Jim put Miracle-Gro and water on the tiny plants as they begin to poke their heads up. Shirley came by every day and gave him a report on what was going on at the airport. Between John and Ralph, they were keeping the flight school going. John was still signing up new students. Ralph was still covered up with repair work. Things were running pretty smoothly right now.

8

TIMOTHY'S TRAINING

Doug walked into John's office and said, "I need to talk to you about Timothy."

"What about him?"

"This kid is driving me nuts. On the ground, he can rattle off the proper response to any question I ask him. Get him in the airplane, and he seems to forget everything he knows. For instance, the last time we flew, he was way too slow on the base leg. Instead of lowering the nose of the airplane and allowing it to pick up speed, he gave it more gas, causing our altitude to balloon up two hundred feet. I didn't say anything. I wanted to see what he would do when he realized what he had done. He turned final two hundred feet too high. I thought, okay, he can still slip it in.

"He didn't. We flew right past the airport two hundred feet in the air. He was still descending when we got to the trees at the south end. If I hadn't grabbed the airplane, he could have killed us both. I turned it back over to him, and the second time, he was able to land. I will be honest with you, this kid scares me."

"Doug, you are there to teach and protect. How many hours does he have in flight training?"

"Twenty one," Doug replied.

"Twenty one. Most people are flying solo by twelve," John said. "I know. In fact, David soloed at ten hours. Doug, do you want me to fly with him or assign him to another instructor?"

"That's a good idea. Why don't you fly with him, John?"

"When is he scheduled to fly again?"

"Friday, at ten o'clock."

. "Let me check my schedule. I can't do Friday because I'm already scheduled to do a presolo for one of Lisa's students. Go ahead and fly with him Friday. But get online, find a slot in my schedule, and plug him into it." John turned to the computer screen.

Shirley tried to keep Jim up on what was going on out at the flight school. He just didn't care. John and Ralph could handle it. He had no interest. He lost Allie, so nothing else mattered.

Jim had gotten rid of the day nurse, but he still had the night nurse. He had even started to drive his pickup to the therapy sessions every other day. He never drove Allie's Lexus. One reason was that with all of the steel cage holding his spine and shoulders in place, it was easier to get into and out of his pickup truck. The other reason, that was Allie's car—he just couldn't drive it.

Everyone thought he kept the night nurse in case he needed something during the night. That was not it. He just couldn't face that big lonely, silent house at night alone. He knew his insurance company would eventually force him to let all of the nurses go, but he just couldn't face the lonely nights yet.

His whole world revolved around the therapy sessions and his garden. Jim liked his therapist. He was a bright young man and really had a lot of patience for his patients. As soon as he was home from therapy, he was out there in the garden. If a weed dared to raise its head in his garden, it was quickly pulled up. Jim often talked to Allie as he worked. "Honey, where should I plant the flowers?" He didn't ask about the vegetable garden that was his. The flowers had always been Allie's, so he consulted her on every seed that went into the ground. "Honey, what should I plant? Where? Do I put the daisies, next to the roses?" His shoulders and back still pained him a lot, but at least he was free of the brace. To every visitor's surprise, Jim had the most magnificent garden. It looked just like one Allie would have planted.

9

THE GARDEN

Lyle, his pastor, stopped by one morning. "Jim, I like your garden. Don't you think it's time to come back to church and thank God for all he has done for you?"

"Not yet, Lyle. I'm still angry with God for taking Allie away."

"Jim, instead of being angry that she's gone, maybe you should be thankful for all of the years you had with her."

"Pastor, right now, working in this garden is the only way I can get through a day."

"Jim, how are things at the flight school?"

"Shirley, tells me things are doing all right. I guess they are. I don't know."

"Jim, this has been a tough year, but you do still have a wonderful family and a business to look after. It's time you started thinking about them."

"Pastor, I know."

Monday after school, Timothy arrived for his scheduled flight with Doug. "Timothy, I've got an idea I would like to try today, if it's all right with you. Rather than fly the trainer today, I would like to fly the simulator. We can do the same maneuvers in the simulator that we do in the airplane. However, I will not be able to log today's lesson in your logbook because simulators only count if you have already received your license and are working on advanced training."

"That's all right with me."

"Let's give it a try. Today I want you to pick a point on the sectional map that's fifty miles from here and plan a fight to that airport. We'll fly the simulator to that airport and back, just like we're in a real airplane. Then the next time you come out, we'll do the same flight in an airplane."

"Okay." Timothy sat down in the simulator and said, "Wow. This is so cool. This looks just like the cockpit of a real airplane. It's like the one we've been training in. The dials and gauges are exactly like those in the airplane."

"Okay, Timothy, set up your GPS and all the other instruments, like you would in the airplane."

"Now reach down and turn the key and start your engine."

Much to Timothy's surprise when he turned the key, the flat black panel in front of him showed a scene like you were looking out the windshield of the airplane. He said, "This's so cool. You can see the propeller turning and hear the engine noise. It's realistic." Timothy had to look back out the door of the simulator to remind himself that he was still in the hangar. He said, "This is like a giant video game. That is way cool."

Timothy advanced the throttle, and the screen started to change. He could see the taxiway on the screen like he would in a real airplane. He taxied out and lined up on the center of the runway.

"Timothy, you are doing great. Now make your radio calls, and let's go flying. Even though we're in a simulator, treat it just like it was a real airplane."

Timothy did everything almost flawlessly. He actually appeared to be having fun. Doug thought maybe this is the answer—get him to fly the sim first, then take him up in the airplane the next time he comes out and do the exact same flight in the airplane.

"Got a minute?" Doug asked as he walked into John's office.

"Sure, whatcha got?"

"I decided to try Timothy on the simulator this morning, and he was flawless. We planned a flight to the Falls Airport, and he flew the simulator perfectly. He actually had fun."

"That's interesting. What made you decide to do that? You know he can't log the flight time in a simulator?"

"I explained that to him. I was thinking that if he did the flight on the simulator today and then we did the same flight in the airplane the next time, he would remember having done it today."

"Doug, I understand where you're coming from. I appreciate your concern for your students, but his old man is already accusing us of padding his hours. When do you have him scheduled to fly with me?"

"I fly with him again Friday, and he flies with you on Saturday."

Sunday morning, Jim took a shower. That was one of the great luxuries of his improvement. He could actually take a shower by himself. It was hard, but he could do it. Standing in front of the mirror, he could see that his hair was a lot grayer and that he had lost weight.

Looking in the mirror, he said, "Old boy, you're just going to have to suck it up somehow." He looked over at the table sitting in the corner, and there stood a framed picture of him and Allie when they married. Tears just started cascading down. "She was unbelievably beautiful and so full of life." Jim limped back to bed and crawled in. When the night nurse came in, he asked her to give him a shot so he could just blot out everything.

"Mr. Colburn, you know I can't do that. Have you eaten anything at all today? I don't see any dishes in the sink?"

10

TODD'S VISIT

The following Sunday, someone rang his doorbell. Jim thought, *That is probably the Jehovah's Witness or Mormons. They chose Sunday morning to catch anyone who isn't in church.*

As he opened the door, he was totally surprised. "Todd, how did you get here?"

"My sister tells me you haven't been going to church, so I came to help you get dressed."

"You came all of the way from Atlanta to help me get dressed?"

"Well, not exactly. I've got to be in Dallas tomorrow morning, so I came early because I knew you couldn't put that brace thing on by yourself. So here I am."

"Well, we have an hour and a half before church starts. Let me show you my garden."

"You've got a garden?"

Walking out into the backyard, Todd stopped. "How did you do all that?"

"When David was here on spring break, he did all of the digging. All I did was drop in the seeds. Then I come out every day, and when I see a weed start to pop up, I get rid of it. Do you think Mom would have liked it?"

"Dad, she would have loved it. What she would not like would be seeing you sit here all day, not going to the airport, and especially she would not like seeing you miss church. You know how much she loved her church."

"Yeah, I've been trying to get up enough courage to go back to church. It's just hard."

"That's why I'm here. Let me help you get dressed."

After church, Jim was in front of the building when a good friend's daughter came over and hugged him, saying, "Mr. Jim sir, I'm so sorry about your wife."

"Thank you. Do you still run those marathons?"

"Yes, sir, I just finished one last week."

Rene, and her two daughters started sitting with him every Sunday, and they started taking him out to eat after church. It was getting a little easier to talk about Allie until one of the girls would say, "If Grandma was here, she would order that. She always ordered that." Then tears would involuntarily show up.

He would still catch himself driving down the road, and a song would come on the radio they had always liked, and he would have to pull his truck over to the side of the road and cry until he was able to see how to continue driving.

Monday afternoon. Shirley came by to give him a report, and he said, "Shirley, I've got something for you." He gave her a basket of produce out of his garden.

"This basket is heavy. How were you able to carry the basket?"

"I didn't. I placed the empty basket here, and I carried one handful of vegetables at a time until it was full."

"Jim, thank you. This's very nice. Where did you get the basket?"

"I found it in the closet—something Allie had lying around."

Standing in the driveway watching her drive off, he thought, *Maybe I should take some baskets of produce out to the people at the airport.* Then he said, "Allie, I'm going to drive to the market and buy a bundle of bushel baskets. Then I am going to fill all of them with fresh vegetables out of our garden."

The next day, he filled all of the baskets with fresh produce from his garden and drove to the airport. He went from hangar to hangar and invited every family to come out to his truck and get a basket. Then he went to the café for breakfast. The whole crowd spoke at once. "Hey, look who's here."

"Man, it is great to see you."

"How uncomfortable is that steel cage you're in?"

"Jim, I am so sorry about Allie."

Again, Jim knew they meant well, but wished they would just mind their own business.

Christie came flying out of the kitchen with both arms full of food. "Wow, look who's back." Quickly setting down the food, she ran to Jim. "I want to give you a hug, but I don't know where to touch you. Are you hurting?"

"I'm much better, thanks. In fact, I get to get out of this straitjacket next week, if I pass the next checkup," Jim said.

Gene, hearing all of the commotion, came out of the kitchen. "Hey, look at you. What brings you out here today?"

"I brought you a basket of homegrown veggies, but you'll have to get them out of my truck. I can't lift the basket."

Looking into the back of the truck, Gene said, "These are great. How did you get them in the truck?"

"One head of lettuce at a time."

"You're kidding, right?"

"Nope. I couldn't lift the full basket. I could lift an empty basket, so that's what I did,"

"These are great. How much do I owe you?"

"How about a trade? I trade you this basket of lettuce and tomatoes for two eggs over easy with ham."

"Boy, you've got a deal. Come on back in, and let me fix you up."

When Jim walked into the café, he stopped to inhale. He had forgotten how much he loved the aroma of bacon frying and biscuits baking coming from the kitchen.

Jim still had not been in the hangar, but someone told John and Shirley he was there, so here they came.

"Are you supposed to be out here?" Shirley stood there with her hands on her hips.

"Jim, it's so good to see you out here again," John said. "When you finish breakfast, you've got to come and see the two new Flightstar trainers. They're the two you ordered before…" He could not finish the thought.

When Jim had finished eating, he slowly and gingerly shook everyone's hand, then walked with John out into the hangar. He had to admit the two new trainers were good-looking little airplanes. They were painted a nice red, white, and blue. Actually, they were white with red, white, and blue trim. They were good-looking little planes. For the first time since the accident, for a brief instant, Jim felt a longing to go fly; then it was replaced by a wave of sadness.

Jim hadn't just lost Allie; he had lost his way. He no longer could pray to the Lord as he always had, because now he wanted to ask God why. Three things had always defined his life: Allie, his faith, and flying. Now he had lost all three.

"Can you climb the stairs up to your office?" John asked.

Jim looked at the stairs and said, "No, I don't think I can with this contraption on. John I'm sorry I've been neglecting you. I'm just not ready yet. There are too many memories out here."

"Jim, don't worry about it. Things are going well. By the way, David just got his commercial license, and now he's logging time in the charter plane. Ann got her instructor's license and is instructing part-time."

"Thanks, John."

11

JIM'S STRUGGLE

As Jim was walking to get in his truck, a new Diamond single-engine airplane pirouetted into a parking place on the ramp. Jim had never seen one before. He had seen pictures of one on the cover of flying magazines, but this was the first one he had actually seen. For sure, this was the first one to land on his ramp. He walked over to get a closer look at the airplane. The canopy popped open, and a very attractive forty-something woman stepped out of the Diamond.

"Welcome to Millport. Do you mind if I look at your airplane?"

She flashed him a beautiful smile and said, "No, help yourself."

"Wow, she is a beauty." He felt his face turning red. "I mean the airplane."

"Thank you, sir, I think."

Jim held his hand up palms out and said, "Which engine do you have in it?"

The pilot smiled at his obvious discomfort and said, "The Lycoming I-O-350."

"This is the first Diamond airplane I've seen. Where did you fly in from?"

"I just flew in from Atlanta. My brother is the pastor at Prairieville Baptist."

"Thank you for stopping in. Our linemen will take good care of your airplane. Enjoy your stay."

"Honey, did I do the right thing by going out there today?" he asked Allie on the way home.

Of course, she didn't answer, but somehow it felt right to ask her. When he went into the house, he picked up his Bible and thumbed through it. His eyes fell on the thirtieth chapter of the book of Deuteronomy verse 19, which said, "Now chose life so that you and your children may live and that you may continue to love the Lord your God. Listen to his voice, and hold fast to Him. For the Lord is your life."

Then he thought of his best friend in the whole world, Reverend John Davis, up in Nebraska. He had not called John even once since the funeral. JR had sent Derrick up in the jet to get John so he could conduct the funeral. Now Jim was ashamed. He had not called him one time since then. He knew from the messages the nurses had taken that John had called several times. Jim walked to the phone in the kitchen and dialed John's number. When John's wife, Ann, answered the phone. He said, "Hi, Ann."

She squealed, "Oh my God, is that you Jim?"

"How did you know it was me?"

"How many people with a strong Texas accent do you think call here? Just a minute. Let me run and get John."

"Hey, Tex, it's nice to hear from you." A deep and familiar voice came on the line. They talked for several minutes, and Jim cried through most of it.

"John, is it all right if I just come to see you?" Jim finally asked.

"Ann and I have been praying for you every day since we first received the call from JR. Come on, and we'll sit in the basement of the church and talk, like we did long ago."

By the time they were ready to hang up the phone, Jim had agreed to come next Monday. It was about a twelve-hour drive, so he would not arrive until late in the evening. John did not ask why he was driving instead of flying.

"Son, I'm going to see Reverend John next week." After he hung up, he called JR. "Dad, that's a great idea. Are you going to have Derrick take you in the King Aire?"

"No, I think I'm going to drive my truck."

"No, Dad, that's not a good idea, not in your condition, especially when you have a jet that can take you."

At lunch Sunday with Rene and her family, they were all excited about Dad/Grandpa going to see Reverend John. The whole family loved John and Ann.

The sun was painting streaks of silver and blue on the eastern horizon on a Monday morning, when Jim pulled out of his driveway and pointed his truck north. He took Interstate 35 all the way through beautiful rolling hills of Oklahoma, across the wheat fields of Kansas and into the Sand Hills of Nebraska.

All along the way, he had described to Allie the things he was seeing. He would say, "Honey, the glass buildings in Oklahoma City are beautiful with the morning sun reflecting off them. Here in Kansas, the wheat fields are reaching from one horizon all the way to the next. Honey, here in Nebraska, the shrubs and flowers are breathtaking. Oh, Allie, you should see the baby calves in the pastures with their mothers." Then he would think how foolish he was to be carrying on a conversation with a wife who would never be there to answer him again. He would pull his truck over and cry great sobs.

The sun was painting the western sky with hues of orange and yellow when his truck pulled into the driveway at the manse.

Reverend John and Ann both flew out the door to meet him.

"Hey, Tex, I see you made it."

Ann ran up and grabbed him and hugged him, saying, "Oh, it's so good to see you. Come on in. You must be exhausted driving all that way by yourself."

"Is this all the luggage you brought? I thought you were going to stay a while?" John said as he reached into the truck and picked up Jim's bag.

They had just sat down when Ann asked, "How long has it been, Jim, since you and Allie lived across the street from us in Omaha?"

"Twenty years. Can you believe it?" John answered for him.

"No, it doesn't seem that long," Jim said, "but I guess it has been."

"We had some fun times when the kids were small and you guys lived across the street from us. Do you two remember the time Allie and I took the two of you with us to see the Amish village over in Iowa?"

"Jim, you haven't been here five minutes, and already you've got us in trouble. She hasn't thought about that in years," John groaned.

"Let me remind you two in case you forgot. Allie and I took you two with us to see the Amish village. Soon after we arrived, Mr. Jim Colburn here said, and I quote, 'I saw a blacksmith shop at the end of the street. Why don't we go see the blacksmith shop while Allie and Ann look at all of the quilts and homemade jelly?' Then on the way to the blacksmith shop, you found a wine cellar where they were giving away free tasting samples of homemade wine. It has never been fully established who was the first one to suggest that you two go into the wine cellar."

Both men pointed at the other.

Ann went on to say, "All I know is that you two were given a small glass for tasting"—holding up her thumb and index finger—"a small glass let me remind you. When Allie and I finally found you two, you were both as drunk as a skunk and you still had not quite made it all the way through sampling every single wine they had down there, but you were well on your way."

"I guess it's time to come clean. I will confess…it was John's idea."

"That's some confession, Jim Colburn. You sit here in the manse and lie your head off."

By then they were all three laughing, which was exactly what Ann hoped to accomplish by telling the story.

"You boys can talk about old times while I get dinner on the table."

It was great just talking with John. It seemed to Jim that John he had a real special relationship with God. It just shined through when you talked with him. That was one reason Jim had always liked John so much, because he never preached at you. He just talked and he listened. John was a brilliant man and had several advanced degrees. John had been a Methodist pastor for many years. Jim thought, *I like the minister at my church. Maybe it was because of the age difference he was much more inclined to think of John as his pastor. Lyle was a minister, John was a pastor, and he wasn't sure if he could explain the difference.*

Jim stayed four nights and, on the fifth day, said, "John, Ann, you'll never know how much I appreciate all you've done for me. John, when I got here, I was just about at the end of my rope.

"Ann, it was so nice of you to bring me into your home. Thank you. This has been so good for me. Now it's time for me to get back in the fight. I have a war to wage against whoever is responsible for taking our Allie from us." After he drove away, he prayed for the first time since the crash, by himself. He said, *Father, I don't know how you interact in our lives, but I know you do. I know that you have been supporting me since that terrible crash. Father, if you can get a message to Allie for me, tell her I have just spent five days with Reverend John. She'll understand. Tell her I'm going home and I'm going to work. Father, please help me to live the rest of my life to honor you and to honor her, and please reunite us up in your home someday. Amen.*

Jim had made up his mind while talking to Reverend John Davis that he was going to find out why a perfectly good engine just blew up in flight. He wasn't going to just lie down and accept defeat without a fight. That engine took away his precious Allie, and he was going to find out why. If it turned out to be an act of God, he would live with it, but if it turned out to be negligence or carelessness on someone's part, they're in for a fight, and a fight's one thing he's good at.

As he drove into his hometown, Jim stopped by the sporting goods store and bought a good pair of running shoes and asked the clerk, "Are you a runner?"

"Yes, sir."

"Can you recommend a good trainer?"

"What do you want to train for?" the young man asked.

"I want to run a marathon next spring on my sixtieth birthday."

The clerk wrote something on a piece of paper. "Here, sir, is the name of an independent running coach."

This started a daily training schedule that would last Jim the rest of his life.

Jim got home at nine o'clock in the evening. Then JR called, "I am hooooome."

12

FAA RAID

Jim had gotten into his training schedule with the same determination that he did everything else. He was up at five o'clock every morning, strapping on his running shoes. He was working with Rodney, who was a great trainer. They had started out slowly at first, but now they were up to five miles a day with a longer run thrown in on Saturdays. The first thing Jim did after buying a good pair of running shoes was take one of Allie's pictures to a tee shirt shop and have a dozen shirts made with her picture printed on the front. Every time he ran, Allie ran with him.

About a month later, he had done five miles, gone home, showered, and was at the airport by eight. Jim rolled to a stop in front of the big overhead door. He was feeling better, but it was hard eating breakfast alone each morning, so he had started eating breakfast at the café.

"Boss, we have a problem." Ralph walked out of the hangar, wiping his hands on a shop towel.

"What is it, Ralph?"

"The FAA is here."

"Okay, well let's meet them," Jim said, still wearing the steel brace supporting his back and shoulders. When he and Ralph walked into the hangar, both could see this small angry-looking man standing in the middle of the floor.

"Hi, my name is Jim Colburn." He stuck out his hand to shake the FAA guy's hand.

"As of this minute, I am grounding every airplane you own until you bring them all up to airworthy standards," the little angry inspector snarled.

Jim was stunned and confused. Ralph was a great mechanic, and he inspected every airplane every one hundred hours. Ralph replaced any part that was not up to standard. In fact, Jim had instructed him to go way beyond what the book called for. Many times they had replaced several items that were technically okay, but he replaced them anyway if they showed any wear at all.

"Sir, if you will give us a list of any squawks you have found, we will be happy to correct them immediately. Since your office is just across the freeway, we can call you as soon as they are completed and you can come back to verify that they are done." Regaining his composure, Jim tried to smile.

"I'm not going to do your job for you. It's up to you, the owner, to make sure these planes are airworthy. I could fine you right now because your own logbooks show that at least two of these planes have been flown with students on board, and I find that they are not airworthy."

"Sir, I'm not a mechanic, but Ralph here is a top-notch mechanic, and as I said, he has replaced many items found to be below standard. I'm not a mechanic but have total confidence in Ralph. Could you at least give me an example of something you have found that is not a hundred percent airworthy?" Jim looked at Ralph, who just opened his hands palm up as if to say *I don't have a clue where this guy is coming from.* Jim looked back at the inspector, who appeared to be getting even madder.

"That is not airworthy because the tag on the seatbelt showing the manufacturer is almost ripped off." The inspector stormed over to the nearest airplane, jerking the door open, and pointed to one of the seat belts. Jim couldn't believe what he was hearing. He had heard of Gestapo cops before, but this was ridiculous.

"That it's not on tight enough." He pointed to the lower left-hand part of the instrument panel to a little tiny knob on the rheostat control that turned the lights in the ceiling inside of the cabin up or down. The inspector reached the door on the next plane, jerking it open so hard that it made the mechanic suck in his breath.

"Sir, we'll immediately take care of anything like the ones you have pointed out. You can see we're not sparing any expense to keep these airplanes in top condition." Jim could feel not only his anger mounting but also Ralph's. Jim put out a hand and touched Ralph's shoulder. Jim looked at the inspector.

"Surely you are not going to red tag all of our airplanes because of a couple of minor discrepancies on these two?"

"As I told you, it is not my job to tell you how to get your airplanes airworthy. You are the owner. The FAA regulations state that you are responsible. It is up to you to see that each airplane is airworthy. I have already shown you more that I am required to. All airplanes owned by you and registered to you are grounded until future notice."

"Wait a minute. Did you say all airplanes?"

"I said all aircraft registered to you." With that, he stormed out the door. Jim was in a mild state of shock when he walked back into the office area.

"What now?" three of the instructors asked.

Briefly, Jim them told what had just happened. They were instructed to get on the phone and start calling the students canceling their lessons until this could be straightened out.

Then he thought to call Bob. He owned his own airport for many years before selling it a few years ago and retiring. He may have some ideas. Jim could feel his hands sweating as he listened to the ringtone on Bob's phone. When Bob answered, Jim explained in detail the unbelievable incident that had just occurred.

"It sounds to me like you have been hit by a new rookie inspector that is trying to make a name for himself. I know the chief examiner over at the regional office. Let me give Mike a call. I'll call you back."

While waiting, Jim wished with all his heart that he could call Allie. She was always the one he turned to when things went wrong. Allie had been his life partner in everything he did.

He kept thinking this is America. *This sort of thing can't happen, could it?* While waiting, he wandered back out into the hangar. Ralph had a copy of the FAA regulations open and was poring over it.

"We've replaced the seat belt on niner niner Zulu, and I've tightened the knob on zero five three. I have been reading the FAA regs again. The guy is technically correct. However, in my thirty years of experience, I've never heard of downing a single airplane for something so minor. Not one of the things found had anything to do with the safety of the airplane. The seat belt's still good. The light rheostat's a nonissue because we have no night flights scheduled for that airplane. If an instructor was going to do a night training flight, the instructor would have found the loose knob in the preflight inspection. I would've tightened it or the instructor could've tightened it. I'm going to make some calls to other mechanics that I know and see if this has happened to anyone else recently. It sounds like we have a rogue inspector out here."

As Jim walked back up front, three customers came in, having filled up their plane with gas and just wanting to stop in and congratulate Jim on the already improved look of the place. The phone rang. It was Bob calling back. "I talked to Mike, the chief FAA inspector. He is going to look into it, and he wants to see you in his office next Monday. I think they are going to dismiss all charges against your flight school."

"Thank you, Bob. Today is Wednesday. Maybe we'll lose only five days." They talked on for a moment; then Bob wished him luck with his new venture. Jim told the instructors who were still there about the meeting with the chief inspector next Monday.

Jim had never felt lower, walking back into his office; he could hear the instructors calling students to cancel their scheduled appointments. At the same time, they took several new calls that were coming in from people inquiring about lessons. *Lord, please help us. We have tried to play by the book. We have not cut any corners. I hired these instructors, and they are depending on students to make their living. Please help us.*

"Boss, I have some good news." Ralph walked into Jim's office.

The first thing Jim noticed was that big wad of chewing tobacco that Ralph always had in his jaw. The second thing was a grin slowly spreading across his face.

"Man, let's have it. I can use some about right now."

"Well, it seems that our inspector from hell was a little too smart for his britches. The way he wrote these grounding orders up, all it takes to get these planes back into the air is for a licensed inspector like me to reinspect them and sign them off as airworthy again. That is good and bad. He could make it hard on me if I sign them back on, and then he comes back here nitpicking again and finds something".

"So here is what we need to do. I have talked to several of my friends who are all willing to work every night, all day Saturday and even Sunday if you will let us. By Monday, we can have all of them with the exception of your airplane relicensed."

"Did I understand you? You can have a couple of them ready by Friday?"

"Yes, I can. Will you let me hire the other guys to help me?" Ralph asked.

"Absolutely," Jim replied.

Jim walked to the door and called the three instructors to his office. "Ralph, tell them what you just told me."

After Ralph had finished talking, every one of them volunteered to help the mechanics starting right now. What could they do? Ralph had them taking off panels, pulling out seats, even checking the air pressure in the tires. Even though they weren't mechanics, they were pilots and flight instructors who had spent a lot of time in and around this type of airplane. A little later, two guys in grease-stained coveralls showed up, carrying toolboxes. Ralph introduced them to everyone there and directed them to an airplane.

One by one, neighbors started showing up. One was a retired airline captain who lived with his wife in an attractive apartment built above their hangar. Another was a retired air force mechanic who owned his own small plane. They explained that word had gotten around the field about the rotten deal the inspector had given Jim.

"Jim doesn't need this," was the first thing Shirley said when she heard about the FAA inspector.

Jim had never been to the local headquarters for the FAA before. The building could be seen from the freeway with the giant letters *FAA* mounted high on the brick front on what appeared to be the fourth floor. The building was in one of those industrial parks where the streets didn't run north and south. They curved around. Jim could see the building, but it was impossible to figure out how to get there. He was starting to get nervous. There was no way he could be late for this meeting.

He was finally parked. Walking into that big imposing building was reminiscent of the first time he walked into Raleigh High School all alone.

When he stepped through the door into the lobby, it was an ominous feeling. Marble floors polished to high gloss, high ceilings—it looked like a hall of justice. Jim just hoped a person could get justice here. Maybe Bob knew what he was talking about.

Looking on the reader board, Jim found Mike's office listed on the fifth floor. Stepping off the elevator on the fifth floor, he was asked of his name by a woman. Then she looked on a printed form she had in front of her (he wondered if it was a list of the condemned). Soon she found his name and announced, "Follow me." Leading off down a hall, she stopped by large double walnut-stained doors.

When he stepped through the door, a man Jim judged to be in his late forties and an intelligent-looking black lady were already seated at a conference table. They both stood and introduced themselves and both produced Federal ID Badges. After shaking hands with each of them, the lady indicated a seat for Jim to take. The black lady turned out to be an attorney for the FAA.

When Jim realized that the FAA had an attorney there, his blood pressure dropped several points. This was more serious than he thought.

Mike spoke first. "Mr. Colburn, we have the report here from Inspector Wilkes. We would like to hear from you just what is going on out there at Millport. How long have you owned the flight school?"

"I have only owned the flight school a little over a year. As you know the previous owner allowed the airplanes to get in disrepair. All of them were not airworthy when I purchased them. I immediately hired an 'AI' to inspect and restore the airplanes. I have used the man before and know the quality of his work. I had and still do have total confidence in his work. We have spared no expense in restoring those airplanes. In many cases, we have replaced parts that were legal to leave on the airplane."

"Mr. Colburn, have you owned a flight school before?" The attorney asked.

"No, I owned a manufacturing plant."

"Have you ever owned any type of aviation business before?"

"No."

"What made you decide to buy this one?" Mike asked.

"I have had an airplane hungered at Millport for many years. Two years ago, I sold my company and retired. I wanted to buy the flight school then, but my wife didn't. So when it came up for sale again this year, she consented. I love flying, and I hated to see a flight school go out of business. Besides I need a place to buy gas."

Mike laughed. "So your real motivation was so you wouldn't have to fly to Alliance to get gas."

"Yes, that did enter into it. However, I did feel sentimental about a flight school going out of business. We are losing too many airports and flight schools."

"If we allow you to stay open, what are your plans for the flight school at Millport?" The attorney asked.

"I am going to make it back into a first-class operation."

"Have you added a café at Millport?" Mike asked.

"Yes, I built it and sold it to a young couple who run it now."

"We know you have a director of maintenance. Are you the chief instructor?"

"No, sir…I'm not an instructor at all. I'm just a pilot. John Samuels is the chief instructor."

"What are his qualifications?"

"John's a retired military pilot, an ex-top gun instructor, and he flew with the Blue Angels."

"Why is he instructing in a small startup flight school?"

"You would need to ask him. I think he just loves to teach, and he loves to fly."

"Did you bring your logbooks with you, like I asked?"

"Yes, they are right here." Jim handed the logbooks over.

There was an uncomfortable silence as Mike looked at the logbooks. Several times Jim wanted to say something, but his father had always told him in a bargaining situation: when there is a silence, the first person to talk loses.

Finally, Mike spoke up. "Mr. Colburn, can I ask you to step out in the hall for a moment and let us talk?"

Standing in the hall, Jim couldn't hear a word they were saying. The thought kept running through his head that they could refuse to allow him to reopen. He knew he could sue, but he had also heard that suits against the FAA could drag on for years.

"Come on in, Jim." Mike motioned him back in.

Jim thought, *Is that a good sign?* He said *Jim* not *Mr. Colburn.*

"Jim, you don't know it, but you have a reputation as a square shooter in the aviation community. I've talked to Bob, and I also talked to the guy who has been working on your airplane for a long time. He tells me you don't try to take shortcuts when it comes to maintaining your airplane. We have also checked out Ralph pretty carefully, and he has a reputation of following the law."

"Mr. Colburn, chief inspector Mike Rogers has recommended after reviewing all of the evidence that all charges be dropped against you and the flight school," the attorney said.

The meeting went better than could have been expected. Mike was a real professional, just what a person would have expected from an FAA inspector, nothing like the jerk who showed up at his hangar. Jim got the distinct impression from both Mike and the attorney that if you were trying to do your job right and not trying to slip something past them, they would work with you. In fact, the impression was that they were interested in helping to promote aviation safety, not out to get you. At any rate, all charges were dropped.

At the moment, Jim was still in business.

13

LOOKING FOR ANSWERS

As Jim was driving home, he thought, *Okay, the FAA distraction is behind me. Now it is time to find out why that engine failed.*

When Jim reached home, the first thing he did was strap on his running shoes and his Allie shirt. He did his best thinking when he was running. Jim kept thinking, *What am I overlooking in trying to find the answer about the engine failure?*

The next morning, Jim walked into Ralph's office and said, "Ralph, give me the books on the Bonanza."

Jim took the logs to his office and pored over them line by line. The logs appeared to be in perfect order. The engine manufacture recommended that it be overhauled every 2000 hour, and according to the logbooks, it had been sent back to the factory for a factory remanufacture just 0400 hours ago. At its last annual inspection, they had sent the oil off for analysis and found no metal in the oil. He checked the compression on each cylinder and found that each cylinder was in the top of the compression numbers. He checked the oil consumption. It was low. Everything in these logs was showing that to be a perfect engine. How could a perfect, well-maintained aircraft engine just blow up in flight?

Jim pressed the intercom. "Ralph, come up to my office."

"What-cha need boss?"

"Ralph, how could a perfect, well-maintained engine blow up and spew oil all over the windshield?"

They looked at the logs together, and neither one of them could find anything to indicate a problem was brewing. Yet it had happened and with devastating consequences.

"You could look to see if they have a higher incidence of engine failures after they have been remanufactured. Maybe there is a problem with the remanufacturing process?"

"That's a great idea. Thanks, Ralph. It at least gives me a place to start digging."

Jim dialed the phone number for Constantine Motor Company.

A pleasant-sounding woman's voice answered the phone. "Constantine Motor Company, how can I help you?"

"Yes, ma'am, my name is Jim Coburn. I'd like to talk to someone who can tell me about any history your company may have had with remanufactured engine failures."

There was a long pause; then she said, "Let me transfer you to engineering."

Jim was shuffled to five or six different departments until it became apparent to him they either could not or would not answer any of his questions.

Jim thought, *Okay that was a waste of time.* But he was even more determined to keep searching.

He got on the FAA website and found the accident report. It was the coldest, most sterile thing he had ever read. It read,

> On September 12, 2006, about 1132 central daylight time, a Beechcraft Bonanza, November 4499 Delta Charlie, operated as a personal flight, crashed onto a roadway west of Macomb, Mississippi, while attempting an emergency landing on said roadway. The pilot on board the airplane, a certificated private pilot who was the owner of the airplane, was severely injured; and a passenger who was a not a certificated pilot was killed. No person on the ground sustained serious injuries. The aircraft was destroyed by impact forces and postcrash fire. Blah...blah...blah.

He couldn't read any more of it, so he put it down. Jim sat and cried for several minutes, getting the front of his shirt wet with tears before he said to himself, "Suck it up.

You are going to find out why." Picking up the phone, Jim dialed the number for Bonanza directly.

A mechanical voice answered, "If you know your party's extension number, you may enter it at any time. Press one for our company directory, press two for parts, three for customer service, four for sales, five to repeat these instructions." Jim felt like throwing his phone across the room, against the far wall. Instead he jumped up out of his chair and walked down to Ralph's office.

"Ralph, I'm getting nowhere. The people at Constantine Motor Company are either incompetent, or else they are hiding something. I can't even talk to a live person at Bonanza."

"Why don't you go to the FAA office and see if the FAA has anything in their files about recalls on Bonanza engines?"

"That is another great idea. I'll go over there right now."

Ten minutes later, Jim walked into the FAA office. He was met by an older woman working behind a sliding glass window.

That old woman looks like she has been weaned on sour lemons, Sam told himself.

"This is the FAA. What do you want?" she said without even looking up.

How about a kind word and a warm smile? Jim thought, but he decided it was a foolish waste of time to ask for what appeared to be the impossible.

"I would like to talk with someone about crankshaft failures in flight."

"Sign in, and have a seat, and somebody will be with ya in a minute."

I wonder if she even knows how many minutes are in an hour, Jim thought.

To his surprise, Mike, the man he had met when he first had an encounter with the rogue FAA agent, walked out.

"Jim, what can I do for you?" Mike stuck out his hand.

"Mike, last September, my crankshaft in the Bonanza failed, shattering the case and blowing oil all over the windshield. I tried to land on a road west of Macomb, Mississippi." Then his voice broke, and tears started to well up in his eyes. Jim pulled a handkerchief from his pocket, wiped tears from his eyes, and said, "I am sorry. My wife was killed."

"Jim, I am so sorry." Mike said, "I saw the accident report but never realized it was your Bonanza. Let me see what I can find, what year was your aircraft built?"

"2005," Jim answered.

"Looking at my computer screen, I see a recall in 1998 and another in 2002 but nothing for engines built after 2002. In the 1998 recall, it states that the problem was caused by an alignment problem in assembly. In the 2002 recall, the problem was caused by the nitride being too thin in the casting process on the crankshaft. Here, let me print off both of these for you. It might help."

"Do the logbooks show any previous problems with that engine?" While the printer was running, Mike asked

"No, they're in order, but something's still not right. I'm not satisfied. Something just doesn't smell right."

Mike got on the microfiche and scanned through the FAA records of incidents and accidents and found nothing on that airplane except the crash that took Allie's life.

"Jim, in this report, it plainly says the crankshaft separated between the second and fourth journals.

"Wait a minute. Mike, if the crankshaft broke, that would explain why the oil sprayed out."

"Jim, I'm so sorry, but you know these things sometimes do happen, and there's no logical explanation. We've got reams of files in here that just don't make sense sometime."

14

COLORADO CRASH

Timothy had endured another humiliating day of football practice. He hated the game and especially the practice sessions. When he walked into the house, he saw his dad sitting in his favorite chair with a beer in his hand and a stack of empties at his feet.

"Boy, talk to me about flight school. Why're you not getting through any faster?"

"Dad, I don't want to get a pilot's license. I just don't like it. It is okay for you and Grandpa, but not for me."

"What the hell do you mean you don't want to get a pilot's license?" Rufus threw the now empty can against the far wall.

"Pilots are real men."

Timothy thought, *Do you really think flying your little one-hundred-mile-an-hour Cessna makes you a real man?* "Sir, I just don't care anything about flying airplanes. I enjoy studying the material. I don't like flying the airplanes. Why do I have to keep going out there?"

Rufus snapped the top on another beer can, pointing it at Timothy. "You little sissy, you will well keep going back until you get your license and until you become a man instead of a wimp."

"But, Dad, I am terrified every time that airplane takes off. I'm afraid of it."

"You are nothing but a little Momma's boy. I'm gonna make a man out of you. It's time you became a man."

Driving home, Jim heard on the radio about a small plane crash in Colorado, killing a family of four. *I wonder what kind of airplane that was.*

As he flipped on the six o'clock news, he came across a plane crash. Jim instantly sat up and listened as the reporter reported that the airplane was a single engine known as a Bonanza; then they went to the stock report.

Jim grabbed his phone and called Mike at the FAA office. "Mike, this is Jim Colburn. Have you seen anything on the Bonanza that crashed today in Colorado?"

"Nothing except what CNN's reporting," Mike replied.

"Mike, I really have a bad feeling about this. How can we find out if his crankshaft broke?"

"There is nothing we can do until the NTSB makes its report. They will tell us if there is anything wrong with the airplane. Jim, you know airplanes crash in the mountains, and almost all of the time, it is pilot error. Either he flew to close to the lee side of the mountain and got caught in a downdraft, or he got ice on his wings."

"How soon can we expect to get the NTSB report?"

"Jim, you know how these things work. It could be three or four months before we get a preliminary report and up to a year before we get a final report."

"Mike, I am telling you. This scares me!"

The next morning, Jim had fixed himself some breakfast and was watching the news on the small TV in the kitchen. All at once, they played the tape between the Bonanza pilot and the air traffic control center in Denver. The pilots voice was plainly heard saying, "I have an engine failure, and oil is all over my windshield!"

Jim was immediately on the phone to the FAA office. All he got was a recorded voice telling him the office hours were 9:00 a.m. to 6:00 p.m. Monday through Friday.

Jim raced out of the kitchen into his bathroom and jumped in the shower. Then he jumped into his clothes, brushed his teeth in record time, struggled into his braces, and was out the door.

Traffic seemed to crawl. Drumming his fingers on the steering wheel was all he could do to avoid switching back and forth between lanes and dashing through all the cars. Finally whipping into the airport, he was held up by three airplanes waiting to take off. Two were his own trainers, and the third was a Bonanza. Jim couldn't help staring at it.

Walking into Ralph's office, Jim said, "Ralph, did you see the news about that Bonanza that went down in Colorado?"

"Yeah, the one with a man and his whole family?"

"Ralph, we have got to do something. They played the tape on the news this morning of the conversation between the pilot and Denver center. He reported engine failure and oil all over his windshield. That can't be a coincidence."

"I have a friend that works for the NTSB. Let me give him a call and see what we can find out."

"Ralph, I want to know what year that airplane was built and the *N* number. See if he can get that for us."

Ralph talked to his friend for several minutes, and the guy agreed to get back to them with the information as soon as he could.

"Ralph, how can we get the engine back off my airplane?" Jim asked as he was pacing the floor in Ralph's office

"Are you sure you want to do that?"

"Yes, I want to get it back, and I want you to find out why that shaft broke. How do we do that?"

"I guess you could call the insurance company and find out which salvage company ended up with it."

Two weeks later, a box of greasy engine parts arrived. Ralph looked inside the box and said, "Ah, is this all that is left of that engine?"

When Jim came in, Ralph met him at the door. "Boss, your engine came in, but I don't recommend that you look at it."

"It's that bad, huh."

"Yeah."

"Is the broken crankshaft there?"

"Yep."

"Then I want you to find a private testing lab and send that crankshaft to it. I want them to tell us why that shaft failed. Can you do that?"

"I am already on it. I talked to Jim Aleszka testing already, and I'm getting ready to ship the crankshaft to them now."

"Tell them this is a rush. Ralph, I'm afraid there are other airplanes out there with crankshafts that are going to fail."

15

BARRY'S FLIGHT

Barry Wright, carrying his black canvas flight bag with his name embroidered in gold on the side of it, stepped up to the counter. "What's happening? Is my airplane ready to fly?"

"For our best customers, we try to comply. Are you going to be back tonight, or is this an overnighter?"

"Just a down and backer. I should be back by three or so."

Barry was a single attorney who lived in an apartment in one of the hangars. He had been divorced for eight years and only handled enough cases to keep him in "flying money," as he liked to say. Since Barry didn't own an airplane, he was one of Jim's most consistent customers.

"She's all filled up with gas and ready to go. Have a good flight."

Two hours later, Barry was blissfully cruising high above the ranches in South Texas, looking down at boats on the lake below when, all at once, he became aware of something else—the extreme quiet. The engine had quit running. He swiftly scanned the instrument panel. Barry was startled when he saw the fuel pressure gauge reading zero pressure. *What the heck?* After a brief moment of sheer terror, his training took over. First checking the fuel gauges, they read full. He switched the fuel selector to the other tank. Nothing happened. The engine didn't restart. The autopilot was valiantly trying to maintain the airspeed and altitude he had selected, but trying to do it without the engine. Barry immediately turned off the autopilot. He was startled at how terrifying the silence was.

"Mayday! Mayday! Houston Center, this is seven seven one two X-ray Charley. We have an emergency." Barry could sense the weight of the airplane as gravity pulled it down toward the earth below. He reached down and started dialing the trim wheel to set the glide speed at ninety knots, the speed the manufacturer's handbook recommended as the best speed to glide with no engine. It was supposed to give you the greatest amount of distance before gravity pulled you to the earth. He switched on the electric back up fuel pump, again hitting the starter. Nothing happened. He turned off all electrical power and moved the fuel selector to both tanks off. Now committed to going down, in his mind that meant crash. "Say type of emergency," the controller in Houston replied immediately.

"We have lost an engine and are going down, need vectors to nearest airport now!" Barry wondered why pilots say "we" when there is no one on board but himself. He guessed it was *because pilots think of the plane as a living thing.*

"Seven seven one two X-ray Charley, say number of souls on board and fuel on board?"

Again, he always wondered why they still used the term souls on board and what difference it made how much gas. The engine was not running! Would it tell the local fire department how big the fire was going to be?

"Just one soul on board, three hours fuel," Barry replied.

"Nearest airfield nine o'clock, twelve miles. Can you make the field?"

Looking at the altitude and rate of decent, Barry did the math in his head. He was at eight thousand feet and descending at nine hundred feet a minute. At this speed, it would take about eight minutes to reach the field area. At this rate of descent, the airplane would lose 7,200 feet in eight minutes. Oh, boy, if he made it? It was going to be close.

"Houston, seven seven one two X-ray Charley, it's going to be close, but it looks like we might make the field."

"Seven seven one two X-ray Charley, report field in sight. Stay with me until on the ground. Good luck."

Barry thought, *I can actually hear concern in the controller's voice.* Straining his eyes to see the airport off out there in the distance, all the while thinking, *Where is that airport?*

Several things were spotted that could be an airport, but as he got closer, it was a road. An airplane could land on one of them. The problem with roads they often have high line wires running beside them, and those wires will destroy a small plane. Barry began looking at the fields and pastures. They were never as smooth as they appeared from the air, often had gullies and ditches running through them, which would destroy a plane and pilot. In all that time, the airplane was getting lower and lower. Trees and poles were starting to look closer and closer. Finally spotting the runways, he called in, "Seven seven one two X-ray Charley has field in sight." He breathed a sigh of relief.

"Seven seven one two X-ray Charley, you are cleared to land any runway, pilot's choice. Winds one hundred and fifty degrees at eleven knots. Good luck."

He stared at the field. It was easy to see that it had two runways: one running east and west and one running north and south. The wind would favor the north-south runway. Was there enough altitude left to make a turn and land on the north-south runway, or would going straight in to the east-west runway be safer? He was one minute from the airport at eighteen hundred feet. Of course the altimeter was reading eighteen hundred feet above sea level. A quick glance at the GPS (he didn't even remember turning it to this airport, but obviously had), it was showing the field elevation as nine hundred feet above sea level. There was no longer an option.

"Houston, seven seven one two X-ray Charley is going straight in on runway niner."

"Local rescue equipment has been notified and is standing by. Good luck."

Things were happening fast now. It was easy to see the end of the runway approaching and fire trucks lining up on the taxiway next to the runway. Dropping the lever releasing the landing gear, he jerked out the handle for emergency landing gear pump. Crossing over the end of the field, he saw three green lights come on, indicating the wheels were down and locked. At the same time, fighting a right crosswind with both hands on the control yoke, his feet were dancing on the rudders. The runway was flying by under the belly of the plane. He kept telling himself,

"Just hold it straight down the runway, and watch your speed." Then he felt the tires gently chirp as they touched down.

As the plane coasted to a stop, a fire engine roared up alongside. Barry sat still for a moment, then reached for the mike to call Houston Center to tell them seven seven one two X-ray Charley was safely on the ground. His hands were shaking from the adrenalin rushing through his veins.

Keying the mic, Barry said, "Houston, one two X-ray Charley is down and safe, guys, thank you."

"Great job, X-ray Charley, have a good day," Houston replied.

As Barry climbed out of the plane, both of his knees felt rubbery. He suddenly realized that his shirt was wet with perspiration and his hands were still trembling slightly. A pickup truck pulled up, and two men stepped out.

"Buddy, are you okay?"

"Yeah, a little shaky is all."

"What happened?"

"Lost fuel pressure and she just quit."

"I'm Cliff Johnson, the airport manager, and this is Carl Turner. He owns the mechanic shop on the field."

"Do you want me to have her towed over to the shop so we can check her out for you?"

"This airplane's a rental. Let me call the owner. I'm sure he'll say yes, but I need to call him."

When Jim answered the phone, Barry said, "Jim, I lost all power on X-ray Charley and had to put her down at a little town called Grosland."

Jim's heart skipped a beat. Jim immediately thought, *Oh no, another crankshaft failure.* "Are you okay?"

"Yeah, sure, it was no big deal. ATC told me where an airport was, and I glided down to the airport."

"Did oil spray up on your windshield?"

"No, but I got gas leaking out of the engine compartment."

After talking with Jim, they had decided that Barry would have the mechanic look at it, and if it could be fixed, he would pay the mechanic on his credit card, and Jim would reimburse him as soon as he returned.

"By the way, do you have a rent-a-car on the airport?" Barry asked.

"Yes, we do. Jump in my truck, and I will take you over to the counter. Where are you going?"

"Just down to Houston."

"How long are you going to be gone?"

"Just a little while. I have to go down for a contract closing, and then I'll be right back."

Jim just knew that they were going to call back and tell him the crankshaft was broken. He thought, *If the crankshaft has broken, there is no fixing it. We will need to buy a new engine.* Jim called Ralph on the intercom. "Ralph, X-ray Charley is down, at a little place called Grosland. I just talked to Barry. He is okay. He was at ten thousand feet and suddenly lost all engine power."

"Did he get any oil sprayed on the windshield?"

"No, but as soon as he lost power, he shut it down. Maybe he shut it down before it cracked the outside of the engine case."

"Maybe, but if he broke the crankshaft, that prop would have been still whirling and it would have destroyed the inside of the engine. Boss, this is probably not a crankshaft failure this time. It could be as simple as a fuel pump. Let me talk to the mechanic down there and find out what they have found. I'll call you back as soon as I talk to them."

Jim was thinking, *What am I going to do if this airplane has a broken crankshaft?* Then he realized he had a piece of paper in his hands and that he had twisted it until it looked like a rope.

A few minutes later, Ralph called Jim back. "I talked to the head mechanic down there, and it just happens that I know him. We worked together at Alpine. He's a good guy. He hasn't found the problem yet, but he is going to call me back as soon as he does. It may be expensive, but he will treat us right."

Jim thought, *The cost of fixing this one airplane is not the problem. The question is, what do I do if this airplane has a broken crankshaft?*

Five hours later, as Barry was driving back into the airport, he could see 7712 X-ray Charley sitting out on the flight line, which was a good sign. They must really be through with her. Stepping out of the car, Barry said, "What was wrong with her?"

"You broke a little fuel line that supplied fuel to the pressure gauge. When that happened, she was pumping all of the gas out the broken line, starving the engine. You are very lucky she didn't catch fire."

"So is she ready to go?"

"Yes, sir, we replaced the gas line, so she is good to go."

"How much do we owe you?"

"One-hour labor and one fuel line. Total, one hundred and thirty six dollars."

"Great, that will make the owner happy. Which credit card do you take?"

"We take them all."

"Here is a Visa. Run it while I dash over and turn in this rental car." After turning in the car and giving them his American Express card, Barry did a thorough walk-around and then filed a flight plan with the FAA. Barry sat in the airplane a moment before buckling the seat belt. He took a moment to inhale the smell of new leather. Then Barry busied himself arranging all of the toggle switches, setting all of the dials, and pulling on his headset.

Taxiing to the end of runway 17, Barry called the tower, and the tower cleared him to take off. It was always a rush when the big engine roared up to full power, and that big propeller blade bit into the air. When the wheels actually leaped off the ground, all a pilot had to do was allow his imagination to run wild and he could imagine that this was a fighter plane roaring off to intercept some bogies coming to attack his country or he was the captain of a 747 full of passengers off to some exotic destination. Today, he didn't do any daydreaming. He stuck to the business of flying.

It was a busy time for a few minutes, pull the leaver to raise the wheels up, throttle set to climb speed, prop set to cruise speed, trim tab set. Altitude selected, call tower, switch to departure control, engage autopilot, and then sit back and enjoy the ride. Of course, he did catch himself checking the fuel pressure gauge every few seconds but guessed that was to be expected.

Barry loved flying over Dallas and working with the Dallas air traffic controllers. They were always busy, but professional. With the speed of an auctioneer, the controllers gave instructions to all of the planes. It was exciting to be part of it. There was everything from big jumbo jets landing at DFW, military fighter planes landing at the military base, to small single-engine trainers. Yet the people at Fort Worth air traffic control center managed to keep it all straight. He watched as a Jumbo Jet with hundreds of people on board glided smoothly across his windscreen, from left to right only a couple of hundred yards. With his headsets on, he couldn't hear a sound except the radio traffic.

By the time 7712 X-ray Charley was north of the Dallas, Fort Worth, the controllers had worked him down to 3,500 feet and slowed down enough that he could watch a high school football team working out and little kids playing in backyard pools.

As he flew down the east side of the airport, it looked so peaceful. One plane was taking off, but that plane was southbound. It was time to get busy and get the airplane ready to land. The big number on the end of the runway was just off his left wingtip. Barry pressed down the lever that lowered the wheels for landing. He pulled back the throttle, adjusting the power to slow the plane to landing speed, pressed down the lever that dropped in the first notch of flaps (flaps are mounted on the trailing edge of each wing to slow the airplane down), and gently rolled the control wheel to his left. Starting the base turn as he leveled the wings, he could clearly see the runway out the left window. Then it was time to gently roll the control wheel left again. As he rolled out onto final, the view of the runway filled the windshield. He loved that scene.

The single engine Cessna floated over the big number on the runway like a giant hawk coming in to roost. The tires barely squeaked as they touched down. Barry never liked to use the brakes. He preferred to let the plane slow down on its own, using aerodynamic braking instead.

Barry rolled to a stop on the ramp in front of the hangar, went through the checklist for shutting down just as the sun was finally disappearing behind the western horizon. The taxi lights and runway lights had just popped on when he looked back toward the runway.

Barry just sat there, breathing it all in. He had to be the luckiest man in the world. He got to live his dream every day.

Jim still couldn't believe his eyes when he saw X-ray Charley taxi up to the parking area under its own power. There was nothing wrong with the engine.

Barry walked into the building, carrying his brief case and his flight bag, and said "Why are you still here?"

"There was no way I was going to go home until you and that airplane were safely back at this airport. Ralph talked to the mechanic down there, and he told us what happened. You're one lucky dude."

"There you go, Jim, confusing luck with skill," Barry said, laughing as he said it.

"Smart aleck, when you first called, I just knew you had a broken crankshaft too."

16

TIMOTHY'S SOLO

The following Saturday, Ann and David came out to the airport, and as they got out of the car and started in, they met Doug and Timothy coming out the door with headsets in their hands.

"Hey, guys, how was the flight?" Timothy asked.

"South Padre was great. You need to do that some time," David said. "When you get back down, I'll tell you all about it. It's a blast to jump in an airplane and buzz down to the beautiful beaches at Corpus Christi. Where are you guys off to?"

"If I can convince Doug that I can get the airplane up and down without him in it, I'm going to solo today,"

David and Ann both said congratulations. "We'll all be here to see it. This's a great day." It was then that they noticed that Timothy's father and an older man was standing to one side of the ramp with a camera in his hands.

"Ann, that's a little odd. His dad is just standing over there, watching like a big cat ready to pounce on a little mouse or something. When each of us soloed, Grandpa and Mom, Dad and everybody were out there hugging us and making a big deal of it."

"Yeah, I know. When a young student flies solo the first time, it is a big deal. The kid takes their life into their own hands for the first time. I will never forget that feeling when you take off with no instructor in there to back you up if you screw up. It's totally up to you to bring that airplane back to earth safely."

"Yeah, but you'll remember it's the biggest thrill in the world when you do it successfully. I'm glad we're here today because Timothy's such a neat kid. I'm proud for him," David said as they walked into the café.

Timothy took off on runway 17 and climbed to five hundred feet made a perfect thirty-degree bank to the left and continued climbing to one thousand feet. After reaching one thousand feet, he executed a thirty-degree bank to the left and came out on a heading that paralleled the runway. He was now on downwind. When he was abeam, the large numbers on the north end of the runway. He pulled back the power to the proper setting, trimmed his airplane to fly at ninety knots, the proper speed for this segment of flight. Everything was perfectly executed, right down to the tiniest detail. Timothy was performing the maneuver perfectly.

Sitting in the right seat, Doug was watching closely. In the back of his mind, there was a little something that was trying to reach his conscience level. He couldn't quite make out what it was. The kid was doing it right on every step of the flight. No student had ever been that perfect before.

Timothy turned base at the exact time, altitude, and speed called for in the training manual. He was a tiny bit wide on his turn to final. He corrected for it perfectly. Doug thought, *That was good. What was different today? Timothy was doing everything by the book.*

The landing was glassy smooth.

"Good job, Timothy."

Timothy didn't say a word. Normally, he would respond to a compliment. Maybe he was just excited. When they taxied up in front of the hangar, Timothy's Dad and the other man were still standing where they had been when the plane taxied out.

Doug turned to Timothy. "Are you sure you ready to do this?"

"Absolutely," was all Timothy said.

"Do three touch-and-gos just like you did these last three. After the third landing, taxi back to the tie down and I'll sign your logbook." Then he opened the door and stepped out, reached back in and shook Timothy's hand.

As Timothy taxied out, Jim, Ann, David, and half of the café crowd were on the ramp to witness this historical occasion. Jim noticed that when Doug got out of the airplane Timothy never once looked over at his father, nor did his father wave to him or do anything to encourage him. He thought, *Timothy is a nice kid, but he sure has a weird family.*

The first takeoff was near picture perfect. The turns were crisp and sharp. Soon he was back on final. Landing number one was great; then he was back for number two. It too was letter-perfect. By now the crowd was milling around, talking, just waiting for Timothy to complete the next landing so they could go through the ceremony of cutting off his shirttail and congratulating him on completing his first flight all by himself.

Someone in the crowd pointed to the sky north of the runway and said, "There he is, on base."

The entire crowd was focused on the little Cessna as it got ready to turn final for his third landing that would officially complete his solo flight. All at once, the airplane seemed to flip upside down. Then it spun around three times and disappeared into the trees on the hill just north of the airport.

Everyone was in stunned shock; then they were running in mass. They were never sure who had the presence of mind to call 911. Jim ran back and got his pickup as he raced toward the crash scene. He slowed as he passed runners and allowed them to jump into the back of his truck.

Jim wheeled the pickup as close as he could to the trees. Everybody bailed out and ran the last hundred yards on foot. What they saw next would haunt their nightmares for the rest of their lives: a twisted mass of metal that had once been a Cessna 152 with a boy trapped inside. Because the trees and ground were wet from recent rain so far, there was no fire.

The men were trying with their bare hands to get Timothy out. The wreckage was upside down, resting on its roof. Several men were trying to talk to Timothy through the broken windows, while others were trying to get a door open so they could get inside. The boy was hanging upside down, still in his seat belt. He was not responding. Jim kept thinking, *Where are the fire trucks?* High-octane aviation gasoline was seeping out of the ruptured tanks and soaking into the ground around the airplane. The entire area was a bomb set to go off any moment.

Jim thought, *All it would take is one spark, and that whole area would become a roaring inferno. If that happens, we'll lose more than just the boy. We'll lose some of the guys that are trying to get him out.*

"Someone asked can you feel a pulse?"

One of the guys trying to talk to Timothy replied, "I think so, but it is very weak."

Soon the fire department arrived on the scene and hosed down the area around the wreckage. Using metal cutting equipment, they had the boy out of the wreckage in minutes. All of the rescuers just stood around in stunned disbelief.

The paramedics loaded Timothy into an ambulance and raced down the hill toward town. One by one, the would-be rescuers struggled back down the hill. Jim saw Doug standing there in a state of pure shock. He walked over and put his arms around Doug.

"Doug, you did it by the book. This is not your fault," John came up and said.

Big, strong, manly Doug broke down and cried. There were many big strong men walking out of those woods wiping tears from their eyes.

The same question kept being asked, "Why? What could have happened?"

"He was doing everything so well?"

The sheriff's deputies took statements from everyone who saw the airplane go down. The TV crews were sticking mics in front of everyone in sight. A news helicopter appeared overhead. It was a zoo around the airport. The FAA people were there, but this was one for the NTSB (National Transportation Safety Board). Nobody remembered seeing Timothy's father after the airplane went down in all of the confusion and shock. He was completely forgotten. The NTSB investigators were there by early afternoon. The sheriff's deputies had put crime scene tape all across the wooded area, so no one was allowed to see the wreckage.

Since the crash was a half mile from the airport, the FAA didn't close the airport. Several students arrived for lessons and found out about Timothy after they arrived. A few elected not to fly today; a few decided to go ahead. By midafternoon, the rumor mill was in full speed. Some were speculating that a control cable broke, causing him to lose control. Some thought he had overshot his turn to final and banked too steeply to correct, thus causing the airplane to stall. Nobody had a clue at this time. All they knew was a beautiful boy had done two perfect landings and on his third and final approach stalled and spun into the woods a half mile north of the airport.

Jim called Mike at the FAA office. "Mike, if the crankshaft broke in the trainer, you need to ground every airplane flying until we can check them out. What's going on?"

Mike made a quick phone call to the lead investigator at the crash site. He then called Jim back. "Jim, I just talked to the lead investigator at the crash site. How quickly can your mechanics get up there and pull that engine off the airframe and put it on a workbench?"

"Let me call you right back." Racing down the stairs two at a time, he found Ralph with his head under the cowling of an airplane. "Ralph, I just got off the phone with Mike over at FAA. They want to know how quickly you can get some guys up there to the crash site and pull that engine off the trainer and put it on a test stand."

"Boss, I can be there in five minutes if they're serious."

"Let me use the phone in your office, and I'll call them right now."

In just a moment Jim stuck his head back out and said, "Ralph, they want it done right now." Ralph and all three mechanics jumped in Jim's four-wheel-drive truck and sped up the hill to the crash site.

In less than an hour, they were back with the engine in the back of Jim's truck. Four big burley men literally picked up the engine and bolted it onto a test stand. A man in a blue blazer with the letters NTSB emblazoned on it said, "Gentlemen, this is very unusual, but because of the seriousness of the situation, I want you to disassemble the engine, but I want to take pictures of every part as you disassemble it."

Three hours later, Ralph called Jim on the intercom and said, "Boss, you need to come down and see this."

———————————

Rufus Arnold was Timothy Arnold's father. Right now, he was like a wounded animal, running to his place of safety as he turned down his street. It suddenly occurred to him he was going to have to tell his wife about the crash. Hitting the garage door opener, he raced the car into the garage, almost hitting the door before it was up; then before he jumped out of the car, he shot his right hand up and hit the remote door closer on the sun visor and closed the world out.

Storming in through the back door, Doris, his wife, met him in the kitchen. He looked like a wild animal.

Doris was frightened by his appearance. "Rufus, what's the matter?"

"They let Timothy solo today."

She thought, *No, surely he is not trying to say what I think he is saying.* "Is Timothy all right?"

He slinked back as if he was afraid she was going to strike him.

Doris screamed, "You cowardly fool. Is my baby all right?"

He just shook his head and started for the den, saying, "I'm going to sue them for millions." He reached to pick up the phone.

She stopped him, saying, "You're not going to call anybody until you tell me about my baby. Is he all right?"

His eyes were on the floor. He couldn't bear to look at her right now. He just slowly shook his head. At that exact moment, the TV that was on in the den cut into their program with breaking news about a student who had been killed on his first solo flight. Doris ran over and turned up the volume, and there on the screen was a picture of twisted metal. At first, it didn't look like an airplane. Then she recognized the tail. Next, she saw the *N* number on the mangled pieces.

She collapsed to the carpet in front of the TV. Doris couldn't stand to watch it, yet she couldn't take her eyes off the screen. They were not churchgoing people, but she had been raised Catholic. First, she called both of her daughters.

They were as shocked as she was. Without saying another word to Rufus, she got in her car and drove to the church.

Her mind was a jumble of emotions and feelings. The quiet sanctuary seemed to have a calming effect on the turmoil going on inside of her. Her marriage to Rufus had been over a long time ago, but because she was Catholic, she had been taught by the sisters when you married you married for life. She had two beautiful daughters her domineering husband had driven from their home. The girls couldn't wait to go to college. It was a way to get away from their father. When her youngest daughter was six years old, little Timothy was born. His mother and sisters thought he was a gift from God. He was always a thoughtful quiet child. He loved his daddy and feared him at the same time.

Timothy always excelled in his grades, but he never measured up to his daddy's expectation for him to be the superathlete Rufus wanted him to be. Rufus never lettered in a single sport while he was in school, so why was he always pushing Timothy? Of course, Rufus's daddy was just like him, or was he just like his daddy?

Doris thought, *I have to pull myself together. Someone needs to plan a funeral for my baby. She got up and walked into the pastor's office. Somebody is going to pay for this.*

Plans had to be made.

17

THE BROKEN ENGINE

Jim dreaded what he was going to see when he walked down the stairs into the shop area. The NTSB guy was busy taking pictures of the engine parts all laid out on the workbench. Ralph said, "Boss, look here."

There laid the crankshaft out of the trainer airplane engine. It was in two jagged pieces. Ralph said, "Boss, you were right. The darn thing shattered—like it was made of glass."

Jim's knees felt weak. He grabbed the NTSB man and said, "You have got to ground every airplane flying until we can find out why these crankshafts are suddenly shattering."

The NTSB man said, "Sir, you don't understand. The NTSB can't ground an airplane. All we do is investigate and advise the FAA as to probable case so they can determine…"

Jim was no longer listening. He was running full tilt up to his office. Grabbing his phone, he called Mike at the FAA office. As soon as he answered, Jim yelled into the phone, "Mike, you have got to ground every airplane until we or someone can find out why these crankshafts are shattering."

"Slow down, Jim. Start over again, and tell me what you are talking about."

"My guys have the engine all apart on the workbench, and the crankshaft is shattered on the trainer that just crashed today. That is what I am talking about. You have got to issue an emergency order grounding every airplane in the nation until somebody can find out why this is killing people."

"Slow down, Jim. I can't do that. A grounding order had to come from Washington. I will call Washington right now and tell them what we suspect, but they will have to issue a grounding order. What year was that trainer manufactured?"

Jim was so frustrated he couldn't think straight. "What year was the trainer manufactured? I don't remember. That was the newest one we bought before the three we got in this year."

"Jim, I need that information. I know when the Bonanza was made. Now find out for me the year the trainer was made. Washington is not going to ground every airplane that has ever been made. Some of those airplanes have been flying for twenty of more years without a problem."

"Mike, what if it is the motor oil? What if something is wrong with the oil we are using now?"

"Jim, we have to let the system work."

A tired, frustrated, and frightened man slumped down in his office chair and pressed the intercom button on his phone. "John, can you and Ralph come up here?"

As soon as all three of them were in his office, Jim said, "Guys, I think we've got to ground every one of our planes. This is a nightmare or something from the twilight zone."

John spoke first. "Jim, this's a traumatic day, and I know why it would be even more traumatic for you."

Before he could say any more, Ralph spoke up. "D——m it to h——ll, boss. Sorry, I know I'm not supposed to cuss."

"Ralph, today I feel like joining you, so go on with what you were trying to say."

"Well, what I was trying to say is, I've been taking care of these planes for years, some of them I have overhauled myself. There is no reason to ground them. This one that crashed today was the newest one of the Cessna trainers. I looked at the logbooks. It was built the same month your Bonanza was built, but by a different company. Your Bonanza was built by Beechcraft, and the trainer was built by Cessna. It doesn't make sense, but there is something about airplanes built in 2005. So I think they should ground every airplane made in 2005."

Turning to his computer, Jim pulled up the Internet. "Let's see what was model of the Bonanza that crashed in Colorado. Here it is, guys. That Bonanza was made in 2006."

"Why would two different airplanes built by two totally different companies experience the same exact problem with the same catastrophic results?" John sat, rubbing his fingertips on his forehead.

"I keep thinking about the motor oil. What if some way they have done something to the oil?"

"Boss, if it was the oil, it would affect the older airplanes before the newer ones."

"Ralph, is there any way to check every crankshaft in every airplane engine we own?"

"Not short of tearing the engine apart and sending the crankshaft to a testing lab. Every time I do an annual on one of our airplanes, I send the oil off for testing to see if there are any metal shavings in the oil that will tell me if there is any part with excessive wear. I looked at the oil analyses report on the Bonanza and the trainer just now. Both were clean."

"Okay, guys, I feel better about continuing to fly our airplanes, because all of the ones we have left were built before 2005. John, I want your instructors to really stress emergency procedures and engine out procedures."

"Boss, I have an extra engine for the trainers. Why don't I have that crankshaft tested, and if it is good, then I'll put that engine in one of the trainers and send the next crankshaft in for testing? It will take a few weeks, but soon I will have every shaft tested without shutting down the fleet." Ralph wiped his hands on a shop rag as he talked.

"That is a good idea. Let's do it. John, do you have any ideas?"

"No, but I'll tell you what I will do. I'll start going through the FAA files, looking for accidents involving crankshaft failure and see if I can find any kind of pattern other than the years 2005 and '06."

"I'm going to call Mike and tell him about the years these airplanes were built and lean on him some more. I'm real frustrated with the bureaucracy at the FAA."

18

GOING FOR ANSWERS

Jim called Derrick on Sunday afternoon. "Derrick, this is Jim Colburn. Can you meet me at the airport at five o'clock Monday morning?"

Derrick was already there with the King Aire pulled out and gassed up.

"Are you ready to fly, Captain?" Jim asked him.

"Yes, sir, where are we going in Wichita, Kansas, that requires us to be there so early?"

"I have an eight o'clock appointment to sit down with the sales manager at the Beechcraft Company. He thinks I'm coming to make a deal to buy a new Bonanza to replace the other one."

"Apparently, that's not why you're going. So why are you going to Wichita?"

"I'm going to squeeze the information out of him about how many crankshaft failures they've had within the past two years. By the way, pilots' talk, is there any scuttlebutt around about airplanes suddenly breaking crankshafts in flight?"

"None that I am aware of."

"If you hear anything, let me know, will you?"

"There is no place prettier than an airport at night. I like just standing here, drinking in the beauty of it. So peaceful and quiet, the blue lights outlining the taxiways, the sparkling white runway lights. The huge silver moon bathing the whole scene in its glow," Jim said as they walked out on the ramp.

"Yes, Jim, and I love the smell of fresh cut hay brought in by the gentle breeze blowing across the fields at the south end of the airport."

"It's time to go. Mr. Jim, do you want the left seat or the right seat?"

"I'll have to take the right seat. I still can't use my left shoulder very well."

When they were all buckled in, Derrick flashed the airplanes lights to signal the lineman that they were ready to start the engines.

"Derrick, these engines don't have crankshafts, do they?"

"No jet engines have driveshafts. Only piston engines have crankshafts—which is pretty much everything else. Cars, trucks, boats all have driveshafts."

When Derrick said that Jim thought, *I wonder if any cars have been experiencing crankshaft failures like airplanes have. At least if you were in a car, you could pull over and call a tow truck.* He put that thought out of his mind.

"Good morning, Fort Worth center. This is King Aire three six five Charley Alpha, with you at three thousand, heading three six zero." Jim keyed the radio mic, as they were climbing out.

"Good morning, three six five Charley Alpha, radar contact three miles north of Millport, climb and maintain twenty-thousand."

"Climb and maintain twenty thousand," Jim read back.

"The night is so dark right outside of the windows. It is as smooth as velvet," Derrick said. "It's like we are in a black cocoon. I can see a few lights on the ground and the soft glow of the instrument panel lights, absolutely nothing else."

All you could hear was the thrum of the big engines. Jim said, "The air is silky smooth. If you didn't see lights moving under the plane way down below on the ground, you would have no sense of movement, and I feel like we are suspended in a black void." He looked off the right wingtip and could see a tiny glow starting to appear on the eastern horizon. Then there it was the first rays of the morning sun, as seen from twenty thousand feet above the Oklahoma ranch land. There was nothing in this world more spectacular than a sunrise as seen from a pilot's view. Then tears came to Jim's eyes as he remembered how much Allie loved sunrises in the air.

"After all, it was moments like this that made all of the work, studying and training needed to become a pilot worthwhile. Wow!" Derrick said as the sun climbed up on the horizon. "It's almost breathtaking."

"Charley Alpha, switch to Wichita approach on one two seven point eight, good day."

Jim was brought back to reality by the announcement on his headset. He instinctively replied, "Charley Alpha going to one two seven point eight, good day." Jim thought, *We can't be here already*. And then he looked at the digital clock on the instrument panel and realized they had been airborne for almost two hours. "Wichita, approach, three six five Charley Alpha with you at twenty thousand squawking two three eight niner."

"Good morning, Charley Alpha, descend at pilot's discretion to one zero. Plan to enter left downwind for runway one seven left, report airport in sight."

Jim read back, "Charley Alpha, PD twenty thousand to ten, direct to Wichita Municipal, enter left downwind."

Jim picked up a rent-a-car at the terminal and went directly to the headquarters for Bonanza. When he walked into the lobby, there stood a white plastic reader board with black letters spelling out WELCOME, JIM COLBURN AND DERRICK DANIELS. Jim thought, *That is a good touch, setting up a welcome board. I need to think about how we could do something like that.* A nice-looking young man who looked to be in his early thirties met them in the lobby. "You must be Mr. Colburn, and I'll bet you are Derrick Daniels. I'm Danny Slaughter. Please call me Danny. Can we get you guys a cup of coffee?" Jim noticed he was wearing an Air Force Academy ring on his right hand.

Seated in Danny's office, Jim said, "Danny, why we are here is because on my Bonanza the crankshaft broke, which then shattered the crankcase and blew oil all over my windshield."

"Mr. Colburn, I am so sorry. I read the file. What can I do for you?"

"Danny, you can do two things for me. Number one, I want to find out why my engine blew. I have tried calling on the phone, and all I am getting is a runaround. Customer service sends me to engineering. Engineering sends me to legal, who sends me back to customer service. Danny, I am not going to buy another Bonanza, but I am going to buy a light twin, and I prefer the Beach Barron. So let's just talk straight here. If you want to sell me a million-dollar Baron, then you need to find some answers for me."

"Mr. Colburn, I'll do everything I can even if you never buy another airplane from us. What is it you want me to do?"

"I want to know how many Bonanzas have experienced a crankshaft failure in flight within the last three years," Jim said. "I know darn well you guys have that information. I am not looking to file any lawsuits. If I wanted to sue Beechcraft, I could already have done that. I lost the most important person in the world to me, and I want to know why."

Danny turned to his computer and started typing. "Mr. Colburn, our records show that within the past three years there have been eleven fatal airplane crashes involving private single-engine airplanes worldwide. Only two were Bonanzas, your airplane and the one in Colorado."

"How many other airplanes use that same engine?"

"Let me see. Your airplane was equipped with an I-O-550. Basically, that same engine is used in the Cessna 206 and 210, the Piper Saratoga, Piper Mirage, the Blanca Viking, the Aerospatiale, the Bonanza, and the Barron."

"Mr. Colburn, let me print this information off for you. Take it with you and after you have looked at it. If you think of anything else I can do for you, please give me a call," Danny said, handing Jim his card.

Jim thanked Danny for his time and his help.

On the way to the airport, Jim said, "Derrick, let's go visit the Constantine Motor Company in Wisconsin."

"You are the boss. Just tell me where you want to go."

Jim called Constantine Motor Company and talked to the vice president in charge of customer relations, who invited them to come on up to the plant. At the Constantine Motor Company, Jim learned that they had only had five broken crankshafts. Jim's and the Bonanza in Colorado were the only two that failed in flight.

"What about the other three?"

"One was broken when the airplane turned too wide on the taxiway and dropped the nose wheel off the pavement, causing the prop to strike the edge of the pavement. One was caused by landing the plane in a farmer's field, and the prop struck a berm. The third one happened when the engine was started, with the tow bar still attached. And the prop struck the tow bar, breaking the crankshaft."

"So three out of the five failures were caused by prop strikes?"

"Mr. Colburn, as you know, all prop strikes do not result in an immediate broken crankshaft. However, if the prop strikes something hard and suddenly stops the engine, it can crack the crankshaft. That's why the FAA requires all engines that have experienced even a minor prop strike to be overhauled. The crankshaft must be x-rayed and tested before being reinstalled in the engine."

Jim thanked Mr. Bojarski for seeing him and thought, *I wonder if the logbooks on the Bonanza show that it had had a prop strike before I bought it. That might explain everything.* As soon as they were back in the rent-a-car, Jim called Ralph. "Do me a favor. Look through the Bonanza logbooks again and see if you can find any reference to a prop strike before I bought that airplane."

"I have already thought of that, but I'll look again," Ralph said. "When are you comin' home?"

"We are leaving now. I'll see you in the morning. If you find anything, call my cell phone and leave a message. I'll have it turned off while we are in the air."

19

THE RECEIPT

Jim took the logbooks for the Bonanza home with him for the weekend. He started to take the logbooks for the Cessna trainer also but decided he would concentrate on one airplane. If he solved the problem for one, he would probable solve it for both?

Jim kept thinking, That airplane had to have had a prop strike. That's the only thing that makes sense. He decided to drive over to Johnny Brown's prop repair shop and talk to Johnny. If anybody in the business had any ideas, it would be Johnny. When he walked in, Johnny was sitting at his desk.

Johnny looked up and said, "What brings you over here today, Jim?"

Jim sat down and told him about the crankshaft breaking and his suspicion that it had a prop strike before he bought it. Johnny looked at Jim for a moment like he was thinking of something; then he asked, "Who owned that airplane before you bought it?"

"I don't remember. Some doctor, just a minute."

Jim pulled out his cell phone and dialed Pete's number. When he answered the phone, Jim asked him, "Who owned the Bonanza before me?"

"Why are you asking, Jim?" Jim told him what his suspicions were.

"Jim, the previous owner was a doctor who lives in Dallas, and his name is Nathanial Dixon, and here is something funny. Right after you crashed, he was around, asking some strange questions about where those logbooks were. He even wondered if you were the type to carry your logbooks in the plane with you."

"He was wondering if the logbooks burned up in the crash," Jim said.

"Jim, at the time, I didn't think much about it, but now that you bring it up. You could be right."

Jim told Johnny the name of the doctor who owned the Bonanza before he bought it. Johnny looked through his files and found no invoice for a Doctor Dixon. "If he had a mechanic order a new prop, then the invoice would be under the mechanic's name. Do you know who his mechanic was?"

Jim called Ralph back and asked him which mechanic had done most of the work on the Bonanza.

Ralph gave him the name of the shop that had done most of the work.

Johnny checked, and he had done a lot of props for that shop, but no Bonanza prop between the time the new engine was installed and the time Jim purchased the airplane.

Jim finally thanked Johnny and left. He was even more certain that he was on the right track, but how many prop rebuilders were in the US?

Jim had gotten into the habit of reading every aircraft crash report that came over the Internet from anywhere in the world. All at once, he sat straight up in his chair. A two-year-old Bonanza crashed in Brazil, killing three people. "The pilot radioed that he had suddenly lost engine power, and oil sprayed all over his windshield."

Jim quickly called Mike at the FAA office. "Mike, look at the accident reports for yesterday. In Brazil, a bonanza crashed, killing three people. Mike, look what the pilot reported just before he crashed."

"Thanks, Jim. Let me see what I can find out."

"Mike, will you call me back when you do find out some more information about that crash?"

"Yes, I will, have you found any more information about a possible prop strike on your Bonanza?"

"No, so far I have not been able to find any evidence of a prop strike—which means there is something wrong with these airplane engines."

"Let me see what I can find out, and I will call you."

Two hours later, Mike called back. "Jim, I can't get any information out of the Transportation Ministry in Brazil. They do not share info with us, sorry."

Jim thought, *This is worse than a nightmare. Real people are dying out there, and nobody will listen.* He picked up his phone and called Senator Thompson's office.

A very professional-sounding voice answered, "Senator Thompson's office, this is Kathy. How can I help you?"

"Kathy, my name is Jim Colburn. I live in the nine-thirty-eighth district, and I need to talk with Senator Thompson. It is very important."

"Oh, Mr. Colburn, I know Senator Thompson would love to talk with you. However, Senator Thompson is in Hong Kong on a trade mission meeting. Can someone else help you?"

"Kathy, who is in charge of Senator Thompson's office when she is gone."

"Oh, that would Samuel Goldstein."

"Can I speak with Mr. Goldstein?"

"Oh, I'm sure Mr. Goldstein would be glad to talk with you, but he is gone to lunch with Senator Baker. Can I have him call you when he returns?"

"Yes, and tell him it is very important that I talk with him right away."

"Can I tell him what this is about?"

"Yes, I'm afraid there is something wrong with the airplane motors built in 2005 and 2006, and nine people have already died. One of them was my wife."

"Mr. Colburn, I am so sorry about you wife, but we can't help you with that. You will need to contact Senator Abernathy's office. He is chairman of the Transportation Committee. They regulate the airplanes." Kathy purred.

If Jim could have reached through the phone, he would have strangled her. Instead, he clicked off the call and threw the phone as hard as he could into the sofa across the room.

Then he got up, walked around to the sofa, and called Derrick. "Can you get us a flight plan to Brazil?"

"Sure, where do you want to go in Brazil?"

"Brasilia."

"And what exactly are we going to be doing while we are there, if you don't mind me asking?"

"A Bonanza went down there yesterday, killing three people, and the pilot radioed that he had lost all power. The oil coated his windshield. I want to find out what we can about that crash."

"Is your passport up to date?"

"Oh no, it is not."

"Since you have had one, you can get it renewed in about a week,"

The next morning, Jim was sitting in the café, eating breakfast when a deputy sheriff walked in and asked, "Are you Jim Colburn?"

"Yes, sir, what can I do for you?"

The deputy handed him a court summons. He was so surprised. "What's this?"

When he opened it, Timothy's father was suing for the wrongful death of one Timothy Arnold. Jim thought, *Well this was to be expected.* He went up to his office and called his insurance agent.

Jim started rifling through a bundle of receipts that came with the Bonanza logbooks. It was just a bunch of receipt for parts that had been replaced since the airplane was new.

All at once, one receipt jumped out at him. It was a receipt for a landing light installed by a small shop up in Oklahoma. Jim thought, *Now why did that get my attention?* He grabbed the logbook and looked on or near the date of that receipt, and there was no entry for a landing light being installed. Then he looked at the date again. The date was just three months before he bought the airplane.

Jim sat there, pondering this new information. *That is very interesting. Because there is no way to break that landing light without hitting the propeller. The way the landing lights are mounted on the landing gear on a Bonanza the light is right behind the prop.*

He thought it through, *If something broke the landing light, that same something could have caused the prop to suddenly stop?*

He picked up the phone and called Pete at home. When Pete got on the line, Jim asked, "Pete, what do you remember about how and when you got that Bonanza?"

Pete thought it about a minute and said, "This doctor just showed up with this real pretty Bonanza and said he needed to sell it. I looked at his logbooks, and they were in perfect condition, so I sent it over for a presale inspection, which I do with all of the airplanes I bring in just like I did on your Centurion. Why do you ask?"

"Pete, have you ever done any business with this guy before?"

"No."

Early the next morning, Jim was in Johnny's office again. "Johnny, check to see if you sold a prop to the shop named on the receipt for a landing light."

"Jim, there is a receipt for a prop sent to that shop on the same week that a new landing light was sent, and better yet the shop owner ordered a prop for a Bonanza N4499Z."

Jim immediately grabbed the invoices and walked over and placed the landing light receipt and the prop invoice both on the copy machine. When he had made a copy of each, he handed Johnny the copy and took the original with him. He then drove straight to the FAA offices and signed in and asked to see Mike. He showed Mike the logbooks and the receipts. Mike took several seconds to study the documents, then said, "Jim, two guys are in big trouble. The aircraft owner and the mechanic could both go to the federal pen over this."

"It won't bring my Allie back."

"No, Jim, it won't, but the guy responsible is not going to get off free either." He picked the phone and called the FBI; then he turned to Jim and said, "I would like for you to wait here a few minutes until a couple of agents get here."

As soon as he was finished talking to the FBI and gave copies of the documents, Jim called JR. "Son, you won't believe what I have found." JR met him the next morning down at the biggest meanest law firm in the state, and together they started filing lawsuits against a big shot doctor who tried to save a few thousand dollars by replacing a damaged prop without rebuilding the engine. The FAA suspended the doctor's pilot's license immediately pending an investigation. They also suspended the mechanic's license immediately pending an investigation.

Later that afternoon, the Dallas Police served a federal arrest warrant on one Doctor Nathanial Dixon, a famous surgeon.

Federal agents walked into the repair shop in El Reno, Oklahoma, produced their badges, and demanded to see the shop owner. Jerome crawled out from under an airplane when his wife told him there were two federal agents there to see him.

The agents again showed their badges and said, "We need to ask you some questions." They showed him the receipts for the landing light and the prop and asked him, "Did you install them on a Bonanza? "

"Yes."

"Did you record it in the aircraft maintenance logs?"

"No, I asked the doctor to bring his logs so I could record it, but he said they were back in Dallas, and if I would make a stick on sheet, he would put it into his logbooks when he got home."

"Did you write the entry on a stick on sheet?"

"Yes, I did, in fact I saved the write-up in my computer because I was a little concerned that he might not do what he said."

"We want to see the write-up, if it is still in your computer."

"Yes, sir,"

Jerome walked into the office, turned on his computer, scanned his saved files for a few seconds, and then printed what was on the screen.

It read,

> INSTALLED ONE THREE BLADE MACAULAY PROPELLER NUMBER 338900SS7113 ON BONANZA 4499Z. RECOMMENDED TO OWNER THAT ENGINE BE TORN DOWN AS PRESCRIBED IN THE FEDERAL MAINTENANCE GUIDELINE. PROPELLER INSTALLED THIS DATE 03/12/ 2006.
>
> INSTALLED REPLACEMENT LANDING LIGHT DAMAGED IN PROP STRIKE THIS DATE 03/12/2006.
>
> Tach reading 3199.6 hours.
>
> Signed
> Jerome Davidson AP #455954458

The agent looking at this document knew that this was done exactly as the law required. The agents then asked, "Do you know what happened, how this airplane came to have a prop strike here at El Reno?"

"Yes, a bunch of doctors came up here to go hunting, and the pilot missed the turn in the taxiway out there and dropped his front wheel off that little covert in the drainage ditch. When the front tire dropped down in the drainage ditch, the propeller hit the concrete culvert, nicking the prop. It just bent the tip of the prop and did not stop the engine, but the FAA requirements are even a tiny nick in a prop tip, and the whole prop has to be overhauled, and they recommend that the engine be overhauled."

The agent asked, "Did it stop the engine immediately?"

"No, he taxied up here after they got it back on the taxiway. I informed the doctor that he should have the engine torn down, but since the engine didn't experience a complete and sudden stop, it was his call," Jerome replied.

The agent went back to his office and filed a report, showing a copy of the log entry printed off Jerome's computer and a sworn statement from Jerome and his wife, who was working the day the Bonanza came in.

Later that day, the FAA reinstated Jerome's license.

20

THE REPORTS

While Jim was waiting for his passport to be updated, he kept scanning the accident report data base, watching for and hoping not to find any more deadly crashes.

JR called and said, "I have a copy of the FBI agents report from El Reno, Oklahoma. Do you want me to fax you a copy?"

"Yeah, send it on over."

When he got the report, he started reading it. All at once it hit him. The Bonanza did have a prop strike, but it didn't stop the engine. Something was still wrong. This was a minor prop strike. Yes, it could damage a crankshaft. That is why the FAA recommended that you overhaul an engine even if the strike is minor.

He quickly called John and Ralph and asked them to come to his office. Handing each one a copy of the report, he said, "What is your first gut reaction?"

"In the military, we would take a brass hammer and tap a small tip bend back in place and keep on flying."

Ralph sat staring at the logbooks and said, "This didn't cause that crankshaft to fail."

"That is what I am thinking. Now if he had had the engine rebuilt, they would have x-rayed and dye glowed the crankshaft and found if it had a tiny crack in it and replaced the crankshaft. But my gut feeling is that had he had that engine overhauled, they would have found some other problem."

"Well, let me show you something else. I was just opening the mail when you called. I was fixin' to come up here anyway, because look what I just got in the mail." He handed Jim the report on the Cessna trainer's engine.

Jim quickly scanned it, then said, "This says that the engine was developing full power when it struck the ground. The crankshaft snapped as a result of the prop slamming into the ground at full power."

"I'm sorry, boss. We were in such a hurry to get it torn down so that NTSB guy could take his pictures that it didn't even occur to me that the crankshaft might have broken after it hit the ground."

"Ralph, that was a very emotional day," John said. "Don't blame yourself for not thinking of that."

"Guys, what're we dealing with here? If Timothy's engine didn't fail, why did he crash? Could the airplane in

Colorado and Brazil have also had a prop strike? Have I just been chasing my tail on the crankshaft business?"

"I ain't buying that about your crankshaft failed because of a little nick in a prop blade. There is a skunk in the woodpile somewhere."

"Gentlemen, we are now back to how could a well-trained student who had made two successful landings and takeoffs crash a trainer that was, according to the NTSB, developing full power when it hit the ground?" John asked.

"Oh, by the way, the slimy lawyers hired by Timothy's father are going to be here Monday, and they want to take everybody's depositions. They also want to look at and make copies of all of the logbooks for that airplane."

"They can look all they want to. Our logs are clean. In fact, I'll take those logbooks and shove them up a lawyer's rear end. "

Jim had to smile at that, but he said, "Guys, tell everybody to be very cooperative. We'll only make matters worse if we get into a fight with the lawyers. Our lawyers will be here. They can do that for us. Why don't we go down to the café and get some lunch?"

Ralph jumped up and said, "Why not? Let's go."

John just shrugged his shoulders.

All during lunch, they talked about Timothy and the crash. John said, "Did you read the newspaper the next morning after Timothy crashed? It never mentioned that he had made two successful takeoffs and two successful landings prior to the crash. The writer obviously was not a pilot. He called it a twin-engine plane when it was little Cessna 152 single-engine airplane. He even said it exploded and fell to the ground when there was no explosion at all."

Jim felt an involuntary shudder go through him when he remembered the horrible sight. Jim said, "I tried and tried to think of any way that a Cessna 152 could just crash, and I could not think of even one. If the engine just quit, all Timothy had to do was do nothing, and the little plane would have glided down to a safe landing in the field north of the airport. If the control cable broke, which was virtually impossible, he could have controlled the airplane by using the rudder if he needed to turn. If Timothy had a seizure, the airplane would have leveled itself and continued flying until it ran out of gas. I guess I was just grasping at straws when I saw that broken crankshaft there on the worktable."

"Yeah, me too. As hard as I tried, I could not think of any possible situation that would cause a Cesena 152 trainer to crash. If it stalled, all you had to do was take your hands off the controls, and it would right itself."

"How do you crash a Cessna 152? Okay, if you flew one into a violent storm, the storm could destroy the airplane. If you were involved in a midair collision with another airplane, that would do it. If you crashed into the side of a mountain? For the life of me, I can think of no way on a clear day, with no other airplanes involved, a Cessna 152 could just tumble out of the sky. Yet I saw it with my own eyes. That crash has destroyed at least two young lives, first Timothy's and then Doug's." John kept asking the same question repeatedly.

"Maybe we should sell the trainers and just concentrate on selling fuel and repairing other people's airplanes?"

"Jim, you can do anything you want. You are the owner. However, you know you love flying as much as any of us," John said. "Yes, you have dealt a horrible blow from flying. Don't give up until we get to the bottom of this. Something is just wrong. You and I have flown and loved flying for many years. It's up to us to get flying back to the fun place it has always been."

21

MILLIE'S NIGHTMARE

Jim and John were walking through the lobby when they heard a panicked female voice on the airport radio. "Mayday! Mayday! Can somebody help me?" They all stopped in their tracks. Every eye was glued to the radio. Then the voice called again and said, "Mayday! Mayday! Can someone help me?" This time, she was even more panicked than earlier. Jim reached the radio first.

"Person calling mayday, say your emergency!" Jim grabbed the mic and said.

"My husband is passed out, and I can't wake him."

"Are you a pilot too?" Jim asked.

"No, I don't know how to fly the plane, and I can't wake him up." This time she was almost hysterical when she screamed her reply.

"Can you tell me where you are?" Jim tried his best to remain calm, but he could feel his hands starting to sweat holding the mic

"I don't know where I'm at," she screamed.

"This is the Millport Airport. Just stay calm. Everything is going to be all right. Can you tell me what kind of airplane you are in?"

"It is a Cessna 172."

Jim thought, *Thank God it is a 172*, and then he thought she sounded a little calmer. Then he asked, "Does your airplane have an autopilot?"

"I don't think so,"

By now, Jim had a crowd around him.

"That's okay. Don't touch anything until I tell you to, okay? Can you describe what you see when you look down? Can you see any lakes or freeways?"

. "All I see is a bunch of pastures," she said. She seemed to panic again.

Jim tried to keep his voice as calm as possible. "That's okay. We are going to get you down. Just stay with me."

"Can you tell me where you took off from?" Jim asked as calmly as he possible could even though he certainly didn't feel calm. Normally in a room full of pilots, there was no such thing as silence. This time the room was deathly quiet. No one wanted to prevent Jim from hearing what the lady said.

"Abilene."

"Which airport are you going to?" Jim pointed to the giant map hanging on the wall. John sprinted over to it.

"Millport," she replied. At least she didn't sound quit so panicked. The last thing they needed was for her to panic and do something that would destroy the plane and both of them.

Jim then quietly asked, "When did you leave Abilene?" Every pilot in the room knew what he was doing. By knowing the type of airplane and the departure point and the airport she was headed for, John could plot the course she should be on and know approximately her location from Millport. That was assuming the airplane was still on course. John drew a yellow line with an erasable marker on the map, starting at the Abilene airport and ending at the Millport airport. The map was drawn to scale one inch equaled one hundred miles. By knowing when they took off and knowing the speed of a 172, they could pinpoint approximately where she was, if the airplane was still on course.

Jim turned to one of the instructors and said, "Call the FAA and let them know what is happening."

She called back and said, "I don't know what time we left. I just can't remember. Please do something." She was starting to panic again.

"Everything is going to be all right. This is the Millport airport. We are going to get you landed here soon. We'll have an ambulance waiting to take your husband to the hospital."

"I think he's dead," she screamed back.

Jim thought, *I can't do this no matter how hard I try to keep her calm. If I ask the wrong question, she panics.*

John spoke up and said, "Why don't I get a couple of planes in the air and fly this line in reverse to see if we can spot her?"

"Go!" Jim pointed to the door and said.

"Ma'am, you are doing fine. Okay, can you tell me what the little compass mounted up by windshield is reading?"

"East."

Jim thought well at least she may be still on course. "That is great," Jim replied as calmly as possible.

"We are doing okay. Now I need for you to look at the instruments on the left side. Can you see the one in the upper-left corner? That's the airspeed indicator. Now count over to the third one from there, and tell me what you see." Then Jim thought, *Oh God, please don't let me lose this plane. There are so many things that can go wrong. Her husband may not be dead yet, but we need to find her and then keep her from panicking and crashing...*

"It has two hands like a clock, and they are both pointing at five."

"Perfect," Jim said. "That tells me how high you are. That is a good altitude."

The FAA was on the other line. They told Jim, "Ask her if she can reset her transponder. If she can, we'll know in a moment which of those blips on our radar screen is her."

Jim keyed his mic. "Do you see a little box on the instrument panel that has the number 1200 in it? Don't panic if you can't. It's not real important, but if you can, it would be good."

"I see it, but I can't reach it. It is located in the lower left-hand corner behind Joe's knee."

At least she wasn't screaming, Jim thought.

The FAA called back and said, "We have an airplane squawking 1,200, nine miles north of Weatherford at 5,500. Its track is drifting southeast."

This was good news and bad news.

Jim thought carefully how he should word his next question. "Do you see a big lake in front of you a few miles?"

"Yes."

Jim thought again, *God, I can't do this without your help.* Because he knew if she continued drifting southeast, she was going to end up right in the middle of the military jets, landing at Carswell Air Force Base, the planes landing at the big and busy Fort Worth Meacham, and right in the middle of the corridor for the planes landing at DFW. He had to turn her back toward Millport. If she panicked now, they would lose her for sure. Now he *was* sweating all over, and the room had really become silent, even though the number of people had grown in the room.

"What is your name, ma'am?"

"Millie."

"Millie, here is what I need for you to do. Listen carefully, and don't do anything except what I tell you, understand?"

There was a long pause, and then a squeaky voice said, "Okay."

Jim thought, *I wish I could land her at Meacham.* Then he decided against it. Trying to get her to change the radio to Meacham could be a real problem. He asked, over his shoulder, "Has anyone called for an ambulance?"

Someone said, "Yes, they're sending an ambulance and a couple of fire trucks."

Jim turned back to the mic. He could feel his hands starting to shake. Adrenalin was rushing through his system by now. "Millie, listen carefully. Take hold of the yoke in front of you with just two fingers on each hand. Just your thumb and index finger only, have you got that?"

"Okay."

Jim thought, *Right now she is starting to sound a little more in control.* Jim said, "Millie, that is great. Now I want you to gently roll the yoke to the left, just a little."

Jim then asked the instructor who was still on the phone with the controller, "Has the airplane's heading changed?"

"They say, yes, it had changed about ten degrees. It is now heading almost due east."

"Ask them to give me a bearing to Millport."

That message was relayed to the air traffic controller on the phone. He said, "Tell her to change to a heading of zero three zero degrees."

Jim thought, *She is never going to understand that.* Jim had been off the radio for a few seconds, sending and getting messages from the controller, when all at once the panicked voice boomed out of the radio.

"Are you still there!"

"Millie, we're still here. You are doing well. Now I need for you to turn the yoke just a little more to your left, using only your thumb and finger to hold it, okay?"

"Okay."

Before he could call her back, John cut in on the radio. "We've got her spotted. She's at my three o'clock and about three miles."

"Fabulous. Millie, did you hear that? Our chief pilot is coming to help you. If you look out your left window, you'll see another Cessna coming to help you."

There was another of those disquieting pauses, and then she said, "Oh, I see him!"

"His name is John, and he is going to talk you all of the way down to this airport, okay?"

John's deep husky voice said, "Hi, Millie, you're doing great. Now I'm going to help you do a couple of things. First, I want you to turn just a little more toward me. Do it just like you did the last two turns. Millic, that was perfect. Are you sure you are not a veteran pilot?"

Jim thought, *Good for you. Your smooth radio-announcer voice is having a calming effect on her, that and the fact she could see him. Of course he couldn't get too close—she could panic and crash into him, destroying both planes. It had happened before, when someone was trying to help a nonpilot.*

John was back on the radio. "Millie, do you see those two black things right in the middle of the bottom of the instrument panel? One is pushed all of the way in, and the other is pulled partway out?"

"Yes."

"Millie, the one on the left is the throttle, and the one on the right is the mixture control. Here is what I want you to do. First, I want you to push the one on the right all of the way in, okay?"

"Okay."

"Great, now I don't want you to ever touch that one again until I tell you to. Now I want you to pull the one on the left out about an inch. No more than one inch, do you understand?"

Jim thought, *No wonder he is a great instructor. Listen to him.*

"Millie, now your airplane is going to go down to a lower altitude, but that is okay. I'll be right here beside you, okay?"

Her voice sounded like a little girl's voice when she said, "Okay."

"Millie, you are doing so good. Now turn your yoke just a little more until the nose of your airplane is pointed straight at the northern tip of that lake,"

Now they were about fifteen minutes out. The fire truck and paramedics were already there at the airport. The most dangerous part was yet to come—when they tried to talk an untrained pilot into landing an airplane.

"Millie, you are doing great. Now do you see that big water tower right in front of us, about five miles?"

"Yes,"

"Keep your airplane pointed right at that water tower. You are doing so good," John said.

Now they were ten minutes out. Jim could see out the window a crowd was gathering in front of the cafe. He thought, *That may not be a good idea. What if she crashed into the crowd? It was two hundred feet from the front of the cafe to the runway, which normally was a long way, but anything could happen if she panicked and lost control of that airplane.*

"Millie, you're doing great. Do you see that little town down there in front of us, about five more miles?"

"Yes,"

"Now, Millie, when we get to that hill, I am going to have you turn to the right a little. I'm going to turn with you. You're doing so good. They've got an ambulance waiting to take your husband to the hospital. Maybe it's not too late. We can always hope, can't we?"

Jim thought, *John, you are doing a fabulous job of keeping her calm. He knows when she makes the right turn he just told her about. She will be lined up with this airport. Jim had always liked John. He was quiet and confident, but his admiration for him had shot way up in the last few minutes.*

"Okay, Millie, I want you to take hold of the yoke with your right hand. I want you to curl your little finger into the palm of your hand and hold the yoke with the other three fingers. Can you do that?"

"Okay."

Jim thought, *My goodness that is smart. By keeping her pinky (little finger) curled up in her palm, she could not get a death grip on the yoke. I would never have thought of that.* Jim looked up and saw two sheriffs' cars racing into the airport. There were two fire engines and an ambulance already sitting there with their red-and-blue lights flashing. Then he looked at the road that ran parallel to the airport on the west side, and there must have been a hundred cars lined up with people sitting on the cars. His first thought was, *How did they get here?*

"Millie, I want you to gently turn the yoke to the right until your airplane is lined up with that highway down there. When you can see the highway out in front, I want you to level the yoke back up for me. Okay, Millie, do it now. I'm going to be right here. I'm going to talk you through it.""

Her voice seemed a little shakier. "Okay, don't leave me," she pleaded.

"Millie, I am right off your left wing. Just keep turning gently. I'm right here."

Several people had handheld portable radios, so everybody in front of the cafe could hear every word of the drama as it unfolded. They heard John say, "Okay, Millie, now straighten it out. Good. Now I want you to pull that little throttle back another half an inch. Do it just like you did before, just pull it out another half inch."

Then they heard a lady's voice, "I'm so scared."

"I know you are, but just hang in there. We are almost home. Now, Millie, do you see all of those white buildings just east of the freeway?"

"Yes, I see them."

"That is the airport. If you look right between the hangars, you will see the runway."

Now the panic was back. "I can't do this. I can't land the plane!"

"Millie, we can do it together. I'm going to move in closer to you. We'll go in side by side. You can do this, Millie. You see, I'm a flight instructor. When we get down, I'm going to get you a logbook and log in your first solo flight and sign it myself. You're doing great. We are descending at the right rate. Move over just a tiny little bit to your left. You know I'm over here, but I will stay out of your way. Just a little tiny bit more. That's perfect. Now you are lined up with the runway, don't turn anymore. I am going to move in a little closer so we can go in side by side. Don't turn your head and look at me. From now on, I want you to only look at the runway."

Jim thought, *He is getting too close. If she jinks left, she will take out both planes. He wanted to yell for John to move back out but decided it would guarantee a midair collision if she panicked and turned hard left right into John's plane.* Everyone in the crowd stopped breathing for two full minutes.

"Millie, you are right on target. There is a big wheel by your left knee. Do you see it?"

"Yes,"

"Take your left hand, and roll it to back one turn. No! Millie, do not turn your head! Keep your eyes on the runway in front of you. Good, good. Just let the plane fly itself on down, and when I tell you to, pull the throttle all of the way back. Wait until I tell you, though," John calmly talked to her.

They came over the fence at the north end side by side. When they were about twenty five feet above the ground, John said, "Now, Millie, pull the throttle all the way back." As he said that, his plane pulled up to go around. She kept coming down for a few seconds; then her plane slammed on to the runway. It bounced at least twenty feet back into the air. It slammed down again, but this time, it was not lined up straight down the runway. So it shot off the runway into the grass on the west side of the runway and headed straight for some of the cars parked on the road. Everything seemed to be in slow motion. Jim saw her plane hit the runway and bounce back into the air; then he saw it angle toward the cars parked on the road.

Oh no, she is going to plough into that crowd beside the cars.

Then all at once, the front tire hit a little drainage culvert. The airplane's nose dipped down. Then the plane stood up on its prop slowly. Then all at once it slammed down over on its back. The two fire trucks were racing across the runway. Several of the onlookers were running across the runway. All at once, Jim looked up, and there was John coming back to land. There were twenty people in the middle of the runway. John added a tiny bit of power and lifted his plane past all of the confusion and landed gently about halfway down the six-thousand-foot runway.

By the time Jim got to the plane, the firemen had hoses trained on it in case it burst into flames, and the paramedics were pulling a lady out of the plane and onto a backboard. Two other firemen were trying to get her husband out of the plane. He thought, *We still don't know if he is alive or dead. At least we know she was alive a few moments ago.* Then he saw a fireman grab an IV and insert it into her husband's vein. Then he thought, *Oh, thank God, they don't put IVs in dead men.*

Then for the first time he looked at the plane, it had been a pretty little 172, but it was definitely totaled now. Jim saw a car driving across the grass, with US Government licenses plates on it. He thought, *Well at least we won't have to call the FAA.*

All at once, he noticed a helicopter hovering over the runway with a news cameraman hanging out the side.

The next day, the salvage company had a large truck with a big crane mounted on it. They lifted the little Cessna up and turned it over. The front wheel had been broken off in the impact. They ran a trailer up under the nose and gently pulled the airplane away from the runway. They efficiently stripped off the wings and then loaded the airplane onto the trailer. Then the wings were loaded on beside her, all efficiently and unemotionally.

Millie had broken a few ribs and a collar bone and suffered a bunch of scratches and bruises. Her husband's story was far from good. He had undergone a triple bypass last night. His chances of survival were pretty good. Horrible of all horrible was that, he now had lost his medical certificate, and without that, he would never be able to fly again. For a pilot, there is one thing worse than death. That is to lose his ability to fly.

All of the way home, Jim kept thinking about that. Joe was only one year older than Jim. Joe had just finished his physical last month and passed with flying colors. Now he was grounded.

As Jim walked into the cafe this morning to get a cup of coffee, John Henry, one of the regular cafe crowd, stopped him and said, "You know, Jim, we have had more excitement on this airport since you bought this place. You opened a cafe?"

22

TRIP TO BRAZIL

Jim started to his office. As he walked through the lobby, they were cutting the tail off a young man's shirt. Jim thought, *That's an old-time tradition when anyone soloed the first time. The instructor would take a pair of scissors and cut the tail off the student's shirt and then write the date and aircraft tail number on the piece of cloth. Then we will hang it up on the wall for the entire world to see. Until he got his license, then we will take down and place it in a picture frame for the pilot to take home with him.*

Jim walked over and shook the young man's hand, congratulating him. Then he told him, "I still have my shirttail in its frame hanging in my office at home. So you have made the most important step in becoming a full-fledged pilot? Hurry up and let us frame it for you."

He then walked back and chatted with Ralph a few minutes. Ralph had the King Aire in the shop. "Ralph, what's wrong with the King Aire?" Jim was a little alarmed to see it in here rather than in its hangar.

"Nothing. We are just doing an inspection. Derrick has been flying her a lot lately. In fact, he has a party going to Las Vegas this Friday."

John walked in and Jim said, "John, before we talk about anything else, let me tell you again what a fantastic job you did talking that lady down. That was unbelievable."

"I didn't do it by myself. You talked to her first and the longest."

"Yeah, and I was terrified the whole time I was talking to her," Jim replied.

"Do you think I wasn't?"

Both Ralph and Jim said, "You sure didn't sound like it."

"Can both of you guys come up to my office a minute? I've got my passport back, so Monday morning, I'm going to make them take my deposition first. Derrick and I are going to take off to Brazil. Kelly and a couple of lawyers from the insurance company are going to be here. You guys just play it by ear. Just handle anything that comes up whatever way feels right."

"How long are you going to be gone?" John asked.

"I don't know. I saw on the Internet another plane crashed in Australia that sounded mighty suspicious. I'm going to stay as long as it takes to find out about that plane crash in Brazil."

The weather was misty rain and low-hanging clouds. Monday morning, Derrick and Jim boarded the King Aire for a flight to Brazil.

Jim was in the left seat, which meant Derrick would be working the radios. As they lined up on the runway, Jim looked over at Derrick. "Is checklist complete?"

"Yes, Captain, we're ready to go. We're supposed to be off by ten minutes after the hour. You are clear to go." Jim placed his right hand on the big throttles. Derrick placed his left hand down on the levers below Jim's hand as a backup. The King Aire roared down the runway, creating a violent spray of water and mist in its wake.

Derrick started calling out speeds. "Sixty, eighty, one hundred, rotation."

Jim never took his eyes off the runway rushing beneath the big plane. When he heard rotation, he pulled gently back on the control yoke and the airplane leaped up into the clouds.

Jim called out, "Wheels up."

Derrick grabbed the lever that raised the landing gear.

"Good morning, departure control, this is King Aire three six five Charley Alpha, off Millport, runway heading assigned, climbing through two four five, squawking sixty-three twelve," Derrick told Fort Worth control center.

"Good morning, three six five Charley Alpha, radar contact three miles south of Millport. Climb and maintain ten thousand. Fly heading one three zero direct to Cedar, then as filed to New Orleans. Expect higher in ten minutes."

"Out four for ten, direct to Cedar, and then as filed to New Orleans, expect higher in ten," Derrick read back.

The airplane felt big in Jim's hands yet as nimble as an eagle in flight. Jim's eyes were fixed on the instruments in front of him. If he had looked outside, he would not have seen anything except the inside of the dark rain-filled cloud. Then like a cork that has been held under water, the airplane popped up out of the cloud into bright clear sunshine.

Jim engaged the autopilot and reached down and snapped the cap off the cup of coffee that Christie had given both of them just before they boarded the airplane. Jim said, "Wow, I can't see anything on the ground."

"We should we should be clear of the clouds when we get in western Louisiana. Should be clear all the way from New Orleans to Miami. You did remember to bring your new passport, didn't you?"

"Yep."

"Charley Alpha, change to departure control on one three two point ninety-two, good day," the flight control center instructed them.

Derrick keyed his mic. "Charley Alpha changing to one three two point ninety-two, see ya'll."

"Good morning, departure control, this is three six five Charley Alpha, at ten thousand assigned, looking for higher."

"Good morning, three six five Charley Alpha, continue at ten until past Cedar, then climb on course to twenty niner."

"Charley Alpha, ten to Cedar, then climb on course to twenty niner," Derrick read back.

"It is funny how we always say *niner*, rather than *nine* on the radio," Jim said.

"They discovered when radios first came into airplanes that *nine* and *five* sound alike over the radio, so someone figured out that by saying *niner* for *nine* the controller and pilots could keep them straight."

"I have never thought about why we did that. It's just the way I was taught to say *niner*."

"Did they take your deposition?"

"Yep, and we took Timothy's dad's. He's one lying scumbag. He swore under oath that he had never pushed his son to learn to fly or pushed him to play football or anything."

"I heard him with my own ears yelling at Timothy to get in there and be a man. He actually told the boy it was time for him to quit being a mama's boy. I felt so sorry for the kid. I wanted to punch the old man." Derrick asked, "Has anybody come up with a plausible theory as to why Timothy crashed?"

"No, that is the scary part. If we knew why Timothy crashed, we could take steps to see that it couldn't happen again. Until we know what happened to Timothy, I am terrified that it will happen to another student," Jim said.

"There is the Cedar radio beam turning to New Orleans and climbing to twenty niner thousand."

The controller called. "Three six five Charley Alpha, switch to Fort Worth Center, on one three eight point five five, have a good flight."

"Charley Alpha switching to enter one three eight point five five, see ya'll," Derrick replied.

They had to wait for a few moments while the center controller was talking to other airplanes. Finally, there was a break. Derrick called in, "Good morning, center, this is three six five Charley Alpha, out of fifteen climbing to twenty niner on course."

"Three six five Charley Alpha, level at eighteen." The controller called back.

"Jim, what is that all about? Why is he making us stay at eighteen?"

"Ask him."

"Center, this is Charley Alpha, we were cleared to twenty nine. Why are we being held down here at eighteen?"

For noise control," the controller called right back.

"What?" Derrick and Jim looked at each other.

Derrick keyed his mic. "Noise control? We are miles from any populated area."

"Yes, sir, but it is going to make a lot of noise if you collide with that seven four seven coming from the opposite direction descending to land at Dallas Fort Worth."

"I gotcha. No more questions."

Jim laughed and said, "That was good."

"Charley Alpha, traffic opposite direction a seven four seven out of twenty five for fifteen, twelve o'clock five miles."

"Charley Alpha, looking. No joy," Derrick answered.

"Jim, I can't see him, but I have a blip on the collision avoidance screen."

They then heard the controller tell the 747 that he had traffic four miles at eighteen thousand from the opposite direction.

"That would be us he just warned the seven four seven about."

Then the heard the captain of the 747 say, "No joy on the traffic, but we do have him on the fish finder."

"I guess that collision avoidance display does resemble the fish finder I have in my boat."

"I have him in sight." He keyed his mic and said, "Charley Alpha has traffic in sight," Derrick said.

"Maintain visual separation with traffic," The controller said.

They heard the airliner say, "Flight four seven six has traffic in sight."

"Maintain visual separation with traffic."

"Derrick, where is he? I don't see him."

Derrick pointed to a tiny silver speck in the sky above and in front of them.

They both sat and watched as a tiny speck grew larger and larger.

"He is going to pass just off to our left. You should get a good look at him from your side," Derrick said.

When the giant airliner was about a mile in front and just to the left of them, he flashed his landing lights in salute. Jim responded by flashing their landing lights, and the giant plane swept by. They could see people in the windows waving at them. Obviously, the captain had told everyone one the left side of the airliner to look out the window, and they would see another plane passing by.

"It's always fun when you see one of those knights of the sky passing by."

The controller called and said, "Three six five Charley Alpha, traffic no longer a factor. Climb to flight level two niner zero."

Leveling off at twenty nine thousand feet over the farms and ranches of Texas, Jim asked, "How far is it from New Orleans to the coast?"

"Huum, maybe twenty miles."

"After we roar out over the Gulf of Mexico, how far will it be before we see land again?"

Derrick quickly looked at the chart on his kneeboard that he had strapped to his right thigh. Derrick answered, "Four hundred and fifty three nautical miles."

"Do you mean that for about an hour and a half we will not be able to see land?"

"Something like that."

"Are you telling me that doesn't make you just a little bit nervous?"

"I just look at the gauges," Derrick said. "As long as we have plenty of fuel and all of the engine instruments are in the green, I'm not the least bit nervous. Now let one of those needles on one of those instruments move out of the green zone. Then you probably would see me getting just a little bit nervous or maybe a whole lot nervous, depending on which needle it was and how far it moved out of the green zone."

"I guess you've got a point there. It's just that I have never flown out over the ocean before. Hey, look at those ships down there. I never realized you can see his trail in the water for a mile or two behind him. That is pretty interesting."

"From up here, you can see there really is a lot of traffic on the Gulf of Mexico. There are a lot more ships out there than I ever thought there were."

"Three six five Charley Alpha, switch to international control one twenty-one point seventy-five, good day," the controller called.

"Charley Alpha going to international on one twenty-one point seventy-five, good day," Derrick replied.

"Good morning, international, this is King Aire three six five Charley Alpha with you at flight level two niner zero."

A deep Southern drawl called back and said, "Goood moornin', Charley Alpha, no traffic observed in this sector at your altitude."

"Charley Alpha, roger."

There were no more radio calls to three six five Charley Alpha for almost an hour.

During that time, Derrick asked, "Exactly what do you hope to find down here?"

"I want to know, did that airplane down here break its crankshaft in flight and had it ever had a prop strike? I still don't believe that minor prop strike is what caused my crankshaft to break in flight. Don't misunderstand me. I hold that doctor responsible for my wife's death, because if he had followed the law, they more than likely would have found whatever problem that engine had before it blew up on me. Once I find who is responsible, unless it was an act of God, I am going to destroy his life. Just like he destroyed mine."

"Did you bring some good old American hundred-dollar bills with you? I understand that you can get all kinds of corporation down here if you have a few of those with you."

"I sure as heck did," Jim said, "because I intend to see those logbooks and that crash investigation report."

"Can you see that dark spot in the water way out on the horizon?"

Jim, looking intently, said, "Yes."

"That is land. That will be Florida."

At that moment, the international controller called and said, "Charley Alpha, descend and maintain flight level one eight zero. Contact Miami center on one one eight point five. Ya'll have a good day."

"Charley Alpha, out of twenty niner for one eight zero, going to center one one eight point five, good day."

Landing at the Miami airport, they followed the little golf cart with the "Follow me" sign up to the private terminal. There, a red carpet was rolled out from the door of the terminal so that when Jim let down the stair door you stepped out of the airplane onto the red carpet. Jim thought, *Maybe I should get some of those red carpet at Millport.*

It took two hours to get through customs and get clearance from the Cuban IACC (the equivalent to the American FAA) to allow them to fly over the island. The fuel tanks were topped off, and water and other emergency rations were stowed on board.

"Derrick, it's not like going to Milwaukee, is it?"

"First stop, Caracas, which is thirteen hundred nautical miles. Which will take us about four hours. I have a hotel reservation there. Then from there to Manaus, Brazil, then direct to Brasilia."

"How far from Caracas to Manaus?"

"One thousand fifty."

"And from Manaus to Brasilia?"

"Another twelve hundred," Derrick said.

"My gosh, do you man we have thirty-five hundred miles to go before we get to Brasilia. That is a lot of flying."

"Hey, if it was easy, the girl scouts would be doing it instead of us he-man pilots."

Jim laughed. "Derrick, that was kinda dumb, but I guess I got the point."

Derrick, laughing, said, "Are you ready?"

"Thank God we have a potty on board."

"Miami ground, King Aire three six five Charley Alpha, ready to taxi." Jim was now in the right seat, so he called the ground controller.

"King Aire Charley Alpha, taxi to runway one six right. Contact tower on one one eight point three."

"King Aire three six five Charley Alpha, with you at runway one six right, ready to go."

The tower called and said, "Six five Charley Alpha, cleared for takeoff. Fly runway heading. Contact departure on one twenty three point eight five. Have a good flight."

"Is checklist complete?"

Jim ran his finger one more time down the checklist and said, "Checklist is complete. Ready for takeoff."

As they roared off into the bright Florida sunshine out over the blue waters of the bay, Jim radioed the departure controller. "Good morning, departure, King Aire six five Charley Alpha out of five climbing to flight level two one zero, squawking three three seven eight."

"Good morning, six-five Charley-Alpha, continue climb to flight level two one. Turn right to a heading of two two oh."

"Continue climb to two one. Turn right to a heading of two two zero."

It seemed they had just leveled at twenty one thousand feet when the controller called and said, "King Aire three six five Charley Alpha, contact Cuban control on one three three point seven seven. Good day."

"Going to Cuban control on one thirty three point seventy seven. Good day."

An ominous sounding voice replied, "King Aire November three six five Charley Alpha, this is Cuban IACC control. Climb to twenty-five thousand, and maintain heading of two two zero. Do not deviate from these instructions. You will get no other warning."

"November three six five Charley Alpha, climb to twenty-five thousand, and maintain heading of two two zero, exact." He then turned to Derrick and said, "That sounded scary."

"Yeah, well look out your right window."

Jim gave a startled "Oh my gosh." There sat a Cuban Mig fighter with rockets hanging off its wings.

Jim reached down and picked up his camera and aimed it out the window and flashed picture.

"Jim, I don't think I would do that again if I were you."

The Mig sat right there for almost an hour; then the Cuban controller called and said, "King Aire November three six five Charley Alpha, you are leaving Cuban airspace. Contact international controller on one twenty-two point five."

Jim let his breath out and said, "I am glad that is over." He looked, and the Mig banked right and away.

They landed on runway 22 at Simon Bolivar Airport, which is located in the town of Maiquetia. It was about a thirty-minute ride in a Black SUV that served as the official airport shuttle service to their hotel in Caracas. All the way, Jim marveled at the beautiful palm trees and flowering shrubbery. Allie would have loved this place.

It was a beautiful city nestled between the coast and the high mountains. They ate at a fabulous seafood restaurant. As they were walking back to the hotel, two men stepped out from behind a large palm tree.

"Money," one said, holding a huge hunting knife, waving it menacingly.

Without thinking about it, Jim shifted his weight to the ball of his left foot and, spinning around on his left foot, did a spinning kick with his right foot. The heel of his right cowboy boot struck the would-be robber squarely on the point of his chin, fracturing his jawbone immediately. This caused the robber to drop his knife, and both robbers turned and ran away.

"Do you want to keep this for a souvenir?" Derrick said as he picked up the knife.

"Let me have it," Jim said. He then walked over to a crack in the sidewalk, pushed the blade down into the crack, and kicked the knife handle, breaking the blade off.

"Where did you learn to kick like you did?"

"Years ago, buddy, and I got a black belt in karate, but it has been so long I am surprised that I could still do it."

"You weren't nearly as surprised as our robber friend was. I heard his jaw break."

———————

"What time do you want to take off in the morning?"

"What time is it now?" Jim asked. "My watch is still on Dallas time."

Derrick looked at his flight watch, which showed four different time zones. "Dallas time is seven thirty. Caracas time is nine thirty."

"I want to get up early and run along the beach. Let's plan on taking off at nine o'clock Caracas time."

"You've got it. Here is our hotel. I'll file a flight plan and leave a wake-up call. Are you going to eat breakfast?"

"No, I'll grab something when I get back from running, good night."

The beauty of the next morning was breathtaking, as Jim ran along the beach. He kept thinking, *there have been three plane crashes. We know of two that crashed after the engine blew and sprayed oil all over the windshield. Those we are investigating. What about Timothy's crash? How could a perfectly good Cessna trainer crash, killing a student? If a control cable broke, it would have continued to fly straight and level. He could have turned with his rudder. We know the engine was still developing full power when it hit the ground.*

As Jim was getting dressed after his run, he flipped on CNN. The lead story was a single-engine airplane crashed in Kentucky, killing two. The pilot reported that he was experiencing engine failure, and then all transmission stopped. Jim froze to stare at the screen with his shirt half on and half off, then looked at his watch. It was only 7:00 a.m. in Dallas. When they landed at Manaus, he would call Mike. His gut was telling him, *The FAA had to do something.*

As they were climbing out, there were clouds building to the southwest. "Boss, we'll be getting rained on when we stop in Manaus for fuel. It rains alone the equator almost every day. Usually the rain is not thunderstorms, like we see in Texas."

They landed in Manaus about one o'clock local time. The flight was uneventful, even if they did have some trouble understanding the controller's English.

"I wonder who decided that all communication with air traffic controllers had to be done in English?"

"I don't know, but I am glad they did, because my Spanish is not that good."

As soon as they had cleared Brazilian customs, Jim used his cell phone to call Mike. "Mike, this is Jim Colburn."

"Jim, how are you?"

"Fine, Mike. I'm down in Brazil. This morning I saw a report on CNN about a single-engine plane crash after experiencing the loss of an engine."

"I haven't heard about it yet. Where did it go down?"

"Bowling Green, Kentucky."

"I don't know anything about it, Jim. You've got to remember pilots crash six airplanes every day somewhere."

————————————

Manus turned out to be a beautiful city of one and a half million people. It was known as the Paris of the Tropics. While the airport people were fueling the King Aire, Jim and Derrick took a courtesy car to a restaurant recommended by the airport personnel.

"Man, I love all of the colors here," Jim said as they drove to the restaurant.

"The rain is letting up. We should have no trouble getting out of here," Derrick commented while driving back to the airport.

Four hours later, they landed in Brasilia.

"Jim, do you know where to go when we get here?"

"I talked to the American embassy, and they are expecting me. I'll start there. While I am going through the diplomatic channels, I want you to hang around the pilot's lounge and talk to pilots. See if you can find out anything."

"Jim, that's a good idea. You know what a grapevine there is in the pilot community."

That evening, when they got back to the hotel,

"All I'm getting is the runaround. How did you do?" Jim said.

"I met the brother-in-law of the air traffic controller who was on duty the day the plane crashed."

"And?"

"And we are going to meet the two brother-in-laws at a restaurant down on the river front at seven."

"Hey, you the man."

Jim called and talked to John, who said, "So far everything is good. We haven't had anything unusual happen here in the last twenty-four hours."

Jim had a handheld portable GPS, so they had no trouble finding the restaurant.

"There's our guy," Derrick said when they walked in. Brazilian beef turned out to be quite good, and the two locals suggested that they try a local red wine, which also turned out to be very good.

"Gentlemen, let me tell you why we're here. I was flying a Bonanza a few months ago that sheared a crankshaft and sprayed oil all over my windshield. While trying to make an emergency landing in a forested area, I struck the trees and crashed." His voice broke when he said, "My wife was killed. I want to find out about the Bonanza that crashed. Did the same thing happen to him? So what can you tell me?"

"Senor, I was on duty when a Mayday call came in. I was the controller that answered the call. The pilot reported that he had suffered a total loss of power and his windshield was completely covered with oil and he had a fire in his engine area."

"The poor guy didn't have a chance. Is there any way you can get me a copy of the tape from that time?" Jim slowly shook his head.

"It would be very difficult, senor."

"I'll pay five hundred American for a copy of the tape between you and the pilot."

"That would be five hundred apiece, senor." The brother-in-law spoke up.

"Five hundred a piece if the audiotape is legible. There is one other thing. Is there any way to get a copy of the accident report?"

"I don't know, senor. I will ask around. I work from seven to three tomorrow. I will call your hotel when I get off and tell you if I have copies of the tape."

The next morning, Jim went running through the streets of Brasilia, past some beautiful old churches, flower gardens, and water fountains. He was struck by the contrast between the ancient buildings and the modern noise of car horns and car engines.

He had just got out of the shower when the phone rang in his room. He answered, "Jim Colburn."

A voice on the phone said, "Mr. Colburn, this is Chauncey Gilliland from the embassy. We have arranged for you to meet with a member of the Brazilian air safety board for lunch today if that is convenient."

"Absolutely. When and where?"

"He'll meet you at his office, at one four three three San Polo Boulevard, at twelve o'clock. His name is Senor Pedro de Manuel. I will personally meet you there to act as an interpreter. I hope this is helpful."

"I'm sure it'll be." Then he flipped on CNN. He was almost afraid to turn on the TV now. He was afraid he would find another plane had crashed, killing more people.

Jim showed up at the appointed time and was escorted into the office of Pedro de Manuel, where he found that Mr. Gilliland was already waiting with Mr. Pedro de Manuel.

Over lunch, Mr. Manuel was very gracious, and Jim liked listening to the tone and cadence of the Portuguese language. It was smoother and slower in pace than the Spanish language, but to his surprise, because he could speak Spanish, he found that he could understand a good bit of what Mr. Manuel was saying before the guy from the embassy interpreted it.

Mr. Manuel said, "I am very sorry, but we are not allowed to give copies of our internal accident investigations to foreigners."

When Jim got back to the hotel, Derrick was waiting for him. "It seems that our newfound friends can get a copy of the report for us, but it will cost two thousand dollars American."

They talked about it a few minutes; then Jim said, "Let's call his bluff. Call him back, and tell him that I just had lunch with Mr. Pedro de Manuel, and he can have a copy for me in three days, and it won't cost me any money."

"No," he said, "I am very sorry, but we are not allowed to share our internal investigations with foreigners."

"So, Jim, you really are bluffing?"

"Yeah, but go ahead, and tell your guy we can get them free in three days. Tell him I am anxious to get back, so I'll pay one thousand dollars if we can get the report tonight. What about the tape?"

"Haven't heard from the controller yet. He gets off work in half an hour."

When they met later that evening with the two brothers-in law, they delivered the tape and a copy of the accident report. The only problem was that the accident report was written in Portuguese. At this meeting, they also found out that a salvage dealer in Sao Paolo had the wreckage of that Bonanza.

When they got back to the hotel, Jim called the salvage dealer, who did speak English. Jim told him that he was in Brasilia on business. He had a Bonanza and needed some parts. Then he explained that he had been told the dealer had a wrecked Bonanza with an engine similar to the one his Bonanza had.

"Yes, senor, I do have a salvage of the type you speak. Can you tell me the parts you need?"

"I would like to talk with you about buying the entire salvage and shipping it back to the United States."

"Come on down, and we will talk."

Filing a flight plan, Derrick calculated that it was 550 miles, which with time to climb and descend would take about two hours.

"King Aire November three six five Charley Alpha, ready for takeoff." Jim called the tower.

"November three six five Charley Alpha cleared for takeoff. Right turn to heading of one eight zero. Climb and maintain ten thousand. Expect higher in ten minutes."

"November three six five Charley Alpha cleared for takeoff. Right turn to heading of one eight zero. Climb and maintain ten thousand. Expect higher in ten," Jim read back.

"Read back is correct."

Derrick pointed the nose up, and they were climbing at a rate of 2,500 feet a minute. In only four minutes, they were level at ten thousand feet.

"November three six five Charley Alpha, level at ten," Jim reported.

"November three six five Charley Alpha, climb to flight level one niner zero."

"November three six five Charley Alpha, climb to flight level one niner zero."

Soon they could see the Pacific Ocean wrapping around the south end of the continent. In about an hour, the controller called and said, "November three six five Charley Alpha, descend and maintain ten thousand."

"November three six five Charley Alpha, descend and maintain ten thousand." Then he turned to look at Derrick and said, "I will be glad when we get back in the United States so I won't have to say the entire call sign every time."

"Yeah, I have been listening to you, and I'm happy that it is you in the right seat instead of me."

"Wise guy, when we leave here, I am going to take that seat and you can deal with these guys."

When they got to the salvage yard, Jim told the dealer, "Sir, I had a Bonanza just like that one out there, and last fall, I had a crankshaft break in flight, rupturing the outside of the engine and spraying oil all over the windshield. I crashed into the forest." Then he pulled out a picture of Allie and showed to the old gentleman. "My wife was killed. I came here because I want to prove that there is something wrong with these engines. Please sell me that busted engine. I want a receipt showing that it came off this airplane. Then I want to load it into my King Aire and haul it back with me."

The old gentleman sat there, holding Allie's picture in his hand, and said, "Your wife reminds me of my Maria. God rest her soul. She died ten years ago, of the cancer. I cannot do anything for my Maria, but maybe I can do something for your Allie. Senor, I will not sell you the engine."

"You won't sell it to me?"

"No, senor, I am going to give it to you. Maybe you can save someone else's wife."

Three hours later, Jim was in the left seat, and Derrick was working the radios. Twenty five hours and four fuel stops later, two tired and weary pilots climbed stiff legged out of the King Aire at Millport.

"I don't know about you, but I'm going to get a hot shower and sleep for about twelve hours," Jim said.

"Sounds good to me, but first we need to get that junk engine out of the King Aire."

"Aye, aye, Captain. Let's go find Ralph."

Ralph looked up as Jim and Derrick walked in and said, "I thought you two were still sitting under a palm tree in South America."

"This time yesterday we were, and you should see that native girls down there."

"Don't listen to him, Ralph. We never saw a native girl closer than a hundred yards away. We do have something in the airplane that we want you to take care of for us."

"Whatcha got? A case of Jamaican rum?"

Derrick said, "We didn't even come close to Jamaica."

"Ralph, we have the tape recording of the pilot reporting that he has had a complete engine failure, and we have a copy of the Brazilian accident report showing that the crankshaft was broken in flight."

"You boys did good."

Derrick said, "Ralphie, that ain't all."

"Don't call me Ralphie, knucklehead."

"Ralph, we have the engine off that Bonanza that crashed in Brazil. I want you to send this crankshaft in for testing and tell those people we want the report back now." Jim spoke up.

"Boss, now somebody is going to have to listen."

"Not until we can prove there is a flaw in the assembly or the oil we are using or something," Jim said.

"I will get right on it. Let's get the engine unloaded," Ralph said. "How did you two manage to get all of this, including the actual engine?"

"Jim went down there and kicked butt."

"Actually, Derrick did most of it. I was trying to go through legal channels. He hung around pilot's lounges and found the people who got the things we needed."

23

THE KIDNAPPING

The next morning, John was filling Jim in on the depositions. "Jim, that father of Timothy is a real piece of work. When they took his deposition, he swore under oath that he had never pushed his son to take flying lessons, and he definitely had never pushed us to let him solo."

"That lying bag of slime."

John sat toying with a desk clock made to look like an instrument from an airplane. "What have you found that is causing the rash of crashes?"

"It's like a plague of airplane crashes. It's frightening. I'm almost afraid to turn on the TV or look on the Internet. I'm terrified that I am going to see another deadly crash every day."

While they were talking, the phone rang.

"Jim Colburn, can I help you?"

"Mr. Colburn, this is Captain Homes from the sheriff's office."

Jim's heart almost stopped beating. He spun around and looked directly at John. John said, "Do you have another one of my airplanes down somewhere?"

"No, sir, why I'm calling is we desperately need your help. A little six-year-old girl had been kidnapped from the elementary school within the last hour. The county doesn't have any helicopters. Could you send one of your airplanes and help look for a suspect in a green Ford Bronco?"

Jim grabbed a sheet of paper and started writing as fast as he could. Jim asked, "What was the last known location of the Bronco? What color? Can you give me a radio frequency that would allow us to communicate with the sheriff's officers?"

"John, how many of our planes are on the ramp right now?" John looked out the window and said, "We have two trainers and both 172s."

"John that was the sheriff's office. A little first-grade girl was just kidnapped from the elementary school. The kidnapper was seen driving a green Ford Bronco. They want to know if we can assist them in searching for the green Ford Bronco."

Then they were both running down the stairs two at a time. When they burst into the pilots' lounge, two instructors were sitting there, talking. Jim said, "Listen up, guys, the sheriff's office just called, and a little first-grade girl has just been kidnapped from the elementary school. The kidnapper was seen driving a green Ford Bronco. They want to know if we can assist them in searching for the green Ford Bronco."

Every man there jumped to his feet, ready to go. They copied the sheet of paper that Jim had written on, and then they took a map and divided it into four quadrants.

"Each pilot, pick a quadrant. And write your name on it," Jim said.

Quickly, each instructor chose a section of the county. Then they assigned a frequency to put in their backup radio so that they could communicate with each other. Their primary radio would be tuned to the sheriff's frequency. There was some hurried planning; then each guy grabbed an airplane key and raced out to the ramp.

Jim stopped to call the sheriff's office and tell them that they had four planes taking off right now. He informed the sheriff's office of the quadrants that each plane would be patrolling in. When he ran back to get a key, the only thing left was a 152 trainer. He thought, *well, it's not fast, but it will fly slow enough to allow a thorough search of the ground beneath her.* Then he climbed in, or as he often thought, he put the little plane on like a jumpsuit. Jim hit the starter, and the little prop whirled over. Then the little 120-horsepower engine came to life.

He did the checklist as he was rolling down the taxiway. At the end of the runway, he did a quick HATS check, and the little plane sprinted down the runway. The sectional map was spread out on the seat next to him. His quadrant was north and east of the last known location of the Bronco. This area of the state was all rural farming and ranching country, with a lot of trees someone could hide a green Bronco under. Jim stayed just a hundred feet above the ground. He first cruised up Highway 59. Right now, he was cruising at 105 miles an hour, which was all the little 152 would do. He would slow down once he was in the area he wanted to really search in.

He could hear the sheriff's cars talking to each other; it was obvious from the transmissions that they knew what his boys were up to. The highway patrol had two cars in the area also. He had told the sheriff that they would have four planes, and they would call themselves Millport One, Two, Three, and Four.

All at once he heard:

"This is Millport One. I have a green Ford parked in a barn off farm road one one seven. All I can see is the front end. Can't tell if it is a pickup or a Bronco." The sheriff's officers wanted to know the exact location; they sent two patrol cars racing to that location.

The dispatcher told everyone else to keep looking until we determined if this was a Bronco or not. Then there was a call from a sheriff's cruiser. "Do you guys have an airplane in the area around Justice?"

"This is Millport Three. I am five miles north of Justice."

"Can you circle over this wooded area just northwest of town?" the officer asked.

"I'll be there in two minutes," Daren, the instructor flying Millport Three, replied.

Jim was trying not to be distracted by the two officers responding to the green Ford in a barn that One had called in and the circling that Three was doing. Now he was slowly circling over a large forested area with a lake in the middle of it. He could see baby calves nursing their mothers, baby colts frolicking in the open fields that dotted the forest area, but no Ford Bronco. Jim thought what he would do if that little six-year-old was one of his grandkids. Then he wished he had a rifle with him.

All at once, he saw a man standing under the shade of a tree, and he appeared to have a rifle aimed at Jim's little plane. Jim saw a puff of smoke from the end of the gun, and then he heard a *thunk*, as something hit the plane. Jim banked the plane to the right, which put the tree between him and the shooter. He looked, and there was a round hole in his left wing just past the gas tank. He was so stunned it took him a minute to gather his wits about him. "Sheriff, this is Millport Four. Somebody just shot a hole in my airplane."

"Say again."

"This is Millport Four. Somebody shot a hole in my airplane!"

"What is your location?"

"I am circling over a wooded area, just north of farm road eleven fourteen and east of farm road twenty-four seventy-one," Jim replied.

"Do you see any vehicles in the area?" the dispatcher asked.

"No, I saw one man with a rifle just before he fired the gun. He was standing under a tree, just southwest of that small lake down there,"

A deep voice came on the radio. "This is Sergeant Snyder. That is probably a meth lad back in those trees. Car 44, why don't you go check it out? Everybody else, keep searching."

"This is state two ninety-six. I am in that area I will back up forty-four."

Jim worked his controls back and forth. Everything seemed to be all right, but he couldn't keep his eyes off that hole in the wing. He wondered what the exit hole looked like. He couldn't keep his eyes from staying to the engine instruments. Now he had a hole in the wing to worry about. He debated with himself about taking the plane back for Ralph to look at, but decided that if that little girl was one of his kids there was no way he would quit searching.

Two other neighboring sheriff's agencies were sending in more police cruisers to help in the search, and the FBI had men in the area.

Jim must have seen a hundred green vehicles, but when he got closer, none of them were Broncos.

All at once, out of the corner of his eye, he saw just the tail end of a green Bronco sitting beside a run-down old house trailer back off the road in a wooded area. He stood the little Cessna on its wingtip and spun it back around.

"Sheriff, this is Millport Four. I am just off Woodland Road, and I see a dark-green Bronco parked beside a run-down old house trailer here."

"Can you give me a better location?" the dispatcher asked.

"No, there are no crossroads right here. I am north of FM two four two seven. I will climb up a little higher, and the cars coming this way should see me circling the trailer."

The dispatcher sent four cars immediately to that area. "Millport Four, watch for cars approaching that area, and when you see one, direct him in."

Jim then spotted a car coming all out from the south. Jim thought, *That guy is flying down that gravel road.* Jim keyed his mic, "Office coming from the south on one seven zero niner, when you get to the next intersection, turn left until that dead ends into Woodland. I am circling over the house trailer."

"I see you now."

Then he got on his radio and started giving coordinates to the other officers responding.

The dispatcher reminded everyone else to keep searching until they knew for sure if this was the right vehicle.

Jim could see three other large plumes of dust, which represented three other officers risking their lives driving that fast on these roads. He was five hundred feet up and had the throttle pulled back so far that the little plane was making almost no sound that could be heard on the ground, so whoever was in the trailer was not likely to even know he was up here. Then he thought, *If they have a gun. I hope they don't know I am up here. One battle scar was enough, thank you.*

He slowly and quietly kept the little trainer in a tight lazy circle over the house trailer area. He watched the officers arrive on the road near the driveway leading to the shabby-looking house trailer. Jim could hear the conversation between the officers on the ground and the dispatcher. The officers on the ground was pretty sure this was the vehicle. They called in the license number to the dispatcher. A few seconds later, the dispatcher called back. It is a stolen vehicle out of Fort Worth.

Now every car in the county was headed for this location. Jim felt so helpless. There was nothing he could from here but watch. He just prayed that this really was the right Bronco and that they were in time to keep anything really bad from happening to the little girl.

All four officers jumped out of their cars and talked just a few seconds; then they all jumped into two of the cars, leaving two out in the road. The two cars with the four officers in them roared down the driveway and, in a cloud of dust, braked to a halt right in front of the trailer. Officers leaped from the cars with guns drawn. One of them had a bullhorn. Jim couldn't hear what he was saying, but as he was talking into the bullhorn, one of the other officers ran around to the back of the house.

Jim heard Millport One say that he was running low on fuel and was returning to the airport. Jim thought, *that's right. They hadn't put any gas in the airplanes so they were sitting there with whatever they had when they last landed in their tanks.* He looked at his gas gauge. It was half full, so he could fly for another hour or more.

Jim looked down and counted seven squad cars here now. He watched as one of the officers fired what looked like a teargas canister through the front window of the trailer, and three officers immediately raced through the front door. At the same time, he saw two officer jump through the back door. Jim didn't realize it, but he was holding his breath. All at once, an officer came running out the front door, clutching what appeared to be a little girl tightly to his chest.

Jim slowly banked his plane to the southwest and advanced the throttle to get back up to cruise speed. He was so proud of his guys the way they responded without question when asked to do it. In his heart, he felt better than he had felt in a long time. Maybe his guys had helped save a little girl's life and a family a lifetime of heartache. Jim prayed, "God, thank you for allowing us to be your instruments to help save a child. Amen."

A few days later, the county sheriff and two of his deputies stopped by the hangar and presented the flight school with a framed citation for service to the community. The little girl was fine. She had not been physically hurt, and she and her family were going to counseling. The bad guy was a three-time loser, so he was not likely to ever get out of the pen again.

24

BILL HUETT'S CRASH

Jim had Ralph start checking with mechanics whom he knew. What he wanted to know was if they had any crankshafts on any engine that they had overhauled that failed to pass when they had them x-rayed.

In the meantime, the lawsuit by Timothy's father was getting to be a real nuisance. It was taking up so much time—dealing with the interrogatories and more depositions.

John came into Jim's office. Jim told John what he was having Ralph do. Then he asked, "John, do you think I am just wasting time? We know Timothy's crankshaft broke after it hit the ground. My Bonanza had an unreported prop strike. What if the lab report comes back and says the engine I brought back from Brazil shows signs of a previous prop strike? Should I just abandon this whole thing?"

"They told us in the military the war ain't over until the last hill is taken. What does your gut feeling tell you?"

"My gut tells me that there is a danger out there that no one is looking at." At that moment, Mike walked into Jim's office.

"Mike, what brings you out slumming with the working class?"

"I guess you haven't heard about Bill Hutt's RV-8."

John, who had turned to walk away, stopped in his tracks and looked back.

"What about Bill's RV-8?"

"It went down yesterday evening out near Spindletop."

"Don't tell me Bill was killed."

"Both Bill and Nancy."

Jim felt cold all over. Like someone had suddenly turned the air conditioner down ten degrees. "Did he lose it on landing or takeoff?"

"No, he was en route to El Paso and lost power over Spindletop. Thankfully, there was no postcrash fire. He went into the side of a hill. The wreckage is badly damaged, but forensics has a lot to work with since there was no fire."

"Mike, check to see if his engine was factory remanufactured. I'm getting a feeling something is going wrong in the remanufacturing process. Are they putting the crankshaft back in without proper alignment?"

"I heard that you went to Brazil and that you actually got a copy of their accident report. Is that right?"

"Yes."

"Why didn't you bring it to me when you got back?"

"Mike, first of all, the report is in Portuguese. I had to have it translated. That's not all. I have a copy of the tape between the pilot and the air traffic controller."

"You have the actual tape?"

"I am not sure if it is the original or a copy, but you can clearly hear the pilot saying he has engine oil all over his windshield. Mike, I also came back with something else."

"What?"

"I have the engine off that Bonanza from Brazil."

"You have the actual engine."

"Yes."

"Where is it?"

"I sent it to Aleszka Testing Labs to have it lab tested."

"Jim, you can't be holding up an ongoing investigation by withholding evidence."

"Mike, I am not withholding anything. I'm a private citizen. I went to Brazil and, with my own money, procured certain items that are of interest to me. I just got back the translation and copies of the tape. I will gladly give a copy to you. When the lab report comes back on the engine, I will give that to you also. Mike, I have a feeling there is something you are not telling me about Bill's airplane. What is it?"

"I'm not sure I should be telling you anything since you are running all over the globe, conducting your own investigation."

"Mike, you told me yourself that you couldn't get a copy of the Brazil accident report. You said they wouldn't share that information with the FAA. I just gave you a copy. Now what is it you are not telling me about Bill's crash?"

"Crash investigators found the windshield coated with motor oil."

25

THE LAWSUIT

The lawsuit brought by Timothy's father was coming to trial in four days. The insurance company offered several times to settle it, but Jim's liability coverage was only for five million; and Rufus Arnold was suing for twenty million, claiming negligence, improper training, and improper maintenance of the airplanes.

"Jim, as your attorney, I must tell you, you have got to settle this thing. If you were to lose, you would be bankrupt. Your insurance will only cover up to five million. You could lose, your business, everything. You have got to let them settle."

"No, I will not pay that man for forcing his son to take flying lessons. We did nothing wrong. His training was good. The airplane was well maintained. No, I will not give in to blackmail."

"If Rufus Arnold were to win, we will appeal, but that would incur more attorney's fees and waste a lot more time."

As soon as Jim hung the phone up, he went back to the pile of documents he had on the engines.

Jim was having a difficult time pursuing all of the possibilities on the failed engines because of the time spent on this lawsuit. Jim was still sitting in his office, going over the reams of material already collected for the suit when David popped in.

"Grandpa, I have something here you need to see." Turning his laptop around so that it faced Jim, he sat it on Jim's desk. "Read that."

Jim didn't know what he was looking at, but he could recognize Timothy's picture on the screen. David pointed to the written words on the screen. Jim started reading, and he was shocked. "What is this?" Jim asked.

"This is called Facebook, where young people can post anything they want to tell their friends. Of course, anyone in the world can read it," David answered.

"Do you mean that Timothy wrote this?"

"Yes, sir, it does."

Jim reread what was written on the screen. It read,

> I hate my life, and I am sick and tired of being pushed around and bullied by my old man. He forced me to take flying lesson when I don't want to, just like he forced me to play football like he did. I wanted to play in the band. There is nothing wrong

with football. The guys are okay. It is just not for me. The people at the flight school are great guys, but I hate flying. What really hacks me off is how he is out there trying to force them to do things his way too. He even had that stupid lawyer of his write a letter threatening to sue the flight school if they don't let me solo. I didn't want to solo. I told them that, and they were so understanding. They told me I could fly forever without ever soloing a stupid airplane if I wanted to."

I know how to fly the airplane, and today, I am going to show that stupid father of mine that I can. Then I am going to end this once and for—all in a fireball.

"When did he write this?" Jim asked.

"Look at the date. Isn't that the day he crashed?"

"Oh my gosh, it is." Jim turned around and grabbed his phone off the credenza and dialed Kelly's number.

Coleen, Kelly's secretary, said, "Mr. Colburn, he is in a meeting with the other partners."

"Coleen, get him out of that meeting. This is important."

In a few seconds, Kelly answered the phone. "This is Kelly."

"Kelly, are you familiar with Facebook?"

"Sure, my daughter uses it all of the time."

"Get to a computer, and look up Timothy's Facebook page."

A few seconds later, Kelly asked, "When did you find out about this?"

Jim told him about David finding it just a few moments ago and bringing it into his office.

"Look at the date. It was posted on Facebook. That is the date of the crash."

"Jim, this is a bombshell. We'll call the court this morning and request an emergency hearing. I will file a motion for dismissal immediately."

Kelly called back two hours later and said, "The judge has granted a hearing for nine o'clock next Monday morning."

Within minutes, everyone in the hangar was looking at Timothy's Facebook page. Someone—- they never knew who, called the local TV station; and the noon news report was showing Timothy's Facebook page on the screen during the noon news. It was then picked up by the networks and flashed all across the country by the six o'clock news.

Monday morning, the judge granted a summary judgment, and the case was dismissed. Jim thought, *This part of the nightmare is over.*

26

THE DIAMOND COMES BACK

Bill Huett and his wife's funeral was Tuesday. Jim and John attended the funeral. Jim said, "John that was the hardest thing I have ever done—partly because I know that if I had found the answer to why airplane engines were failing in flight, the Huetts could have been saved."

"I used to get aggravated at the FAA service bulletins and Advisory Directories Service bulletins when they came out telling me that I had to replace a part that seemed to be working just fine. I never dreamed that someone went to a lot of trouble to get that service bulletin sent out," Jim said.

While they were attending the funeral, Jenifer landed her new Diamond airplane at Millport. The lineman waved her into a parking place and placed a set of chocks under her tires. "Welcome to Millport. Have you been here before?"

"Once."

"How long are you going to be with us?"

"I'm visiting my brother and his family, so I'll be here three or four days. Is that a problem?"

"No, ma'am. Do you want me to top off your fuel?"

"Yes, please do, and can you put the airplane in a hangar?"

"No problem, ma'am. Just leave your name and a contact phone number with the lady at the front desk. I'll take good care of her."

"Thank you." Then she gathered up her bags and walked into the building. After giving her name and cell number to the receptionist, she walked down the hall to the café. Jenifer thought, *this hall is nice. Look at all of the vintage airplane pictures here.*

Christie saw Jenifer walk in and said, "Hi, grab a seat anywhere. I'll be right with you." Sitting a glass of water in front of Jenifer, Christie said, "I think I have seen you in here before, right?"

"Yes, I came through a couple of months ago."

"Where did you fly in from?"

"California."

"Well, we are glad you came back. What can I get for you?"

At that moment, Jim walked through the door. He stopped and looked at Jenifer and said, "You are the lady with the new Diamond out there, if my memory is correct."

"Yes, that's my Diamond D-50.'"

"Do you still like it?"

"Oh, I love it."

Jim stood there like he was thinking, then said, "Your brother's the pastor over at Fowlerville."

Smiling, Jenifer said, "Close. He is the pastor at Prairieville."

"Sorry."

"That's okay. You get the prize for being close."

Jim realized that Christie was waiting to take the ladies' order. "Oops, sorry, Christie. I'll bet you were just trying to take her."

When Jim walked away, Jenifer said, "Christie, who is that good-looking cowboy?"

"That is Jim Colburn. He owns the FBO."

"He sure seems nice, and he is darn good-looking."

"He is a nice guy, and it is so sad about his wife."

"What about his wife?"

"He and his wife were in a plane crash about two years ago. She was killed. It almost killed him, physically and emotionally, but he is slowly coming back."

27

WHAT IS THE ANSWER?

Jim walked into the hangar and said, "Ralph, it has got to be in the remanufacturing process. All of the newer planes that have never had their engines rebuilt are not experiencing catastrophic failures."

"Boss, that is a possibility, but we have three other airplanes out there on the ramp that have had their engines rebuilt by that same company. In fact that 152 right there"—he pointed to one parked in the hangar—"was rebuilt five years ago. It is almost time for it to be rebuilt again."

"When will we hear back from the lab?"

"Should be any day now."

"I wish they would hurry every time I see an airplane take off. I'm worried that it won't make it back."

28

THE BUS CRASH

Jim had spent a long and lonely night. He hated the sounds the house made in the night. You could hear boards creak. The ice maker made strange sounds in the night. It was strange he never heard these sounds when Ally was here. Getting a cup of coffee, he flipped on the TV in the kitchen. The lead story was a bus crash in California where sixteen people died. What caught his attention was when the reporter interviewed the driver of the car that was following the bus.

The reporter asked, "Can you tell us what you saw?"

"It was horrible. We had just topped the ridge at the top of the pass, when all at once smoke came out of the back of the bus. You know, in the part where the motor is. Then spots of oil started to cover my windshield. I put my brakes on because I couldn't see with all of that oil on my windshield. Then the bus started picking up speed. I was stopping, and he was going faster. It was like his brakes quit working or something."

The reporter looked into the camera and said, "You heard it first here on channel 5. Apparently, something was mechanically wrong with the bus before it crashed in the canyon."

Jim froze, staring at the TV.

Harold was sitting in front of the TV, but he obviously wasn't watching it. Juanita said, "Baby, what is the matter?"

"Sweetie, I'm scared. Every day I just know I am going to hear about another airplane crash. I don't know what to do. I need this job. If I go to the authorities, whom would I go to? You know what historically happens to whistle-blowers."

"Harold, you do what you think is right. Don't worry about anything else. In three more weeks, this baby is due. If they fired you next week, the insurance would still pay for the baby." Then she thought, *I hope that is right.*

"Sweetie, if I tell anyone, I will get fired and I could get blackballed so that no other company will hire me. If I don't tell anyone and an airplane full of people crashes." He shook violently, with a deep shudder. "I hate this position I find myself in. I wish I had not found the bad parts."

"No, baby, you don't wish that because innocent people could lose their lives. All of their hopes and dreams could be lost forever if one of those engines broke down. What if that airplane had little children on it?"

Harold said, "I just don't know what to do. If I wanted to warn somebody, whom would I talk to? How would I go about it? What about you and our baby? I cannot lose our insurance right now. I don't know which way to go!"

Juanita reached over and pulled his head down on her ample breast and said, "Don't worry, baby. You are a good man. God will show you the way. Let's pray that no one gets hurt by one of those engines,"

Jim threw his jacket over the back of a chair and walked into the office in his house and powered up his computer. As soon as he was on the Internet, he looked up the story of the bus crash. A man was talking to a reporter. "I was following this bus about two car lengths behind him, when all at once I saw black smoke come out of the back where the motor is. Then all at once my windshield started to get coated with black oil. I couldn't see anything, so I slammed on my brakes. My car kinda skidded sideways in the road. I saw the bus hit that guardrail down there, and it just vaulted over the rail. It was the worst thing I have ever seen in my life. I jumped out of the car and ran to the edge of the interstate where the bus went off the road, and I just froze. I'll tell you, I didn't want to go down there and see what I was fixing to see. Then all at once, this highway patrol man ran up beside me and said, 'Come on. Let's go,' so we both ran down there."

The reporter asked, "What was it like when you got down to the bus?"

"The cop jerked open the back door, and it looked like a garbage dump in there. Some of the seats had broken loose from the floor. They were piled up, and suitcase and people were all piled together. The highway patrol man grabbed a seat and passed it out to me. Then he picked up this girl and handed her to me. All at once, a lady ran up to me and said she was a nurse and asked me to put the girl on the ground so she could see about her. Then the officer handed me a boy, whom I put on the grass beside the girl. Then the officer waved for me to come in the bus with him. Then other firemen and police started arriving. We all worked as hard as we could to get 'em out."

The reported asked, "When the professionals arrived, did they make you get out of the bus?"

"No, me and that first cop were the last two out of the bus. I don't know about him, but I am afraid that I am going to have nightmares about what we saw today for a long time."

"What do you think happened?"

"It looked like something blew in the motor area and he lost all of his brakes."

Then the reporter looked at the camera and said, "You heard if first on channel 5, folks."

Jim thought, *My God, what is happening out there? This was not an airplane engine. This was a diesel bus engine.* While he was sitting there, he pulled up the NTSB reports on the most recent airplane crashes, and sure enough, there was a report of a seaplane that crashed in the Bahamas when the right engine failed soon after takeoff, killing five. The accident had happened several months earlier, but the report had just come out. As he read the article, he *jumped*, like he had been shot with a volt of electricity when he read that the investigators had found that the crankshaft had broken between the number three and four journals.

Jim kept thinking, *What can I do? Who else can I talk to someone has to listen?*

29

THE BABY IS BORN

Juanita shook Harold about three in the morning. "Wake up, baby. It is time to go."

Still half asleep, he said, "Huh, go where?"

"To the hospital. We are going to have a baby."

Now he was fully awake. He shot out of the bed. Okay, don't panic," he said as he tried to shove his feet into the sleeves of his shirt.

"Honey, you are the one who needs to calm down. Let's get in the car." Juanita was up and had her gown on.

"Yeah, the car." He ran out the kitchen door and started to jump in the car. Then he remembered he had forgotten Juanita. Racing back into the kitchen, he met Juanita walking slowly toward the garage door.

Putting his arm around, her he helped her into the car, ran around to the driver's side, and jumped in.

"Harold, you need to get my overnight bag. It is on the foot of the bed."

"Oh yeah, the bag," he said as he raced back into the bedroom.

Juanita looked at him and said, "Harold, you have got to calm down. I can't drive myself to the hospital, and I don't want you to have a wreck on the way."

Miraculously, they made it to the hospital, and three hours later, a beautiful baby girl was curled up next to a tired but very happy mother. A very relieved father was sleeping in the recliner in the corner of the room.

Rene was on duty the next morning while making her rounds. She looked in on the family. When she walked in, Juanita was awake. Rene said, "Hi, my name is Rene. I will be your nurse this morning. How are you and little Janica doing this morning?" She picked up Juanita's chart and studied it for a minute, then said, "Did she nurse at all during the night?"

"She tried. I'm not sure how much she got."

Harold woke up and looked around.

"Well, I see that Daddy survived."

Juanita laughed and said, "It was touch-and-go for a while, but he survived."

Rene smiled and said, "They usually do. Let me take her and weigh her and check her over. We'll be back in a few minutes."

Juanita looked at Harold and said, "Daddy, have you called our parents?"

"I woke 'em all up. They are excited to know that you and the baby are okay. You are okay, aren't you?"

"Yes, we are both okay. I'll be a little sore for a few days, but did you look at her? Isn't she beautiful?"

"Sweetie, what can I do for you?" Harold asked.

"Baby, that nice nurse is going to take good care of me and the baby. Why don't you go home and take a shower? Then you will need to get a box of cigars, but get the candy ones so you can stop by the office and pass them out."

Harold stood there for a moment; then he said, "I'm getting so that I don't want to go to that office. What if I quit and found another job, with a company that wasn't making airplane engine parts?"

"Baby, you are tired. You have had a stressful night. Don't make any decisions today. Just go home and take a hot shower and pass out some candy cigars. Then hurry back to see your daughter."

Three hours later, Harold came in with the biggest grin she had ever seen, carrying a four-foot-tall teddy bear... Juanita had to laugh.

"What's so funny?"

"You are. If you put down that bear, I'll let you hold your daughter."

"Do you think I can do that? I don't know how to hold a baby."

"Come here and cradle her in your arm. Just be sure to support her little head." She placed the tiny little bundle in her daddy's arms.

Harold stood there, looking like he was holding a fine crystal. Then he said, "Sweetie, she is beautiful."

"Yes, she is. She is going to be a daddy's girl."

After a few minutes, he said, "Maybe I better give her back to you."

After handing her the baby, he sat down in the chair and said, "Tell me, sweetie, how are you feeling?"

She looked down at the tiny bundle in her arms and said, "I have never been this happy before in my whole life. Everything is perfect. I have you and I have her."

"Sweetie, how much life insurance do we have on you and me?"

"We have a lot, but why do you ask that?"

"I was just thinking we should have wills made up so that she is protected."

"Harold honey, that's a good idea."

Rene walked into the room. "Am I interrupting anything important?"

"No. Harold suggested we need a will, since we have the baby. Do you know a lawyer?"

"My brother is a lawyer. I'm sure he could draw one up for you."

"Can you give us his name and number?"

Rene picked up a notepad on the table. "I'm writing his office number and my cell phone number. If for some reason you don't get him, give me a call. I'll tell my little brother to call you."

"Your little brother. How old is he?" Juanita asked.

"He is only two years younger than me, but all his life I have been reminding him that I am the oldest, so what I say goes."

After Rene left the room, Harold said, "That will is a good idea. I heard on the radio that there was another airplane crash today. I am getting scared."

"When the baby and I get out of here, let's give her brother a call."

Harold took two steps over to the movable table that the hospital used to serve food to the patients. Picking up the piece of paper that Rene had written on, he said, "Do you think I should call him?"

"Yes, your daughter and I would both feel better if you called him."

"Should I call him right now?"

"No, wait until we get home. Then we can make an appointment to go see him. Maybe you could talk to him about the things going on at work?"

"I don't know. What if he tells me to go to the authorities? I sure can't afford to lose my job now."

30

HAROLD MEETS JR

Jim got in his truck and went straight to Mike's office at the FAA regional office. When he walked in, he met Mike in the lobby. Mike walked over and shook Jim's hand. "Jim, what can I do for you?"

"Mike, do you have a minute?"

"Sure, come on in. Do you want a cup of coffee?"

As soon as they were in Mike's office, Jim said, "Mike, look at the NTSB report that just came out about the seaplane that crashed in the Bahamas."

"What about it?"

"Look at what the NTSB said caused the engine to fail."

"Jim, that is interesting, but do you know how many airplanes crash every year? Last year, civil aviation in the US alone had one thousand five hundred and sixty-five airplane accidents that we had to investigate. Most of those are when someone hits another airplane while taxiing or runs into a hangar, but of those, two hundred fifty-six were fatal accidents resulting in four hundred fifty-eight deaths. Jim, I appreciate what you are doing, but somewhere in the fifty states, we crash six airplanes every day. Now to put it into perspective, four hundred and fifty-eight people died in airplane crashes last year, but over thirty thousand died in car wrecks."

"Mike, I know all about the statistics. I know that statistically a person is more likely to fall in the bathtub and get killed than in an airplane crash. Mike, I have been flying for a long time, and I am telling you something is wrong."

After Jim left, Mike told one of his associates, "Poor guy, he lost his wife in a crash last year, and he just can't accept it."

A week later, Harold called JR's office and talked with JR's secretary. "My name is Harold Johnson. My wife has just had a baby. I guess I should say my wife and I have just had a baby. Well, she sure did most of it. Anyway, her nurse is Mr. Colburn's sister, and she recommended I call him. Is he in?"

"I think so. Can I tell him what this is about?" she asked.

"We need a new will made out since we have a baby."

"Let me see if he can take your call."

"This is JR. I understand you know my sister. How can I help you?"

"Mr. Colburn, my wife and I have a new baby, and we need to have a will made out."

"How do know my sister?"

"She was my wife's nurse at the hospital. Like I said, my wife just had a baby."

"Congratulations, are they both doing well?"

"Yes, they are. Thank you."

"I had a court case scheduled to start today, and it just got postponed. Do you want to come over this afternoon?"

"That would be great. What time?"

"Can you make it at three?"

"I have to take my wife and daughter back for a checkup at eleven. That gives me plenty of time to get them home and get back to our office."

"Do you know where my office is?"

"Yes, your sister gave me the address."

"I'll see you at three then. Congratulations on the new baby."

31

JIM'S RUNNING ACCIDENT

Jim got in from work and put on his running shoes. He was up to five miles a day except Saturday. That was okay because he did his best thinking while running. The air was cool this afternoon as he ran down Shenandoah Street. It was funny how the shadows created by the trees almost gave him vertigo as he ran in and out of the dark shade areas. As he ran, he talked with Allie, whose picture was on the front of the shirt he was wearing.

"Allie, I don't know if there's any way you can get a message from me or not, but, darling, I miss you so much. Everyone tells me it'll get better, but I don't see how it can. I hate the way the house makes creaky noises in the night, which I never heard when you were here. I hate waking up in that big king-size bed all alone. There's not much I do like without you. The garden was good. Your flowers are beautiful. I'm hitting a stone wall with trying to find out why the engine quit." Tears started to fall down his face. "I'm so sorry I wasn't a better pilot."

A squirrel being chased by a small dog chose that moment to race across the sidewalk. Jim leaped to his left to avoid hitting both animal, and when he did, his foot hit the curb. He fell and crashed his left knee into the concrete curb. The pain was instant and intense. He looked down at his knee. The skin was badly lacerated, but the joint was swelling rapidly. After a moment, he tried to get up and immediately fell. Now what was he going to do? He didn't want people to see him lying out here on the sidewalk. Finally, he took his cell phone and dialed 911.

"Nine one one emergency. Say type of emergency."

"I fell while running in the nine hundred block of Shenandoah. I need an ambulance."

"Are you bleeding, sir?"

"Yes, but that is not the problem. I think I broke my knee."

"Sir, stay on the line with me. We have an ambulance on the way. Do you have a family member you want me to call?"

"Yes, call my daughter." Jim gave her Rene's number.

A few moments later, the operator said, "Sir, your daughter is going to meet you at the emergency room."

While she was talking, Jim could hear the siren coming. Soon it stopped beside him. Two paramedics jumped out. The driver said, "What's the problem, sir?"

Jim just pointed to his knee.

The paramedic looked at his knee and said, "Looks like you banged it pretty good. Let's get a splint under it." While he was working the splint under Jim's knee, the other paramedic was taking his blood pressure and counting his pulse rate. Then he shined a light into Jim's eyes. All of the time, the first paramedic was carrying on a running conversation, asking Jim all kinds of questions.

While all of this was going on, a police car pulled up. Now Jim could see people standing on their front porches, looking at all of the commotion out in the street. The policeman asked, "Sir, do you have any identification on you?"

Jim managed to get his wallet out of his pocket.

"Sir, do you still live here at twelve oh eight?" the policeman asked.

"Yes."

"Can you tell me what happened?" The policeman pulled a pad out of his uniform pocket.

"I was running, and a squirrel ran in front of me. I tried to dodge it and tripped over the curb."

"Officer, we are ready to transport."

The officer handed Jim back his wallet. "You guys go ahead and take him to the hospital. I'll come by there later and finish filling out this report."

JR's cell phone chirped. He looked down at it and said, "Whatcha got, sis?"

"I'm up here at Mersey Hospital. Our father was out jogging this afternoon and fell. He has torn the tendons in his knee, and they are getting ready to take him to surgery."

"You have got to be kidding. He doesn't need that. Where are you?"

"We are still in the emergency room."

"I'll be right here."

———

Jim's pastor walked into the hospital room and said, "Well, I see you are going to have some railroad track scars on your knee like mine. I got mine while playing Canadian football. You got knocked down by a squirrel."

"I didn't get knocked down by a squirrel. I was trying to protect the little squirrels of the world, and I tripped."

"If that is your story and you intend to stick to it." He was laughing as he pulled up a chair and sat down. "Seriously, what can I do for you?"

"Pastor, you could do me a favor?"

"Just name it."

"Could you go by my house and get my laptop so I can continue doing some research while I'm lying up here in this bed?"

"How do I get into your house?"

"There is a keypad on the garage door. I'll give you the code."

After a few minutes, Pastor Lyle said, "I have two other patients to see here and one over at memorial, so it will be after lunch before I can get back. Do you think you can you keep your sanity until I get back?"

At that moment, Rene walked in. "Well, how's our patient this morning?"

"Bored silly," Jim answered.

She smiled and said, "Well, old man, I guess that's a good sign."

"Watch who you're calling an old man."

"Are you stuck with nursing this crotchety patient today?"

"Actually, no, I'm working the maternity floor. I thought I would just pop down and make sure he wasn't driving the nurses down here crazy."

After they left the room, Jim turned on the TV. Every time he turned on a TV, he was afraid that he was going to see another airplane disaster. He flipped through the channels until he found a rerun of *Gunsmoke*.

The phone rang. It was JR calling. "How are you feeling?"

"Bored. I'm sitting up here in a hospital bed with one of those designer gowns on, watching an old rerun of *Gunsmoke*."

"Don't you just love those gowns?"

"It was one sadistic person that designed these things."

"Dad, how much pain are you in?"

"Not too much, as long as they keep giving me those pain pills every four hours. Of course I can't walk on it for a while, but I can get to the bathroom with the crutches. To do that, you need four hands, one on each crutch and two hands to hold this stupid gown closed. Otherwise, you've got a cold wind whistling up your north side. Tomorrow I'm going to get out of here."

"Dad, I called to tell you I just got a report that Dr. Dixon pleaded guilty and was sentenced to five years for failing to report that prop strike."

"He should have, even though I still don't believe that prop strike was what caused my engine to fail. If he had done the right thing, they would have caught whatever problem that engine had and prevented it from failing. So I do hold him responsible for causing your mother's death."

"I do too. That's why I'm filing a wrongful death suit today against the good doctor."

"JR, I don't want any money."

"Dad, it is the principle of the thing. I'm going to hit that arrogant joker hard. If I win, why don't we take the money and set up a scholarship fund in Mom's name?"

"I like that. If I ever find out who's responsible for that engine failing, you can include them in your suit."

"No, Dad, if you're right, that'll be a class action suit. We'll include every person who has lost a family member because of an engine."

"That's fine, but you know winning a lawsuit and getting some money has nothing to do with why I want to get to the bottom of this. There's something wrong. If we don't find it, soon there are going to be more engines failing. Did I tell you about the bus in Tennessee?"

"No, what about a bus in Tennessee?"

"He topped a mountain, and his engine blew. He lost all of his brakes and crashed off the interstate, killing sixteen people."

"Dad, that was a diesel engine, not an airplane engine."

"I know. I don't see any connection. That bus engine was built by Michigan Engine Company, and the airplane engine was a Constantine engine."

JR sat there, staring out in space for a few minutes, then said, "Dad, I wonder if those two companies could have a common supplier—someone who supplied crankshafts to both of them?"

"That is a thought. I'll get busy and find out. Maybe it's some new supplier that they both just started using."

"I wonder how you could find that information."

"I don't know, but I'm going to start digging. That's an avenue we haven't considered. It could explain everything."

"I could sue Constantine and force them to turn over who their suppliers are."

"That wouldn't tell us if that same supplier sold parts to Michigan Motor Company."

"No, but I guarantee you there are lawyers lining up to sue that bus company. If I could make contact with one of them, I could get them to request a list of Michigan's suppliers. Then we could see if there was a name that appeared on both lists."

"Son, it's a long shot, but it might work. Let me see what I can find out. I'll let you know."

32

FINDING A LEAD

Ralph walked into John's office and said, "What's this I hear about the boss falling down and busting his butt?"

"You're so crude. He fell down and broke his knee, not his butt."

"How long is he going to be laid up?"

"Knowing him, not long."

"John, I got the lab report back on those two crankshafts."

"Really, what does it show?"

Ralph handed him a copy of the two reports. "It is a lot of gobbly goop, but what it boils down to is this. The crankshaft on Jim's Bonanza was slightly twisted, causing a weak spot in the shaft."

"Really, so the prop strike really did cause the thing to fail."

"That added to the failure. The real problem in both crankshafts was the nitride coating was too thin, making them weaker than they should've been."

John thought a moment, then asked, "Were they both I-0-520s?"

"No, the one from Brazil was an I-0-470. But they were both made by Constantine."

"I don't have a student until three. I'll take these up to the boss at the hospital. He'll want to see them right away."

John walked in Jim's room at the hospital and said, "You're looking chipper this morning."

"I'm just lying here, trying to think up some evil things I can do—to the guy who invented these hospital gowns."

"They are a little airish, when you walk down the hall. Jim, I have the lab reports back on the two crankshafts."

"Really. What does it say?"

"The crankshaft in your Bonanza had a slight twist in it, causing a weak spot. Probably caused by an earlier prop strike."

"I was so convinced that prop strike couldn't have caused the catastrophic failure. What about the Brazilian plane?"

"Jim, you didn't let me finish. The lab reports that the nitride coating was too thin on both crankshafts, causing them to be weak."

Jim had been looking down at his bed; his head snapped up. "What did you say?"

"I said, both crankshafts were defective. The lab reports say the nitride coating was way too thin on both shafts."

"Wait a minute. One was an I-0-470. The other was an I-0-520."

"Yes, but they were both Constantine engines."

Jim thought for a moment, then said, "But we have five other airplanes out there with Constantine engines on them."

"I know. It doesn't make sense."

"Thanks for bringing those down here. I assume you are going to leave them with me."

"Yeah, these are for you. Ralph has the originals back at the hangar."

"Hello, everybody," Lyle said as he walked in with Jim's laptop.

"John, have you met my pastor before."

John stuck out his hand to shake hands and said, "Sure, how are you, Pastor?"

"Great! Good to see you again. How are things out at the flight school?"

"We are very busy," John said. "In fact, I've got to run. I have a student at three."

"Thanks for bringing these reports."

"Jim, here's your laptop. Are you supposed to be working? Didn't you just have surgery?"

"Preacher, if I have to watch one more rerun of *Gunsmoke*, they'll have to move me down to the psycho ward." Holding up some papers in his left hand, Jim said, "Lyle, these reports that John just brought to me show both the crankshaft on my airplane engine and the one I brought back from Brazil were defective. The nitride coating on both crankshafts was defective."

"What does that mean?"

"It means that they failed in flight because of a factory defect. Here's the problem. They're not the same engine. That means that the crankshafts are not interchangeable. It seems to rule out a bad batch of parts. It is enough to make you want to scream or throw something. It is maddening."

"Jim, have you prayed about this?"

Jim wanted to throw something at him.

"No. I haven't."

"Then let's pray about it, Almighty God, we know you know the answer to all of the mysteries this world holds. As we struggle in our finite ways to unravel the mysteries that surround us, we beseech you to guide our paths. Give us wisdom and give us insight to understand the clues that are before us. Father, we search not for fame or personal glory in this matter. Our goal is to find the answers so that we can help alleviate human suffering and pain. Father, if there are criminals involved, may they be brought to justice. If it is bad design, may it be found and corrected. We ask all things in the name of Jesus, your Son. Amen."

Jim was stunned. He said, "Why have I not thought of that before?"

"Sometimes, we're so busy trying to put out the fire. We forget to call the fire department."

Soon Lyle had to leave. Jim was still a little embarrassed. The idea of praying for help in finding a solution had never occurred to him. Rene popped into the room.

Jim looked up and said, "Hi, sweetheart. How is my favorite medical person today?"

"The question is, how is the patient doing since I left."

"Are you already off work?"

"Yes, I got off at three today. How is your pain level?"

"As long as they keep me on those pills, I'm doing okay. John brought the lab reports from the Bonanza engine and the one I brought back from Brazil."

Rene stopped straightening his bed covers and said, "What did they say?"

"Both engines had defective crankshafts. Sweetheart, I'm so sorry. I know how much you loved your mom."

Rene ran over and put her arms around him. They both cried when she said, "Daddy, we both love her, so don't tell me you know how much I loved her. You loved her too."

"Yes, I still do love her. I'm so sorry I couldn't land the plane." Jim struggled to get words to come out.

"Daddy, I have read the reports. I know that no one could have landed that airplane, that day. Stop beating yourself up. Go beat up the bad guys that put a defective part in your plane."

"If I ever find him, God help him." He wiped tears from his eyes.

"Now that sounds more like the daddy I know. I've got to go pick up Katy. Can I get anything for you before I go?"

"No, honey, thank you."

The door opened a few minutes later. David and Ann stepped in.

"How is the number one grandpa in the whole world?" Ann said.

"You guys have got the wrong room."

"I don't think so. There is a sign on the outside saying beware of old grouch in here," David said.

"Come over here and give me a hug." They both climbed up on either side of him in the bed.

"David, be careful with his knee."

"Grandpa, how is the landing gear after the overhaul?"

"It hurts like the devil when the pain pills wear off."

"Grandpa, you can go around in shorts and make up exciting stories about your old football injuries."

"You don't think I should tell them I was tackled by a squirrel?"

"No, Grandpa. I think you need to work on your presentation a little more."

"Can we borrow one of the Cessnas and fly down to South Padre Island this weekend?" Ann asked.

"Sure, who's going?"

"Just David and me, unless you want to go with us."

"Real funny, Ann. Have you got a fork lift we can use to put him in the airplane?"

"No, but several people on the airport have one."

Jim smiled and said, "No, thank you. If I go, someone has to ride in the backseat, and it's not going to be me."

"Well, Ann, that means you."

"I don't think so, little brother. Since I am the oldest, I get priority seating."

Jim laughed. "You two sound just like Rene and JR."

33

THE WILLS

Harold walked into JR's office at three. The receptionist said, "Good afternoon, sir, how can I help you?"

"I have an appointment to see Mr. Colburn at three."

"Please have a seat. I will let Mr. Colburn know that you are here. Can I get you a soft drink or a glass of water?"

"No, thank you, I am fine."

A few minutes later, a tall, good-looking man walked out of one of the offices down the hall to his left. Sticking out his hand, he said, "Hi, my name is Jim Colburn, but everybody calls me JR. You must be Harold?"

Harold liked his handshake. It was firm but not crushing. "Mr. Colburn, I am Harold Johnson."

"Come on in, but call me JR."

Walking into JR's office, he thought it looked like a successful attorney's office. In one corner stood a large expensive globe. On the walls were expensive-looking

Western art. On the credenza was a bronze statue of a bull rider holding his rigging like he was getting ready to ride. Two walls were covered in leather-bound books.

"Have a seat, Harold. How's the wife and baby?"

"They're great. I just dropped them at home a while ago. Her mother is with them. The baby's the first grandchild on both sides. We shouldn't ever have any trouble finding a babysitter."

JR leaned back in his leather chair and smiled. "No, if they are anything like my parents were, you won't have any trouble."

Harold noticed something dark come over JR's face as he mentioned his parents.

"Tell me what this is all about. Let's see if I can help in any way."

"I am an engineer for ACE Foundry, and our company has a rather large life insurance policy on me, and we bought a large policy on my wife. We have been thinking since the baby that maybe we should have a will drawn up."

"That's good thinking. Let me make some notes. How much life insurance do you have on yourself, and how much do you have on your wife?" After making notes for a few minutes about how they would like a will structured, JR asked, "Is there anything else I can do for you?"

Harold was tempted to tell him about the things going on at the foundry, but he said, "No, sir. That's all."

"Harold, this is pretty straightforward stuff. I should have it ready for you and your wife to come in and sign by next Monday. Just don't let anything happen to you before Monday."

"I promise. I'm going to do my best—to stay out of trouble."

When Harold arrived at home, Juanita met him at the door. He said, "It's done. JR's going to have the papers ready for us to sign by Monday."

"Did you talk to him about things at work?"

"No, sweetie, I didn't. I thought about it, but I just got cold feet. I couldn't do it."

"Why not? You know that's what you have to do. Harold, people are going to get killed if you don't tell someone. You may not have caused it, but you are letting it happen."

"Look, honey, I grew up in a poor black neighborhood. I worked waiting tables on rich white people so I could go to college. I am not going to have our baby grow up like that!"

Juanita was surprised. He had never raised his voice at her before.

"All that maybe true, Harold, but you still can't allow those defective parts to be put into airplanes."

"Do you know what kind of people buy airplanes? Rich white folks. I'm not going to sacrifice my baby's future to protect a bunch of spoiled rich white folks. It's not going to happen. I'm sorry I told you, but that's as far as it goes. We've got our wills made up. We will sign them Monday and get on with raising our baby."

34

PHYSICAL THERAPY

Jim thought, *I don't need anybody to take me to physical therapy. I can drive myself.* Trying to put on his sweatpants by himself turned out to be a challenge.

"Wait a minute. If I lay the pants on the floor and step my left foot in, then my right foot, I can then pull them up by leaning my butt against the bathroom counter. Mission accomplished."

Getting the crutches, he hobbled out to the truck. Opening the door, he banged the door into his left crutch, knocking it out from under his arm and down on the floor. By getting into positions that Houdini never dreamed of, he was able to retrieve the fallen crutch. Then turning his back to the seat, he was able to slide up into the cab of the pickup. Then he managed to knock the mirror all askew and get the crutch jammed between the steering wheel and the passenger door. Eventually, he was able to start the engine and back out of the garage without running over anything.

After therapy, he went home, showered, changed, and got back in his truck without an incident to head for the airport. When he started to pull on to the interstate, he saw Lyle's wife's car on the side of the service road. Stopping, he got his crutches and hobbled up to the side of her car.

"Carrie, are you all right?"

"Am I glad to see a familiar face? No. The car made a loud clunking sound, and then it just quit. I can't reach Lyle because he is counseling a family about a funeral that he is supposed to do tomorrow."

"Let me take a look at it. Pull the thing that releases the hood." Looking at the motor, he said, "This is not good. You have water dripping out of the motor. Let me call a tow truck for you. Then I will take you home."

"This is not good. We can have a tow truck take this old piece of junk to Roy's garage, but can you then take me to someplace to get a rent-a-car? You see, Baylee is a candlelighter in a wedding Saturday, and I've got to go get her dress. Then I have to help with the flowers, and then I have to help arrange food for the funeral. I can't be without a car right now."

Jim pulled out his cell phone and dialed a wrecker service that he had used before. Soon, the wrecker arrived to tow the car.

"Rather than take you to get a rent-a-car, Carrie, I want to loan you Allie's car. It is just sitting in the garage. It is not being used. Why don't we go get it?"

Carrie and Allie had been close friends, even though there was twenty-years' difference in their ages.

"Do you mean the Lexus?"

"Yes."

"Oh, Jim, I couldn't do that."

"Why not? It is a good car?"

"But it was Allie's car."

"If Allie was here, don't you think she would let you borrow her car?"

"Well, I am sure she would, but she is not here."

"Let's go see if it will start. It is only two blocks to my house. Come jump in my truck."

The garage door opened, and a shiny Pearl White Lexus was sitting there just like Allie left it a year and a half ago.

"Let me get the keys and see if it will start." It started as soon as he pressed the Start button.

Jim handed Carrie the electronic Start button. "You press this to open the doors, and then as long as this thing is in the car with you, all you have to do is touch that button, and it will start." Looking back at the dash, he said, "It is full of gas, so jump in and off you go."

"Jim, as soon as Roy gets my old car running, we will bring it right back."

"Carrie, I don't want it back. After all you and Lyle have done for my family, this is the least I can do. I don't have any need for this car, and you obviously do have a need for a car. So get going tell Lyle that I'll bring the title over tomorrow."

Carrie just sat there as if she didn't know what to do next.

"Where were you going when your car broke down?"

"To pick up Baylee's dress."

"Then get going. Put that thing in the middle console on *R* for reverse."

Jim watched as Carrie backed the car out of the garage, and he felt good.

Getting back in his truck, he started to the airport again. This time as he approached the interstate, he looked at the Harley Davidson dealer on the corner. As he hobbled in on his crutches, a nice-looking young man approached him.

"Yes, sir, welcome to Midtown Harley Davidson. How can I help you?"

"I haven't ridden one of these since I was in college."

"Was it fun then?"

"Yes, as a matter of fact, it was."

"Well, sir, it will be even more fun now. These new bikes have electric starters, fully integrated circuitry. Antilock brakes and a far superior ride than those twenty or so years ago."

"Either you are being very kind, or you can't judge people's age very well, because it has been a lot more than twenty years since I was in college."

One hour later, he was the proud owner of a beautiful maroon Harley Davidson.

Three weeks later, he was enrolled in a three-day class to get his motorcycle license. After motorcycle class, he walked into the hangar and went straight to Ralph's office. Ralph looked up.

"How is the knee, boss?"

"It is getting better every day. This little therapist is good. Did you find out which company makes crankshafts?"

"Yeah, they both do. So I still don't know which one is the culprit."

"Ralph, I want you to order one crankshaft for an I-0-520 from one of those companies and then order a crankshaft for an I-0-360 from the other one."

"You want me to then send them to the testing lab."

"Yes."

"Boss, let me remind you of two things. One, remember it will take six to eight weeks to get them back after I send them in. Two, those things cost twelve thousand dollars each, and they will not be worth a plug nickel after the lab gets through with them."

"Order them, but don't send them to the testing lab. I'm going to take them to the lab. Ralph, I'm now monitoring every airplane crash anywhere on the planet. This morning, there was a story about a commuter plane taking off from Sidney who lost his right engine and had to go down in the bay."

"Was anyone killed?"

"No, thankfully they were all rescued."

"Does it say that his crankshaft broke?"

"No, this story doesn't say what happened. I guess I'm just paranoid, or maybe I'm just losing my mind?"

35

TRIP TO CALIFORNIA

Jim had just finished his morning run when his cell phone rang. Looking at the view screen, he saw it was Ralph.

"Good morning, Senor Ralph."

"Boss, I've got the second crankshaft in."

"Good. I'll be right out there. Look up the phone number for that testing lab, and see if you can find the president's name for me."

"You've got it, boss. Are you going to ride the Harley today?"

"Yeah, I think I will. See you in a few minutes." After showering and getting dressed, Jim jumped on the big Harley Davidson. The ride was beautiful on the Harley. He could smell the fresh mown hay in the fields along the road leading to the airport. Jim thought, *I love the rumble of that big engine.*

When he wheeled it into the corner of the hangar that Ralph kept reserved for the Harley, Ralph walked over to meet him.

"Were you able to find the president of that lab's name for me?" Jim asked.

"Yep, here it is." He handed Jim a piece of paper with the following written on it:

James C. Aleszka
Failure Investigations
4718 Renovo Way
San Diego, CA, 92124
Phone: (858)560-5530

Jim called James Aleszka in San Diego. "This is Jim Aleszka. Can I help you?"

"Mr. Aleszka, my name is Jim Colburn. I own the FBO at Millport Airport here in Texas. Last year, I had a crankshaft break in flight, resulting in a crash that killed my wife. Two months ago, I sent two crankshafts to you. Your report states that both were defective, which is exactly what I suspected. Your company does very good work, which is why you have an enormous backlog of test being run. I have a gut feeling that some company has been putting out defective crankshafts and more people are going to get killed if we can't find who it is and get a recall on those parts. I have purchased two new crankshafts from two companies that are suspect. We can't afford to wait two more months for these shafts to make it through your backlog. If I get in my airplane and bring them to you, can you personally walk these two through and get back to me?"

"Mr. Colburn, let me ask a couple of questions. Why haven't you shared this with the FAA and or the NTSB?"

"Oh, believe me I have been. I have worn out my welcome over at the FAA regional office. I have been there so many times. The problem is all I have at the moment are my suspicions. I need something that I can take to them and get a recall sent out."

There was a long pause. Then Mr. Aleszka asked, "Were you flying the plane when the crankshaft broke?"

"Yes, it shattered the crankcase and instantly blew hot oil all over the windshield. I was over a heavily forested area in Mississippi. I tried to land on a small road that ran through the forest, but I struck a pine tree with my left wingtip."

"I am so sorry. I lost my wife in an automobile accident two years ago. How are you coping?"

"I am sorry about your wife. The answer to your question is one day at a time."

When they got off the phone, Jim called Derrick. "I need to make a quick trip out to San Diego and back."

"Jim, I can't I already have a trip scheduled with Doctor Elders. Why don't you get David to fly with you? He can do it."

"Okay, thanks, I'll see if I can find David."

David looked down at his phone. "Hi, Grandpa."

"David, I need to make a quick trip out to California and back in the King Aire. Can you go with me?"

"Sure, but where's Derrick?"

"He's on a trip with Doctor Elders."

"When do you want to go?"

"As soon as I can run home and throw my shaving gear into an overnight bag."

"So we'll be spending the night then."

"Yes."

"Hey, I am on it. See you in about an hour."

When Jim got back to the airport, David had the plane sitting out on the ramp.

"She is all gassed up and ready to go."

"Have you already filed a flight plan?"

"Yes, sir, westbound. We are going to have a hundred miles an hour headwind above twenty thousand feet, so I filed us at eighteen."

"That was good thinking. Let me check in with John. Why don't you get Ralph to help you load those two crankshafts on board, and we can go as soon as I get back out here?"

"They are already on board. Do you want to fly pilot or copilot?"

"Why don't you fly left seat going out, and I'll fly it coming back."

"Done deal." He mounted the stairs up into the plane.

Three hours and forty three minutes later, they were landing at San Diego.

"Wow, look at all of those beautiful boats in the harbor."

"Captain, you look at the runway. I'll look at the boats."

Jim and David went straight to the testing lab. When they walked in, the receptionist greeted them warmly. "Good afternoon, how can I help you?"

"Hi, my name is Jim Colburn. I talked with Mr. Aleszka earlier today about some crankshafts we need to have tested."

"Yes, we have been expecting you. One moment. Let me get someone to assist you." She paged a person named Juan. "Gentlemen, have a seat. Juan will be right with you. Can I get you some water or a cup of coffee?"

"No, thank you."

"A glass of water would be great."

She smiled and said, "how about a bottle of water?"

David grinned and said, "That would be even better."

She disappeared around a wall. Within a few seconds, she returned. She had just handed David a bottle of water when a nice-looking young man in a lab coat appeared.

"Hi, my name is Juan. I understand you have some parts for me."

"Yes, they are in the car. Do you want me to bring them in this door, or would you rather I bring them around to the loading dock?"

"What are they?"

"Two new crankshafts."

"Can we carry them, or will we need a forklift?"

"No, I put them in the car. If you could get one, I can get the other."

While they were unloading the car, another young lady appeared. "Are you Mr. Colburn?"

"Yes."

"Hi, my name is Susan. I am Mr. Aleszka's administrative assistant. He is sorry that he can't be here to greet you. He's testifying in court. He asked me to see if you need anything. Do you have a hotel reservation?"

"Yes, thank you. We have a reservation at the Hilton on Harbor Island."

"Have you stayed there before?"

"Yes, I have."

"It is beautiful on the island. Do you need dinner reservations or directions to anything?"

"No, thank you."

"Mr. Aleszka wanted me to tell you we have put a priority rush on the material you have brought. If you could meet him here in the morning at ten, he hopes to have some information for you."

As they were leaving, David said, "Wow, that Susan is cute."

"Really. I kinda noticed that myself."

"You are way too old for her, but I think she likes me. After all chicks go for dashing young pilots."

"Wait until I tell her I own a Harley. Then we'll see who she likes."

That night, they stayed at the Hilton on Harbor Island. At ten the next morning, they were at the testing lab.

Susan said, "Good morning. How was the island?"

"It was great watching the boats come in and go out," David responded.

"Gentlemen, please go in. Mr. Aleszka is expecting you."

When they entered his office, James Aleszka stood and shook hands with them and said, "I have the test reports on the two crankshafts that you brought in yesterday. I have a crew that worked all night on them so you could have the reports this morning."

"Mr. Aleszka, thank you. You may never know how many lives you have saved by doing this."

"Mr. Colburn, there's a problem."

"What is it?"

"Both of these crankshafts are perfect."

Jim dropped into a chair. "Did you say that they both were perfect?"

"Yes, they are both perfect. There is no flaw in either crankshaft."

Jim sat in stunned silence for a moment, then looked at Jim Aleszka and asked, "Since you lost your wife, have you ever had moment when you thought you were losing your mind?"

"Yes, I have, but I don't think you are. I went back and pulled the testing report on the first two you sent out here. They were definably faulty. Could it be that you just have not found the right foundry this time?"

"I'm so sorry that I asked you guys to jump through the hoops for us. I was so sure that one of these two was the guilty party."

Flying home, Jim felt a dark depression trying to settle over him. What were they missing?

Somewhere over Arizona, Jim's cell phone rang.

It was Pastor Lyle. "Jim, we can't just take your car. That thing is worth a lot of money."

"Pastor, I'm kinda busy right now. I'm flying the King Aire at twenty-nine thousand feet somewhere over Arizona. How about you keep it as a loan, and I will call you when I get back home?"

"Oh, I am so sorry. I didn't know you were out of town."

"Just let Carrie drive the car, and you and I will talk about it when I get home, okay?"

"All right. Call me when you get home."

36

HAROLD TELLS JR

Juanita called her mother. "Mama, I am worried. Harold is late getting home, and he was not answering his cell phone."

"Baby, maybe he had to work late on a project or something."

"Mama, he always calls when he is going to be late. What if he has been in a wreck or something?"

"I am sure he will show up in a few minutes, and everything will be all right. I get that panicky feeling every time your daddy is out of pocket too. How is my grandbaby?"

"Mama, she is beautiful. She is growing every day."

An hour later, Harold pulled into the driveway. As soon as he walked through the door, Juanita knew something was wrong. "Harold, are you okay?"

He slurred his words when he tried to answer, "Suure, I juss stopped for a little drink on my way home. It's all."

Juanita looked at him and thought, *He has never drank before. Something is wrong.*

Jim turned on the morning news and was horrified, along with the rest of the world to see scenes from a small town in Canada. An eighteen-wheeler had lost his engine on a hill, roared down the hill, and wiped out a school bus stopped to let children off.

The reporter was interviewing witnesses.

"This big truck just came over the hill up there, and instead of stopping, he seemed to pick up speed as he came down the hill. The driver started blowing his horn about halfway down the hill, but kids were getting off the bus. So the bus driver couldn't do anything. It was horrible that big truck just slammed right into the bus full of kids."

The pictures showed little bodies scattered all over the grass around the wrecked bus.

The reporter said, "So far, there are twenty-one known killed, including the bus driver. The driver of the truck has been taken to the hospital. We understand that he is in a state of shock."

"This is Melody Carmichael with CNN News."

Jim felt sick at his stomach. He raced to the sink and gagged, but nothing came up.

Juanita called Rene. "Hi, this is Juanita Johnson. You were my nurse when Janica was born."

"Oh, hi, how is the baby?"

"She is wonderful. It is my husband I am worried about."

"Is he okay?"

"Could we meet for lunch someday soon?"

"Sure, I'm off tomorrow. I look forward to seeing little Janica again. You live in Fowlerville, don't you?"

"Yes."

"Do you want to meet at the Soup N Salad on State Street?"

"That would be great. Is eleven o'clock all right?" Juanita said.

That evening when Harold came in, he did not stop at a bar on the way home. Juanita handed the baby to him when he sat down in his recliner. He looked down at the cute little face, and tears came into his eye.

"Hi, baby girl. How was your day? Did you know your daddy loves you?"

Juanita busied herself with dinner, but all of the time she was watching the interaction between Harold and the baby.

"Okay, you two, dinner is ready. Let's put her in the baby sling so she can sit at the table with us."

As they sat down, Harold said, "Sweetie, I am so sorry about last night."

"Harold, let's eat supper. Then you can tell me what is wrong. I would like to say grace. Do you want to do it?"

"No, sweetie, you do it. I can't."

"Lord, we thank you for your divine protection over our lives. Sometimes when we can't see the way, we just have to look to you who is the way. Amen."

After dinner, Juanita and Harold cleaned up the kitchen just like they did in old times. They bathed the baby and put her in her crib. Then they sat down.

"Sweetie, I'm so sorry I came home half drunk and said the things I said to you the other night. Please forgive me."

"Oh, baby, I love you so much. In fact there is now two of us who love you. Did you see how your daughter was looking at you when you were talking to her?"

"Juanita, I'm terrified. I don't know which way to go. Every time I flip on the news, I just know that they are going to be reporting another plane crash, but at the same time the thought of me not having a job so that I can support you and the baby is even more terrifying."

"I know, baby. It wasn't a plane crash, but did you hear about that truck that ran into a school bus full of kids?"

"No, where did that happen?"

"I don't remember. I'll turn on the TV. I'll bet they are still talking about it."

The TV came on with scenes from the bus crash and the anchor person talking.

"Eyewitness describes how the truck just seemed to go faster and faster as he came down the hill, wiping out a school bus full of kids. It is the worst school bus accident in Canada's history. The death toll is up to twenty-one, and authorities believe it will go higher. Let's go to Greta on the scene. Greta, are you there?"

"Yes, Chip, we are here at the scene of the worst school bus accident in Canada's history. Authorities tell us now that the engine on the truck blew just as he topped the hill. He lost his brakes, and he lost the ability to use his gears to slow the monster rig down. They are telling me that there probably won't be any charges against the driver. However, they are looking into the maintenance records for the truck. Back to you."

"This is Greta for Canada National Television."

Harold started to shake like he had a fever. He kept repeating.

"I waited too long. I waited too long."

"What is the matter, baby? That was a horrible accident, but you had nothing to do with it."

"Sweetie, you don't understand. We make crankshafts for trucks too."

Juanita sat in stunned silence for a few minutes, then said, "Harold, I'm having lunch with Rene, our nurse tomorrow. I'll talk to her, but you've got to go see JR. You have got to tell him and let him tell you what to do."

"Sweetie, I'm so scared."

"Baby, don't be. JR's a good man. He'll know what to do."

Harold came into JR's office at the time of his appointment. The young receptionist recognized him.

"Good afternoon, sir, how is the baby?"

"She is fine, thank you."

"Have a seat. I'll let Mr. Colburn know you're here. Can I get you a glass of water or a soft drink?"

"No, thank you."

Within a few minutes, JR walked out of his office. The first thing he noticed was that Harold wasn't sitting—he was pacing.

"Hello, Harold, good to see you again. How is that baby girl?"

"All right," Harold mumbled.

JR thought, *This is not the same man I made a will for last month. The other man was bright and confident, excited about being a father. This man is clutching a small briefcase like it held the deed to all of the oil in Texas. He has not made eye contact even once.*

"Come on in. Let's see what I can do for you."

When Harold sat down, he opened the briefcase and took out a small laptop.

"I have an e-mail that I want you to read. Look at the date of the e-mail." He slid the laptop across so that JR could read the screen.

JR started to read the screen. Then you could see the color drain from his face.

"Your company makes crankshafts for airplane engines?"

"Yes, we also make them for other things."

JR sat staring at the screen for several seconds. "If you weren't already my client, I would turn you down on this.

If for any reason this matter ended up in court, I can't represent you. You see, my mother, whom we all worshiped, was killed last year when my dad's crankshaft failed, and they crashed in Mississippi."

"Mr. Colburn, I am so sorry, I didn't know. I wanted to say something before, but my wife was expecting a baby, and I wanted to keep the insurance. I'm so sorry." He started to rise.

"Sit back down. I can't represent you in court. I would have too much conflict of interest. However, you do need somebody to represent you. Let me give you a couple of names that I think would help you."

37

JR CALLS GREG

When Harold left the office, JR sat staring at the wall. *Those bastards. How could he use this information?* Then he picked up the phone and dialed a newspaper reporter that had been in his class at the university.

The phone was picked up on the second ring. "This is Greg."

"How much is a Pulitzer prize worth today?"

"Heck, it is worth a cold beer at TO's any day."

"Meet me there in thirty minutes," JR said.

When JR walked in, he thought, *I know why I seldom drink. I can't stand the cigarette smell in here.*

He had just sat down in one of the booths and looked around. The place was almost deserted at this time of day.

Greg walked in. "What is all of cloak-and-dagger stuff if you just wanted a free beer? You could have said so."

"Sit down and take a load off. I may have just accidentally stumbled on to something that could make your career."

"Do you mean I might get off writing about church garage sales and bake sales?"

"Yeah, you might promoted to covering the Bingo games after this."

"My goodness, I'm all ears. Can I get us two beers, or is this too hot to wait?"

"You're going to owe me a lot more than a beer," JR said.

Greg turned and yelled to the bartender, "Skip, pull two lights for us."

When he sat back down, he said, "Okay now what's this all about?"

"Do you remember when my dad's plane crashed and my mom was killed?"

"My God, yes, everybody loved your mom. What does that have to do with this?"

"My dad has been trying ever since the crash to prove something was wrong. In fact, the doctor who sold him the airplane has been arrested for not reporting a prop strike. Dad kept saying that little prop strike didn't cause the problem."

"I know. He talked to me about it."

"Greg, I'm going to put you on to something, but you can never know the source of the information. I can't ever reveal that to you. Are we clear on that?"

"We are talking deep throat stuff."

"I want your word that you will never use my name. Just like I am not going to tell you the name of my source. Do I have your word?"

"You are serious, aren't you?"

"Yes, do I have your word?"

"Yes, you have my word, that I will never name you as the source."

"Here is the deal. You know that big foundry out east of town?"

"Sure, you mean ACE Foundry?"

"Two years ago, they intentionally reduced the amount of nitride coating on all of their crankshafts to cut operating cost by millions."

"Why would they do that?"

"To make the fourth quarter report look better and to make the top executives bonuses bigger."

"Do you mean that they would put people's lives in jeopardy just to get a bigger bonus?"

"Yes."

"You can't tell me where you got this information."

"That is right."

"JR, if I didn't know you so well, I would get up and walk out of here right now. You actually believe this is for real?"

"Yes."

"If your parents weren't involved, would you have called me?"

JR stared at his beer, then looked up and said, "I probably would not have reacted as quickly, but I would like to think that I still would've called you. Do think you can dig into this thing?"

"Can I start with your dad since he has already been pursuing this thing?"

"Yes, but you cannot tell him you got it from me."

The next day, Jim was lying with his knee elevated above his bed when Greg walked in. Hello, Mr. Colburn, how are they treating you?"

"They're treating me all right. I just don't have time to lie here all day long."

"What are you doing that can't wait until you get back on your feet?"

"You remember when my engine blew over Mississippi and I crashed? Well, I think something stinks about that engine failing, and I'm out to prove it before anyone else gets killed."

"Sir that is why I'm here."

"Greg, what are you talking about?"

"I've got a source that tells me that the ACE Foundry right here in our city makes crankshafts for airplanes and two years ago they reduced the amount of nitride coating on the ones they shipped out in the last quarter to make their bottom line look bigger and the top boys get bigger bonuses."

"Where are you getting this information?"

"I can't reveal my sources."

"You think this source is reliable?"

"Yes."

Jim lay staring at the wall for a long time; then he said, "Now it all makes sense."

"What makes sense?"

"Greg, go to the NTSB web page, and look at all of the airplanes crashes within the past two years, and see how many were the result of a crankshaft breaking. Derrick and I flew all of the way to Brazil and brought back an engine off a plane that crashed down there. I had it and the crankshaft off my Bonanza tested, and in both cases, the nitride coating on the crankshafts was too thin."

"Then just before I fell, I had Ralph purchase two new crankshafts, and I took them to the lab. Guess what they were—perfect. Call Ralph at the flight school, and he can give you the name and number for the lab. Then look at a bus crash in Tennessee. It also had a crankshaft failure. If you could prove all of those crankshafts came from here."

"Why haven't you been able to put it together before now?"

"I couldn't figure out why thousands of airplanes are flying every day and only a few were experiencing crankshaft failure. Don't you see? All of the crankshafts shipped before they reduced the nitride coating are fine. The crankshafts that are failing are the crankshaft with the thin coating.

That explains why there are thousands of engines out there with no problem.

I have got to get out of this bed." Jim was visibly agitated.

"Why don't you share with me all you have looked at up until now, and I will take it from here? Newspaper men can often get doors open that might not normally be opened."

"I'll be out of here tomorrow. Why don't you come over to my house, and I'll show you everything I have done so far? Greg, this is great, if we could prove those crankshafts all came from one source. We can nail some jokers. If I could prove that some idiot killed my Allie just so he could get a bigger bonus, I just might kill him."

"If we can prove it, we can do better than that. We can destroy him."

When Greg got back to his office, he went to the archives and started looking for everything he could find on the foundry.

First, he found that the company was an old, established company with a stellar reputation in the industry whose stock has been languishing in the market for several years.

Then in the summer of 2006, they brought in a hotshot new president. All at once, their stock starts to shoot up. Why? Who was this new guy? Where did he come from?

38

THE FUNERALS IN CANADA

The next morning, when Jim got to the airport, everybody in the café was talking about the bus accident in Canada.

As Jim, John, and Ralph sat down at a table, Ralph said, "If they find out that the crankshaft on that truck broke and caused that wreck, somebody needs to find a tall tree and a short rope to put around his neck!"

John said, "It is horrible, but maybe somebody will wake up and start looking into what Jim has been saying for months."

"Guys, it is like somebody stuck a hot knife in my gut. I was hoping so hard that when I took those two shafts out there to California that one would be the bad one. Did you notice that one of those foundries was right here in town?"

"Yep, it is just out east of town about two miles."

"There is a manufacturer out there somewhere that is putting out bad parts. I just don't know how to find him."

A few days later, Jim came in from his morning run and turned on the TV in the kitchen. As he was pouring a glass of juice, he looked at the TV. At that moment, his youngest daughter Kay called,

"Dad, are you watching the TV?"

"I just flipped it on."

"Isn't that the saddest thing you have ever seen?"

The TV anchor person was speaking in a hushed tone. It made Jim think of the way announcers talked at a golf tournament.

"All of the funerals were held in the school gym because there was no other building large enough to hold the crowd. All six church pastors officiated: Catholic, Presbyterian, Methodist, Lutheran, Baptist, and Christian."

Another voice cut in. "We are told that every funeral home for miles around have been brought in to handle this many bodies."

"Yes, there are twenty-seven funeral coaches from twenty-seven different funeral homes in this procession as it winds its way through the treelined street to the lone cemetery here in Regina. We are watching as one by one the funeral coaches arrive in the cemetery. One by one they unloaded one normal-size coffin and twenty-six little coffins."

"Tom, we are told that the mayor is going to say a few words at the close of the ceremony."

The camera moved over the ground from one family saying good-bye to a child to the next until it had shown all twenty-seven grieving families.

"My fellow Canadians, today, we stand on hallowed ground. There is not one family in the region that has not been touched by this tragedy. My own granddaughter lies right here beside where I stand."

Then his voice broke, and giant tears cascaded down his rugged face.

"We Canadians have faced hardships before. We will weep for a while. Then we will pick up our task and move on. This day will never be forgotten. We will wonder why. Why would a loving God allow such a senseless tragedy to occur? I have no answers. The city council in emergency caucus last night voted to erect a marble statue with the names and ages of all twenty-seven victims written thereon. Grief counselors are here in our city, ready to talk with each family member. They are being paid for by the Canadian government. Do not be afraid to use them. Now I am going to be with my family to mourn the loss of our little Elise. I bid you Godspeed."

The anchor person came back on. "This has to be one of the saddest days in the history of Canada."

"Tom, I do have an update on the truck. It appears that something inside the engine broke and parts from inside the engine broke through the outer shell and ruptured his break line. With no brakes and no engine compression, the driver had no way to slow he eighty-thousand-pound rig as it careened down the hill."

"Dad, I cried all the way through that whole service. It was just awful."

They talked for a few minutes more; then they hung up. Jim just stood there feeling cold. He asked himself, *Why didn't I cry too? Am I losing my feelings for other people's misery?* Then he thought, *No, it is because I am angry. I know what caused that terrible tragedy, and, so help me, God. I am going to find the people responsible, and I am going to destroy them.*

39

THE BICYCLE PEDAL

Jim didn't feel like eating, but his trainer had stressed the importance of a good breakfast after each run. He thought, *I don't feel like messin' with frying eggs this morning. I'll just pop two in the microwave while I shower.* He took a plate, placed two eggs in the center, and covered them with a paper napkin and set the microwave on three minutes.

Just as Jim was making coffee, he happened to look back at the microwave. He couldn't believe what his eyes were telling him. Those two eggs were swelling. They looked as big as a pair of footballs. Then he ducked as the microwave door, rocketed across the kitchen, knocking down the chandelier in the dining room. What he saw froze him in midstride.

The door on the microwave was imbedded in the far wall, and there were egg particles everywhere. You would have thought he had put a hundred eggs in that thing. The whole inside of the microwave was coated with egg confetti, and the countertop was coated. Jim grabbed a paper towel and stepped with his bare feet all in the broken eggshells and goo covering the floor. Then with the paper towel, he proceeded to smear a thin layer evenly over the surface of the countertop. Then he ran out to the garage and got a pail, filled it with hot water, and barefooted in his underwear. He proceeded to start scrubbing the egg confetti off everything in sight.

When he finally had some semblance of cleaning done, he got dressed and called a handyman who did home repairs.

Ralph walked into Jim's office, carrying a set of bicycle pedals.

"Boss, look at this. My boy was riding his bike yesterday, and look what happened." He handed Jim a broken pedal off a kid's bicycle.

"Ralph, why are you bringing this to me?" Jim looked at the two pieces.

"Boss, look at it. That's a crankshaft, and the darn thing broke. When was the last time you saw the crankshaft on a kid's bike break right in two?"

"I have never seen one break before. What does this tell us?"

"Maybe it tells us there is something wrong with the metal that they are using to make crankshafts with?"

"But don't forget the two I took to California. They were perfect."

"Yeah, I hate that."

"Leave this broken pedal with me. I am going to call Jim Aleszka out in California and talk to him about this."

40

TRIP TO HAWAII

Flight 4469 was boarding at gate 18 at 10:20, from New York LaGuardia bound for Honolulu, Hawaii. The aircraft was a two-year-old Airbus 380 with a crew of 11 and 395 passengers getting on board.

All were excited about spending a few relaxing days in Hawaii.

As the giant plane was being pushed back from the gate, the overhead speakers came on. "Good morning, ladies and gentlemen, this is Captain Steve Armstrong. I will be in command of Flight 4469. Assisting me today will be First Officer Curt Billings and nine very competent flight attendants. This is a nonstop flight from New York to Hawaii. Our flying time will be eleven hours and fourteen minutes at an altitude of thirty-seven thousand feet. Now sit back, and make yourself comfortable for your flight to the beaches of Hawaii. If there is anything we can do to make your flight more enjoyable, please let us know. Welcome aboard."

Reverend John Davis turned to his wife and said, "Ann, I'm glad you talked me into going on this trip. I wonder how much Honolulu will have changed in twenty-five years."

"Probably not as much as we have changed in the twenty-five years since we were here on our honeymoon."

"I don't know I think you are just as beautiful now as you were then."

Ann smiled. "Wrinkles, gray hair, and all. Could it be your eyesight has gotten a little older too?"

"Ann, I love you. This is the perfect way to celebrate our twenty-fifth anniversary."

"Mrs. Davis, these are for you." The flight attendant handed Ann a dozen long-stemmed red roses. Ann looked at her, then looked at John, who was grinning back at her.

"Mrs. Davis, if you would like, I'll be glad to put those in the refrigerator for you until we land."

"Oh, could you?" Holding the roses up to smell the delicate aroma one more time before handing them to the flight attendant.

"Reverend John Davis, I love you," she said, smiling at her husband.

Harold wrestled with what he should do all weekend. Monday morning, he had made up his mind. Purposefully, he walked into his office and went to the files. Pulling out the file drawers on his filing cabinets, he was shocked to find that all the files he wanted were gone.

He thought, *How can they be gone? They were just here.* He quickly glanced around the room to see who was watching him. Then he told himself, "You've got to calm down. If anybody were to see you now, they would know that you are scared out of your mind." He sat the briefcase under his desk and went to the drawing board.

Jim Aleszka answered the phone. "Hello, Jim, what have you got?"

"I have the crankshaft off a kid's bicycle in my hand that snapped in two yesterday evening while a six-year-old kid was riding his bike."

"We have seen those before, but I'll admit it's rare. Usually, only on a racing bike."

"Do you mean like Armstrong rides?"

"Yes."

"I can see that, but how many six-year-olds are strong enough to break a steel crankshaft?"

"You have a point there. Send that thing overnight to me, and let's take a look at it."

"I'll get it out overnight today. You should have it before noon tomorrow."

As soon as Jim hung up, he raced down the stairs and into Ralph's office.

"Can we get this shipped overnight to Jim Aleszka's lab today?"

"Sure, boss, no problem. I have his address."

"Ladies and gentlemen, Flight fourteen sixty-nine is now boarding at gate twelve from Dallas to Honolulu. Please have your boarding passes out for the flight attendant at the door. Have a good time in Hawaii."

"Mom, Dad, this is a cool way to start the summer. All four of us going to Hawaii. Thank you," David said.

"Yes, Mom and Dad. I want to thank you too."

"You two are gone all year to school, so Dad and I thought we would capture you for a week before you race off to your summer projects."

"You can capture me in Hawaii anytime you want," David said.

"Mom that is one time I agree with my brother. I volunteer to be captured in Hawaii or Disney World. Either one is fine."

"Who chose our seat assignments? Dad, you and I are in row thirteen seats A and B? Mom and Ann in row twelve seats A and B."

"I thought you guys could sit together. Ann and I could sit together."

"Mother, haven't you ever heard that thirteen is an unlucky number?"

"Don't give me that junk. Just get on the airplane. You'll probably sleep all the way anyway."

"Well, I see the guys in row thirteen made it just fine," Kay said eight hours later.

"I was ready to run up there and help the pilot if he needed any help all of the way."

"Like you could fly an L-10-11. I don't think so," his sister said.

One hour later, an Airbus 380 landed from New York.

"Ann, you may have to go get a wheelchair for me. I don't think I can stand up after sitting for eight hours."

"Oh, you'll do just fine. Look out that window. The tropical breezes and sun await you."

The next day, John and Ann were browsing through the shops when they heard.

"Look, Mom, there's Reverend David and Mrs. Davis!"

"Oh my gosh, is that you, Kay?"

"Yes, and this is our Ann."

"You are kidding." Hugging Ann, she said, "Look at you. You are all grown up."

"Where is the rest of your family?" John asked.

"The guys are gone to get tickets to a harbor cruise. When did ya'll get here?"

Ann Davis laughed and said, "Listen to that Texas drawl. We got here yesterday. When did you get here?"

"Yesterday, and we are going back on Sunday. How long are ya'll going to be here?"

"We are going back on Monday."

"Unless we decide just to stay here," John said.

"Sir, I'm with you. I told Mom we should just move out here."

"How was your flight over?" Kay asked.

"Long."

"He wanted me to get a wheelchair for him when we got here."

The younger Ann spoke up and said, "The flight won't be as long going back."

"Why is that?" John asked.

"The jet stream is flowing eastbound. We'll have a tailwind going home."

"Reverend John, I forgot to tell you both my son and my daughter here are pilots. Ann is a flight instructor at her grandfather's flight school."

41

THE FURNACE

James Aleszka called and said, "Jim, it appears the foundry that made this bicycle pedal is using the old Bessemer furnace to produce steel."

"What does that mean?"

"Those old furnaces are very expensive to run. They were originally coal powered, but most have been converted to run on fuel oil. They use a lot of oil to operate. Most steel factories have gone to the newer electric-powered furnaces.

To melt off all of the impurities in the pig iron before it becomes steel, it must be fired at three thousand degrees for thirty minutes. If the furnace ran less than thirty minutes, you have a weaker product."

"Let me make sure I understand this. If I'm making steel, a major cost is the amount of fuel it takes to run those furnaces. So if I run them less than the full thirty minutes,

I would have a product that would look the same, but it would not be as strong?"

"That is correct."

"So if I wanted to pad my bottom line, all I would have to do is shorten the cycle on my furnaces, and I would save a lot of operating cost."

"Yes. You would also be violating all kinds of laws."

"So I need to find out who made that crankshaft for the bicycle pedal."

"I already know it was made right there in your town."

"Do you mean ACE Foundry?"

"Yes, the manufacturer's part number is stamped right into it."

"Mr. Aleszka, thank you. I have got to find a way to prove that they are the same people that made those other crankshafts. It keeps coming back to those two new shafts that you tested. They were perfect. How can that be if they are putting out bad stuff?"

"What if they are not doing it all of the time? What if you wanted to cheat the system and you shortened the cycle on some batches and at other times you didn't?"

"Oooh, that would make it hard to catch, wouldn't it? If I ever find proof that they are doing that, I'm going to shut that place down. I'm going to see that they never make another part again ever."

"If I can help, let me know."

Greg's Porsche roared down the ramp into the underground parking garage. He was talking to Jim Colburn on the phone. You are telling me that the bicycle pedal revealed that someone had short cycled the furnace melt time and that made the metal weaker."

"Yes, that's what the lab is saying. Here's the kicker. It was done right here at ACE Foundry."

Greg let out a low whistle. "I am here at the office now. Let me get up to the office and start digging."

He thought as he rode up the elevator, *the first thing I am going to do is see who is running that place.*

Looking at the computer, a few minutes later, he said, "That is interesting, in the summer of 2006, they brought in Horace Thorn as president and CEO. Then in the fourth quarter of 2006, their earnings report shows a significant increase in profits. I wonder what magic he did to turn things around so quickly. Or was he just in the right place at the right time?"

Looking further, he found that their stock had been languishing at around seventeen dollars a share, and now it was up to twenty-seven dollars a share an all-time high. Greg thought, *This is strange. Their sales have not gone up, yet the profits are way up? Let's see what I can find on this Horace guy. Where did he come from?*

Digging a little deeper, he found that Horace Thorn had grown up in a small town in Michigan right in the middle of the steel-making industry.

Then he found his college transcripts. Greg spoke out loud to himself. "This guy almost didn't graduate. His grades were so bad. In fact, it took him five years to get his BA. Hummm, this is interesting. He is getting a divorce from his third wife."

Greg asked himself, "Why would the board of directors hire him?"

Harold came in from work, carrying his empty briefcase.

"Sweetie, it's all gone."

"What's all gone?"

"The files...I went to copy the files that show what I found, and they are all gone. Someone has gone through my files and removed every bit of proof I had. Why would they do that? Did I do the wrong thing by telling JR about it?"

"You are never wrong by doing the right thing. If somebody removed the files, that means they are running scared. If I have to, I can always go back to teaching. Did you call any of those other lawyers that Mr. Colburn gave you?"

"No, sweetie, I wish he could be my lawyer. I trust him."

"I know, baby, but since it was his mother that was killed, you can see why he needs to bow out."

"Yes, apparently, they have or had a pretty close family."

"Thinking about close families. Daddy, you have a little girl who has been waiting to see her daddy. Why don't you go see your daughter while I finish dinner?"

"First, I want to kiss the baby's mother." Harold pulled her close.

"Don't start anything now. You go play with the baby."

Harold lifted his daughter out of the crib.

"Hi, baby girl. My, you look so beautiful. Did you miss your daddy today?"

"Juanita, I'm finding a lot more. It's more than just shortening the nitride coating. Somebody's shortening the furnace cycle sometimes." He walked back into the kitchen, carrying the baby.

"Harold, what does that do?"

"It keeps the furnace from smelting out all of the impurities in the steel, which makes the product weaker."

"Do you think someone is doing it intentionally, or is it just sloppy work?"

"There appears to be a pattern to it. I haven't put my finger on what it is yet. I just don't know what to do with the information once I get it compiled."

"Call one of those lawyers."

42

THE 757

Jim sat down with John and Ralph. "I think we are close to finding the truth on these crankshafts, but I am running out of ideas. I can't figure out where to go from here."

"There's a tavern near the front gate where I understand all of the guys go after they get off the three-to-eleven shift. I could start hanging around there a couple of nights a week and listen to the bar talk."

"I am not going to ask you to do that. At least not yet. What other ideas can we come up with?"

"Have you run a Dun & Bradstreet report on them?" John asked.

"Yeah, but it didn't tell me very much, just that they pay their bills on time most of the time."

"Why don't you purchase a few shares of their stock? Let's see if their annual report gives us any clues?"

"John that is a good idea. What else?"

"Do we know anybody that works out there?" Ralph asked.

"I don't. Do you, John?"

"I don't think so."

"I'm getting paranoid. We haven't heard of any major crash in the last few days. That thing up in Canada was horrible."

John looked like he was lost in thought.

"I wonder what other products they make out there."

"What are you thinking?"

"Could they also make bridge support beams? Do you remember that bridge that collapsed somewhere a couple of years back, killing all of those people?"

"You don't suppose the Russians are doing it, do you?"

"Doing what? Ralph, you have lost me," John said.

"You know, sending us bad stuff over here. Look at those two buildings in New York that fell down after them two airplanes hit 'em. I still don't see how an airplane hitting the top of a building can make the whole thing fall down. It was like one of them implosions, you know, where they set the dynamite just right and the whole building just falls down. If the Russians or the Chinese were sending us bad steel, would more buildings be fixin' to fall down?"

"Guys, the problem is we know that at least one of the crankshafts that failed was made right here in our town. Does that mean they all were?"

"I just don't know."

While they were talking, one of the flight instructors poked his head in the door.

"Flip on your TV. There is a 757 inbound for DFW that has lost his right engine."

Jim flipped his chair around and picked up the remote. The screen came on with a picture of a 757 in flight. The pictures were obviously taken from another airplane.

All at once, John exclaimed, "Look, his right engine is gone."

"Look at that. The engine fell off," Ralph said.

"What does that do to the handling characteristics of that airplane?"

"It is sure going to screw up his weight and balance," Jim said.

The reporter was saying, "Somewhere over the ranch lands of West Texas, the right engine departed from the jetliner. I wonder why they didn't have him land at Abilene or Wichita Falls. Why did they allow him to continue into the crowded Dallas–Fort Worth area?"

Another anchor person said, "We have Captain Wilkinson, a retired Piedmont Airline captain, with us on line one. Good morning, Captain, what can you tell us?"

Ralph snorted and threw an empty diet coke can in the trash can sitting over in the corner. "Where do they get these broken-down windbags?"

Captain Wilkinson was saying, "As you know, these airplanes are designed to fly on only one engine. That was assuming the nonworking engines were still attached to the airplane. I have on more than one occasion shut down one engine in flight as a precaution if it was overheating or losing oil pressure. I have never had an engine just quit on its own, and I certainly have never had one fall off before."

"What kind of problem does this cause the pilot?"

Captain Wilkinson said, "I am not sure anybody knows. This much I can tell you. One of those engines weighs over seven thousand pounds. That airplane is balanced if you have a seven-thousand-pound engine hanging off each wing. It is definitely not balanced if one falls off."

The anchor person said, "Would it be like if I was walking with a ten pound bowling ball in each hand and I dropped one?"

"It would be more like the scene where you were walking on ice with a hundred-pound bowling ball in each hand and you dropped one."

"That is probably a pretty accurate assessment," John said.

Captain Wilkinson went on to say, "The problems are going to come when he tries to land. He obviously has been able to trim the plane to compensate for the uneven weight distribution, at this speed. No one knows what is going to happen when he slows down to land."

The anchor person asked, "Why do you think they allowed him to come on in to the Dallas-Fort Worth area?"

"There was no reason not to. He has the aircraft under control or at least appears to in the picture you are showing.

If he is going to crash and we are all praying that he doesn't, he is going to crash in the vicinity of an airport when he slows to land. The big airport at DFW is better equipped to handle major emergencies than any of the smaller airports."

"Listen," John said as he picked up his handheld radio and turned up the volume.

The controller was saying, "American nineteen forty-seven, you are cleared to land runway one four left. Can you make that runway?"

A calm, steady voice replied, "If I can make any runway, that one is as good as any."

Another airplane made contact. "DFW tower, this is Delta 3366 at one four left, ready to depart."

The controller came back. "Attention, all aircraft, I am halting all departure until American nineteen forty-seven is on the ground. Everybody, stand by."

———————————

The phone rang. Jim answered. "This is Jim Colburn. Can I help you?"

"Hi, Dad, you will never guess who we ran into over here in Honolulu?"

"Don Ho or Elvis?"

"No, silly. Reverend John Davis and Ann."

"No kidding. How are they doing?"

"They appear to be great. They are celebrating their twenty-fifth anniversary. We had dinner with them last night. Can you believe we'll be coming home in just forty-eight hours? It seems like we just got here."

"How long are John and Ann going to be there?"

"They got here the same day we did, and they are going back on Monday."

"Well, y'all continue to have fun, and tell John and Ann I said hello. We'll see you when you get back."

Jim turned his attention back to the 757.

John had turned down the volume, when Jim picked up the phone and turned it back up. The controller was saying, "American nineteen forty-seven, you are cleared to land use one four left or one four right, pilot's discretion."

A calm clear male voice said, "One four left or right, pilot's discretion. We are taking one four left."

"I would too. Look at where all of the fire trucks are."

The three of them sat glued to the radio and the TV screen as the big plane came closer and close to its destiny. After what seemed an eternity, the big plane touched down. All three men started to let out the breath they had each been holding when all at once the airliner careened off the runway, plowing up the grass between the runway and the taxiway—crashing into a fire truck that had been running alongside of it. It took a few seconds for the dust and smoke to clear; then you could see firemen racing to the crippled airplane, and then the slides popped out, and people started sliding down. At the same time, the stairs came down and rescue personnel started running up into the airplane.

The announcers were saying, "He is on the ground. We don't know how many injured we have. The fire rescue personnel were right there. In fact, when he veered off the runway, he crashed into one of the fire trucks. We don't know if any of the firemen were injured. Stay tuned. We will keep you updated as we receive information from the scene. It is time for a station break."

"It could have been a whole lot worse. Ralph, what holds those engines on a plane like the seven fifty seven?"

"A series of large bolts through an attach point."

"What would happen if you had inferior bolts?"

"You would lose the engine just like he did, but those bolts are tested and retested many times."

"What are the odds that they will ever find one of those bolts?"

"Oh, you may be surprised. When I was in the military, we had GPS that would tell us exactly where he was when it turned loose. They will find the engine for sure. With some of the equipment the military has, it is possible they will find the actual bolts. They are pretty big."

"Yeah, each one is bigger than your thumb and about six inches long," Ralph said.

"Wow, they may find some dead cows. It would be like fifty-caliber bullets coming from the sky."

43

THE BAR

Greg pulled his Porsche into the Lamp Lighter parking lot. He had ran home and put on jeans and a sweatshirt. He knew that dressed in his normal work clothes, he was going to stand out like a diamond in a bed of coal. The air was filled with blue smoke, and the jukebox was about twenty decibels too loud, but the place had a comfortable feel about it. Greg thought, *This is a working man's bar.*

Looking, he saw there was an opening at the right end of the bar. He just slid onto the stool when a pretty little brunet plopped a napkin down in front of him and asked, "What'll ya have?"

"What do you have on draft?"

"Miller Lite, Coors, and Bud Light."

"Make it a Bud Light."

She was back in a moment with a frosty glass. "That'll be two fifty."

Greg handed her three ones and said, "Keep the change." Greg had learned you never want to appear as a cheapskate, and you do not want be known as a big tipper either. Because both stand out and he wanted to blend in. Greg had done his homework. He knew that the old-time foreman out at Ace had retired two years ago. Most of these guys looked to be in their twenties, so that meant that they could not have worked there more than four or five years.

Four of five guys were playing pool after sipping his beer for a few minutes. He wandered over to the lighted area around the pool table. "Mind if I watch?" Greg asked no one in particular.

"No. Make yourself at home," a couple of the guys said.

Greg watched and, after a few minutes, said, "Whatever happened to ole Otto?"

One of the guys looked at Greg and asked, "Did you work for Otto?"

"No, my old man did before I went to Afghanistan."

One clean-cut-looking young man looked up from taking a shot. "What unit were you in?"

Greg thought quickly of a unit he had written a piece on last year. "Armored cav."

"Did you ever get to Iraq?"

"No, all we ever did was drag a heavy artillery piece up a mountain and lob high explosives down on bad guys."

"You were the guys that had the patch that said *death from above*."

"That was us."

The young man walked over and shook Greg's hand and said, "Larry McConnell, one hundred and first."

Greg wanted to change the subject, so he asked, "Can anybody play?"

"Sure, just put your quarter on the table, and you can play the winner. We are playing for beers. You lose, you buy."

"Buy for the guy who beat me or the whole bar?"

"Everybody in this light circle."

"So all a guy has to do is sit in this circle, and he can drink free all night?"

About six guys spoke at once. "No, it don't work that way. You ain't playing, you ain't stayin'."

Greg lost but just by a couple of shots. He didn't want to appear to lose too easily. "Good game." Then he turned and yelled to the bartender, "Miss." When the girl looked up, he waved his finger in a circle to mean to include every man in the light circle.

"So they suckered you into buying, huh?" she said when she brought the tray with all of the beers on it.

A chorus of guys said, "Brenda, you hush. We got us a newbie here. Don't run him off."

"I lost, so they said I had to buy."

"They have the table rigged. You can't win. All you can do is buy."

Greg made this exaggerated concerned look and said, "In that case, you better bring us another round. I'll just go ahead and buy and save all that sweat."

The next day, Greg called Jim.

"Mr. Colburn, this's Greg. I hung out at a bar where the workers go after the shift finishes. They were telling me some interesting things."

"That is funny. Ralph suggested yesterday that he would be willing to hang out there and see what he could learn. What did you hear?"

"Not much yet, but there is some undercurrent. Something's going on that the old-timers don't like. They were a little reluctant to talk about it. I'm certain that if I hang out there a few more nights, I can win some of their confidence and get them to open up."

"Let me tell you what we have learned. That bicycle crank that we sent to the testing lab—was made right there."

"Wait, what bicycle crank?"

"I'm sorry. I thought we told you. Ralph's kid was riding his bike the other day, and the pedal crank broke in two pieces. We sent it to Jim Aleszka's testing lab, and he said it was made at Ace. He also said that the test showed that someone had short cycled the furnace during the smelting of the steel and didn't burn off all of the impurities—which made the steel weaker. That's why it broke when a six-year-old kid was riding it."

Greg thought for a moment, then asked, "Why would someone do that?"

"James told me that they use the old Bessemer furnaces out there, which are very expensive to run. It costs hundreds of dollars a minute, so if you shorten the smelting time, you lower the cost to make that batch of steel."

Greg was quiet for a minute, then said, "The old-timers would notice that the time had been short cycled, and they would know what it did to the product."

"That would be my guess."

"I think I'll wait until Friday night and stop in there again. It'll look suspicious if I start showing up too often."

"What's your girlfriend going to think about you hanging out in bars every night?"

"Right now, I don't have a steady girlfriend, but there is a hot little bar maid there at the bar."

"Oh, I see, so your interest is not totally journalistic. Let me know what you find out."

John walked into Jim's office.

"Guess who the production manager out at the foundry is?"

"I give up. Who?"

"Timothy Arnold's father."

Jim sat straight up in his chair. "You are kidding!"

"No, I was talking to Christie down in the café, and she happened to mention that her sister was the secretary to the production manager. Then she said, 'You know Timothy that crashed, it is his father.'"

"I wonder if her sister would know what's going on out there."

"I don't know. We've got to be careful, because if we start asking questions, it'll tip him off that we're looking."

"I just talked to Greg. He hung out last night at the bar that Ralph volunteered to go to. He tells me that he got the feeling there is something going on out at the foundry that the old-timers don't like. The feeling was that there was something that they didn't want to talk about. He is going back Friday night."

"Jim, when are your kids coming back from Hawaii?"

"They are coming back Sunday. I wish they were back. After that 757 lost the attach bolts the other day, I have been worried about their flight back."

"Look at it this way. First off, American is flying the L-10-11 on the Hawaiian route, so those engine mount bolts have been on there a while. Second, the L-10-11 has three engines one on each wing and one sticking out of the tail of the plane. So if he lost both engines on the wing, he could keep flying."

"That's a good point. I wonder who my friend John flew with to get over there. I hope they have L-10-11s also."

"That is not likely. Most airlines are phasing them out. By the way, did you buy any stock in the foundry?"

"Yes, and I received their last annual report. It has been a stable old company for the past sixty years. It's also by far the largest employer in our area. I'm going to shut that sucker down as soon as we can prove they knew they were putting out bad parts."

"If we find proof?"

"No, we are going to find proof. I feel that we are getting close. I suspect Greg is going to find something out there at that bar. I'm still trying to think of an angle on Christie's sister. I haven't got that one figured out yet."

"Jim, you know Christie and Allie were real close. In fact, the last person Allie talked to before ya'll took off was Christie. Who knows, Christie might convince her sister to help us."

"That's a good point. Let me keep thinking about it. How's the student count right now?"

"It's way up. It always is this time of year. I think we should retire those two oldest Cessna 152s next spring and replace them with two more of those new trainers. Those things are performing well."

"Okay, just keep me posted," Jim said.

After John left his office, Jim said, "God, I couldn't stand it if something happened to Kay and her family or John and Ann. Please let those two planes make it home from Hawaii."

44

TAKING THE BABY TO HOUSTON

Juanita said, "Baby, my parents are going to Houston next weekend to see my grandmamma, and they want us to go with them so grandmamma can see the baby."

"Sweetie, when do they want to go?"

"Next weekend."

"Sweetie, I can't go. We're taking inventory at the plant. I'll have to work Saturday. There's no reason you and the baby can't go."

"Baby, will you be all right here by yourself?"

"Juanita, I'm six feet tall. I weigh one hundred and eighty pounds, and I can run like a gazelle. I'll be just fine."

"Yes, but you can't find your socks in the morning, so, Mr. Macho Man, my question is still, will you be all right?"

"I could find 'em if you would quit movin' 'em on me."

She laughed. "They have been in the same drawer for five years. Of course you can always call me, and I will give you directions over the phone."

"Yeah, well, it is a good thing your daddy is driving, because you and your mother would never find Houston if you didn't have one of us men along to find the way. Who was it that called me last month when the mother and grandmother couldn't find the doctor's office so they could take the baby back for a checkup?"

"That was different. They had construction in the way."

"Seriously, sweetie, I think you should go and take your camera so you can get a three-generation picture. After all, Grandmamma may not be around long enough for Janica to get to know her, but you can always show her the pictures."

That evening, when Harold came in, Juanita said, "Sweetie, Daddy said if you can't go with us, he would like to go Friday. If it is all right with you, I would like to attend our tenth high school reunion Friday night. Mom, Jim C. and Grandmamma can watch the baby. I would like to see Lawna and LaQuisha and the whole gang again and come back Saturday so we don't have to miss church Sunday. Is that all right with you?"

"Sweetie, I wish I could go with you. I would like to see the look on all your old high school boyfriend's faces when they see how beautiful you are now. I would like to see them when they realize what they let get away."

"I wish you could go with me, because I would love to see the sheer jealously on the women's faces when they see what a handsome devil I married."

"Sweetie, you go see Grandmamma and have a good time. Going Friday is fine because you and the baby will be back in time for church also."

Friday morning, Juanita's parents were there early. While Grandmother and Mother were fussing over getting the baby ready to go, Harold and his father-in-law attached the baby's car seat into the Buick.

"Harold, how are things at the foundry?"

"Oh, Pops, it is all right. They have me designing collars for some big oil well drilling equipment. You would be surprised at how much pressure there is in one of those things. If we don't get it just right, that thing will blow and it would be awful to be anywhere around that thing when it blew."

"Are these drilling rings on platforms out in the gulf?"

"Mostly, but some are used on land also, depending on how deep they have to go. What is scary is how they are drillin' right in neighborhoods. They are drillin' right on the school yard over on Fifth Street."

Soon they had the baby loaded into her seat. Juanita turned and kissed her husband.

"Don't let anything happen to Janica's daddy while we are gone."

45

THE FLIGHT HOME FROM HAWAII

Kay had her whole crew on board. They were seated like before. The guys were in row sixteen A and B, while she and Ann were seated in row seventeen A and B.

David turned around and said, "Mom, are you sure we have to go back now? We could get off and stay another week."

"That would be fun, but, no, we have to get back."

The plane started to push back from the gate. Kay's husband, Danny, was sitting, looking out the window and watching the man with the orange flag walking by the wingtip. All at once, the airplane lurched and then stopped moving. He turned to David and said, "What was that?"

"I don't know, but it wasn't good whatever it was."

At that same instant, Ann asked, "What was that?"

"I don't know. I was just telling Dad. Whatever it was, it wasn't good."

———————

Jim tied his running shoes and headed out the door, then stopped and went back for his cell phone. Today was Sunday, and his training schedule called for a twelve-mile run today. Looking down at the picture on the front of his shirt, he said, "Okay, Allie, let's do it. Today we are going to run all of the way around the lake."

Hitting a fast but comfortable pace, he headed down Shenandoah Street and headed for the entrance into the state park jogging path that ran around the lake. Talking to the picture on the front of his shirt, he said, "Allie, I love these morning runs. The air is clean, and it is not yet hot. There are not too many runners out yet. I feel good. We are going to have a good run today."

Just as he turned the corner into the state park, his cell phone rang. Looking at the display, he could see that it was Kay calling.

"Hi, sweetheart, are ya'll on your way home?"

"Dad, there is a problem."

Jim felt his pulse quicken. "Sweetheart, what is it?"

"Dad, we were on the plane backing out from the gate when something broke, so they made us all get off, and they tell us we can't get another flight until tomorrow."

"What happened?"

"Here, I'll put David on. He can tell you."

"Grandpa, the steel pin on the nose gear that they used to attach the tug to the airplane broke, and they don't have another one here on the island, so we have to wait until they can bring one from the mainland."

Jim let out the breath he had been holding ever since he heard he words, "There is a problem."

"I'm so sorry for you, David. What a terrible thing to happen? You're going to have to stay another night in Hawaii."

"Yeah, Grandpa, it is rough over here—the palm trees, the bikinis, and island music. It is rough, but we'll survive."

Jim was laughing at his grandson. "Call me when you know when you are coming home."

"Allie that was the kids calling from Hawaii. A steel pin that attaches the airplane to the tug broke. They're going to be stuck there another day." Then he thought, *another steel pin broke that is never supposed to break?*

46

GREG RUNS INTO HAROLD

Greg had gone into the office. This morning, he was still looking into the foundry. He had gotten a list of all the employees, hoping to find a way to talk to someone who could tell him exactly what was going on out there. One thing he had learned by hanging around the bar was that there was a really great bunch of guys who worked out there. He thought of Charles Ray. He and his wife were trying to adopt a baby. Billy Joe was working, trying to save enough to go to college in the fall. He was convinced that they were not the cause of the problem. He doubted that they even knew a problem existed. Even though he was certain that they knew something was going on that they did not like or approve of, but what?

Just as he turned into Wall Street, his cell phone rang. He reached down to pick it up off the seat beside him, then looked up and said, "Oh dangit!"

When he reached for the phone, he took his eyes off the road and his Porsche slammed into a minivan that stopped at the traffic light.

There was a hollow thump, followed by the sound of glass and metal falling to the street.

Greg jumped out of his car and started for the driver's side of the van. The door opened, and a nice-looking black man emerged from the van.

"Sir, I'm so sorry. I looked down to pick up my phone, and then when I looked up, there you were. I'm so sorry. Are you all right?"

The driver of the van said, "I am fine. I don't think your car is, though."

Greg looked back at the Porsche. Being smaller and sitting lower to the ground, it had gone under the back of the minivan. The van had some damage, but the worst of the two was the Porsche.

"Sir, I am so sorry. Let's get the cars out of the road so other cars can go by, and I'll give you my insurance company. We'll repair your car. It was all my fault."

When they were safely over to the curb, Greg removed the insurance papers from his glove box, and he took a card from his wallet.

"Sir, again, I'm so sorry." Handing him his card, he said, "My name is Greg Standefer. I work for the news."

The other driver handed him a card that said *Harold Johnson Engineer* ACE FOUNDRY on it.

Greg stared at it for a moment, then said, "You work for the foundry?"

"Yes."

"Oh, here's the name of my insurance company and the policy number. Is your car drivable?"

"Yes, I can drive it. Are you okay, man? You seem shook up."

"I need to call a wrecker for my car." He was staring at the card he held in his hand, "Harold, I'm working on a story that I think you could help me with. As soon as the wrecker gets here, would you have time to grab some lunch somewhere? That's if you could give me a ride."

Harold looked back at the card he was holding in his hand and asked, "What kind of story are you working on?"

"Harold, I would rather answer that over lunch if we could. It is a complicated story, but I think you could really help me put some missing pieces together. What do you say?"

"Well, since we just bumped into each other and I haven't had lunch, so what the heck."

As soon as they were seated in the booth, Harold said, "Okay, Mr. Reporter Man, what is this big mystery that you are working on?"

Greg held up Harold's business card and said, "This's what I'm working on. Let me tell you where I am and see if you can fill in some blanks for me."

Then he proceeded to tell about the plane crash that killed Allie, the bus crash, the school bus crash, even the bicycle crank, and all of their suspicions. He saw this pained expression come over Harold's face.

"That explains something."

"Explains what?"

"JR Colburn is my attorney."

Then he went on to explain how he had tried to get JR to help him expose the things he had found wrong at the foundry and how JR had said he couldn't represent him anymore because a conflict of interest.

Greg's eyebrows shot up. "You know JR?"

"He drew up the wills for my wife and me."

"You are the mystery source."

"What do you mean?"

"JR came to me a few weeks back and was telling me about problems at the foundry, but he would not tell me where he had gotten the information. He got it from you."

They talked for another half hour; then Greg asked, "Do you have time to meet with JR and his dad?"

"My wife and daughter are gone to Houston. They won't be back until late this evening. So, yes, I can meet with them."

"Let me call them."

First Greg dialed Jim's phone. "Mr. Colburn, this is Greg. I'm sitting here in Denny's, talking to a gentleman that you need to talk with. Can you meet with us right now?"

"Sure, Greg, do you want to come by my house, or do you want me to meet you somewhere?"

"Sir, your house is fine. Can you call JR and see if he can meet with us also?"

"Greg, this must be important. I'll find JR. How long will it take you to get here?"

"About half an hour."

"Come on. I'll call JR right now."

Half an hour later, when he pulled up into Jim's circle driveway, JR's car was already there. Greg rang the doorbell, and Jim's voice came over the intercom speaker box. "Come on in, Greg. It is unlocked. We're in the kitchen."

When the two walked into the breakfast area, JR looked up and stopped for a moment, then said, "Hello, Harold."

"Mr. Colburn, I want to introduce Harold Johnson. He's an engineer for ACE Foundry. I literally ran into him this morning."

Jim shook Harold's hand. "Glad to know you, Mr. Johnson. Do you boys want a cup of coffee?"

"Harold, don't be offended by that remark. Dad calls all males under fifty boys. It has nothing to do with race."

"No offence taken." Then he turned back to Jim. "No, sir, we have been sitting in a Denny's for four hours. I've had enough coffee."

JR looked at Greg. "Where did you 'run into' Harold?"

"At the corner of Wall street and Fifth Avenue."

JR looked confused.

Harold spoke up. "I was stopped at the light on the corner of Wall Street and Fifth when this guy in a Porsche tried to drive under my van."

"So, Greg, you literally did 'run into' him?"

Both men said, "Yes."

"JR, Harold tells me he is the source you couldn't tell me about."

"He can tell you that I can't."

"I understand. He and I have been comparing notes for the past four hours. That is why I asked you two to meet with us. If we decide we want to and if we have enough to convince my editors to run the story, we can still make the Sunday edition."

"Mr. Johnson, apparently you have met both of these guys before this, but you and I haven't met. Would you mind telling me what you have told them?"

"Sir, please call me Harold. About two years ago, I was doing some research and discovered that the nitride coating we were putting on our crankshafts for aircraft engines was too thin. I went to the production manager, and he blew me off."

"Then what did you do?"

"I went over his head and went to the CEO."

"Did you get in trouble with your boss for going over his head?"

"Sir, I am an engineer. The production manager is technically under me."

"Why do you say technically?"

"Because production is supposed to follow engineering exactly as it is drawn. After I got back to my office, I sent an e-mail to my wife. Here it is." He passed his laptop to Jim.

Jim looked at Greg. "Can you run with this?"

"There is one problem, Dad. Right now, it is Harold's word against theirs. If Greg runs a story about them with only that e-mail, only two things are going to happen. Harold will get fired, and the newspaper will get sued."

Jim looked back at Harold. "Can you get any proof and bring it to us?"

"There is problem. All of my files are suddenly missing."

"My editors will never let me run a story without more proof than we have."

"I bought two new crankshafts and flew out to California and took them to the testing lab. They were perfect. Harold, how do you explain that?"

"If you look at my e-mail, it says the CEO told me to fix the problem. I drew up new specs on all of the crankshafts going out after that date."

Jim thought for a moment and said, "That is when they started short cycling the furnaces."

"Sir, today is the first time I have heard about that. If they are doing that, they are absolutely not following the plans drawn up by the engineering department. I can routinely do a quality control check on some parts and see if they pass inspection, but if they are not doing it all of the time, it will be the luck of the draw if I get a batch that was short cycled."

JR spoke up. "Even if we found a bad batch, then the production people would start pointing fingers at the engineering people and the engineering people would be pointing at the production people. Nobody would take the blame. The real culprits in the front office would go on TV and promise a thorough investigation, and the whole thing would be swept under the rug."

"Here is what we know. Allie is gone, then the four in Colorado, the three in Brazil. Sixteen people died in the Tennessee bus wreck. Then twenty-nine school children died in a school bus accident in Canada. All of these were caused by an inferior crankshaft that came from this foundry. Guys, we have got to stop this madman before a jetliner filled with people crashes, killing several hundred or who knows what else. Guys, what can we do?"

Saturday afternoon, David and Ann ran into John and Ann again.

John said, "Hey, I thought you guys left this morning."

"We liked it here, so we decided to stay," David said,

"I can understand that I have been trying to get Ann to do the same thing."

"As much as we would like to stay, the reason we're still here's when they tried to push our plane back this morning, a little steel pin that attaches the tug to the airplane broke, and they have to bring one from the mainland. So we're now scheduled to leave tomorrow."

"What a terrible thing to happen. You're forced to send an extra day in Hawaii."

Ann Davis said, "Gee, I hope this's not a bad omen."

47

FINALLY GOING HOME

The L-10-11 from Hawaii landed at DFW Airport at ten thirty Monday morning.

David said, "I loved Hawaii, but I don't like sitting in the backseat of a jetliner for seven or eight hours."

"It would be easier if you were sitting up there where the dials and gauges are," his sister said.

"I don't care where you sit. Seven and a half hours, it's too long for me."

"Wonder if Reverend John and Mrs. Davis have made it home yet?" Kay said.

"No, they were not leaving until two hours after we were, and they had to change planes in New York. They won't get home until sometime this afternoon," David said.

"I am glad we ran into them. They are such nice people. You two were just little kids the last time they saw you. I hope they get home safely."

Harold had told Juanita all about the meeting at Jim Colburn's house.

Monday morning, he kissed Juanita good-bye and said, "Wish me luck in finding some concrete evidence that we can use today."

"Sweetie, you be careful. This is starting to scare me."

Not long after arriving at his desk, Harold told his assistant, "I am going to the archive and do some research on these well casings." Once there, he started digging through stacks of old disks.

At the end of the day, he had found nothing incriminating. Whoever was doing this was covering their tracks well. Harold thought, *Where have they slipped up? They can't cover every track.*

Skimming through electronic files, he saw something that stopped him cold.

The 737 was cruising at thirty-three thousand feet from New York, bound for Omaha, Nebraska, when all at once the airplane shuddered and flames shot out the back of the right engine. Everyone seated on the right side could see the flames. The captain immediately activated the fire suppressant system, and the flames died. Then the intercom came on. "Ladies and gentlemen, this is the captain speaking. We have experienced a failure in the right engine. There is no need for concern. This airplane is designed to fly on one engine. However, I have decided to make an emergency landing in Chicago, which is only thirty minutes in front of us. We are contacting the operations people in Chicago right now, so they can be making arrangements to get you on your way to Omaha as quickly as possible."

Several people started to cry. Some started to swear. "I am going to miss my connecting flight."

"We are going to get stuck here in Chicago."

"I have an important meeting tomorrow morning. I think I'll get a car and drive."

Ann turned to John and said, "Do you think he will be able to land this airplane in Chicago all right?"

"I don't know. He said he could fly on one engine, so I guess he can."

The flight attendant stopped by John's seat and said, "The flight manifest says you are a minister. Is that right?"

"Yes."

"We are supposed to be making sure everyone stays in their seats, but some of the people are near panic. Would you mind coming up front and leading a prayer?"

John reached down and unbuckled his seat belt. "I will be glad to."

Following the flight attendant to the front of the cabin, he thought, *It is a good thing this plane doesn't have a first-class section.* When they reached the front, the attendant looked at her seating chart and picked up the microphone.

"Ladies and gentlemen, this is Reverend John Davis. He is the pastor at Fairview Methodist Church. I have no doubt that our captain is more than qualified to fly this airplane. However, I have asked Reverend Davis to lead us in prayer for a safe landing."

She handed John the mic. John said, "Feel free to pray with me.

> Our Father who is in heaven, hallowed be Your name. Your kingdom come. Your will be done on earth as it is in heaven. Give us this day, our daily bread. And forgive us our debts as we also have forgiven our debtors. And do not lead us into temptation, but deliver us from evil. For Yours is the kingdom and the power and the glory forever. Amen."

John then paused for a few seconds, then continued, "Holy Father, we beseech you on behalf of all on the airplane. Father, we know that we are all terminal, and one day we will all die and stand before you. On behalf of our families, we ask that you guide this crew that is piloting the plane. Give them courage and wisdom and skill. Father, may we the passengers use this experience to look deep inside of ourselves and know that we are always in need of your protection in everything we do. Amen."

With that, he handed the mic back to the flight attendant and started back to his seat. Almost everyone reached to shake his hand and thank him for the prayer.

When John and Ann were safely on the ground at O'Hare Field, the first thing they did was call their kids and let them know that they were safely on the ground at Chicago. Soon they were booked on another flight bound for Omaha.

Before they boarded, Ann said, "Should we call Jim and let him know that we are okay and boarding a new flight home?"

"Probably a good idea. Something like this might make CNN or something, and he might see it."

48

THE CLASS ACTION LAWSUIT

Jim hurried to get home because JR, Harold, and Greg were meeting at Jim's house at eight this evening. Greg arrived first. Jim could hear that powerful engine on his Porsche when he roared up the circle drive. Jim thought, *Greg goes like he is on the way to put out a fire everywhere he goes.*

As Greg mounted the steps, Jim opened the door. "Come on in, Greg. What news do you have?"

"I don't have any more than the last time we talked. Maybe one of the other guys have something new. Have you come up with anything new?"

JR and Harold arrived at the same time. JR pushed open the front door and yelled, "Is anybody home?"

"Back in the kitchen."

As soon as they were all sitting around the table, Harold said, "I may have something here." Opening his briefcase, he pulled out four copies of a graph.

"What am I looking at, Harold?" Greg asked.

"It may be nothing, but what you have there is a graph from the electric company showing the electric uses hour by hour for the last three months. You see the sudden drop in usage every so often. I went back and found these." He handed another set of graphs. "This is the same graphs from two years ago. There are no sudden drops in usage during that time period."

"So this shows that they are short cycling the furnace every so often?"

"It sure looks that way. That smelting equipment uses thousands of kilowatts per minute when it is running, so shutting it down would certainly drop the kilowatt usage for that time period."

Jim said, "Harold, you are an engineer. Can you testify to that fact?"

Before Harold could answer, JR spoke up. "Just a minute. They could say that they shut down the equipment for cleaning or maintenance. You notice that almost all of these drops are on the night shift."

While everybody was venting their frustration about their inability to pin anything on the foundry, Jim was quietly making a list on a legal pad in front of him. When he had finished, Jim handed his list to Greg and said, "Greg, here is a list of the accidents that we know of where people died. Do you have the resources to find the name and address of the family of each victim?"

"Give me a couple of days. I'll bet I can."

"Dad, what are you thinking?"

"In a civil lawsuit, we don't need the burden of proof that we need in a criminal indictment, right?"

"Yes, that's right."

"How much would it cost to file a class action suit for all the victims' families?"

"Dad, it is not that easy. We would have to contact all of the families and get a number of them to agree to be a party to a suit."

"How hard would that be?"

"If Greg can find them, then getting them to agree to be a party to the suit should not be hard. As to how much would it cost, a suit of this magnitude is more than our little firm could handle."

"You could be lead council, then hire Kelly and his crew to assist you."

"Well, in theory, that is true. If they agreed to participate."

"How much money are we talking about?"

"Dad, you are talking about a lot of time. I would guess that you are talking about a hundred thousand to get started. You know those other victim's families are not going to pay a dime."

"If you file a class action suit, I can run a story on that, can report that a suit has been filed and what the suit is alleging."

"Guys, we are running out of time. Every time I turn on the TV, I am expecting a major disaster caused by bad metal from this foundry. I am going to close that sucker down before some more innocent victims die. Harold, I will help you find a new job, but that thing is going to go down.

"Here is the way I see it. If we file a suit, then we can get people under oath and start asking questions. Greg, if you write an article about a multimillion dollar class action lawsuit, what are the odds that the national media will pick it up?"

"Oh, I can write a story that will guarantee to be picked up."

"There is one other thing I want. I don't want my name on the suit anywhere."

"Mr. Colburn, I understand how you feel. I want the problem fixed as bad as anybody. However, there are a lot of innocent people working out at the foundry. They are not the ones causing the problem, but they are depending on that foundry for their living."

Six weeks later, JR called Jim. "Dad, I filed the suit this morning. Now the stuff will start to hit the proverbial fan."

The next morning, above the fold on the front page of the newspaper was a story the head line read, "ACE Foundry Suit for One Hundred Million."

———————————

Horace Thorn stormed into the conference room, threw the newspaper on table, and demanded, "What do we know about this?"

Sara Delgado, the vice president and corporate council, said, "Horace, we just got served the suit papers this morning. We haven't had time to study it yet and see what kind of response to file."

"Somebody better get on top of this thing. Our stock closed yesterday at thirty-three dollars, and something like this could kill it!"

Turning to the public relations guy, Horace said, "Get a press release out today and say this is a nuisance suit and we look forward to seeing them in court. Then make a lot of noise about frivolous lawsuits and how they are killing our country. Then get that congressman on the line. I want to talk to him."

Rufus Arnold said, "This reporter is quoting some pretty sensitive material from the lawsuit. Where are they getting their information from?"

"That is a good point. Find out who the mole is. I want him or her out of here now."

49

HAROLD GETS FIRED

Later that evening, Harold's phone rang at home. When Juanita answered, she listened quietly for a moment, then walked over and handed the phone to Harold. When he answered, a female voice said, "Harold, my name is Carrie. I am Rufus Arnold's assistant. My sister Christie and her husband own the café at the Millport Airport."

"I know your sister. What can I do for you?"

"I'm just calling to warn you they found out that you copied some of those files that are being used in the lawsuit."

"What if I said I don't know what you are talking about?"

"It wouldn't matter. They're going to fire you in the morning when you show up for work. I just felt like you should be warned. If you are helping the guys with the lawsuit, I can provide you with some more documents."

"How can I get in touch with you?"

"I will give you my cell phone number, but you have got to promise me that you will not tell anybody that I'm giving stuff to you because I can't afford to lose my job."

When Harold hung up the phone, he immediately called Jim and told him all about the phone call.

Jim listened quietly, then said, "Harold, go to the bank in the morning and apply for a twenty-thousand line of credit before you go to work. That should hold you over until this thing gets settled."

"Mr. Colburn, I don't have any way to pay back the loan even if they gave it to me."

"Harold, you have got to trust me. When this is all settled, that will not be a problem. Everything is going to be all right. Just call in, and tell your office that you are going to be running a few minutes late, then go to the bank while you are still employed."

As Harold hung up the phone, he thought, *That is easy for you to say. You are rich, and you don't have a wife and young baby to support. Besides you are not a young black whistle-blower. Why did I ever get involved?*

50

TAKING DEPOSITIONS

Rene came into Jim's office the next day. When she walked in, Jim said, "Hi, sweetheart, how is my girl?"

"Dad, I need to talk to you. Have you got a minute?"

"Honey, you know I always have time to talk to one of you kids. What have you got on your mind?"

"Dad, I read that article in the paper about the lawsuit that JR filed."

"Okay, what about?"

"Dad, I know you too well. I see your fingerprints all over that lawsuit. You are out to shut that foundry down, and I don't blame you. It was my mom that died, but, Dad, there are hundreds of good families in this town that depend on that foundry to make a living. Go after the ones that are guilty, but don't shut down the plant."

Jim looked at his daughter for several seconds before answering; then he said, "Rene, I know it hurt when you lost your mom, but you still have your family. I wake up in a cold lonely house every morning. Worse, there are fifty plus other family members of people who have died as a result of their sloppy operations or worse their criminal activity. This lawsuit is our only way to get people under oath and try to find out who the guilty parties are and who is not. Sweetheart, we have just got to let the chips fall where they fall."

Later that day, Jim rode his Harley Davidson home—strapped on his running shoes and pulled on his Allie tee shirt. As he ran, he kept thinking about the things Rene had said. He thought, *I have no desire to punish any innocent people. Enough innocent people have been hurt already. How do you separate the wheat from the weeds?* As he ran, a plan started to come together in his mind.

JR and his team started moving aggressively on taking depositions. The whole idea was to find sufficient evidence to get the justice department to open an investigation into the foundry. Slowly but surely a story started to emerge. They did not start with the top executives; they started with the people working on the plant floor.

Horace Thorn said, "Sara, do something. You are the company lawyer. Do something. Keep those clowns out of my foundry."

"Horace, the law is very specific. They have the right to interview any person they want so long as the testimony relates to the case. If we try to interfere with them, all he has to do is complain to the judge and she will send the marshals out here with them."

Horace spun around and slammed the piece of paper that he had balled up down into the bottom of the trash can. "I don't want them here!"

Jim typed in the three-letter identifier for the foundry into the computer and pulled up the latest stock quote. The day before the lawsuit was filed, the stock was selling for thirty-three dollars a share. Today, it was at nineteen.

He then typed a letter to the company stating that he owned ten shares of stock and demanded a meeting of the stockholders. He then posted his letter online at a popular chat room. Then he sent a letter to the editors demanding a meeting of the stockholders. Three days later, the whole editorial page was covered with letters from other stockholders, demanding a meeting of the stockholders.

Horace came into the office. Sara thought, *His eyes are all bloodshot and puffy looking. Either he is not getting much sleep, or he is hungover. Either way, it is not a good sign for the captain of the ship to be losing control at this time, when a steady hand is needed.*

"Good morning, Horace."

"What is good about it? Have you looked at our stock this morning?"

"No, I haven't looked this morning. What is it today?"

"It is down another five bucks—that's what it is. I have lost over a million dollars already since this started."

"Where do you think it is going to stop falling?"

"Who knows? I even got a call from a Fox news reporter asking me if there was an investigation by the justice department."

"Have you seen today's paper?"

"No, what does that rag have in it today?"

She handed the paper to him. It read, "Federal Aviation Agency starts investigation into ACE Foundry products used in airplane engines and other parts."

"I don't care what this crummy newspaper prints. They just want to sell papers."

"I have already received a call from a lawyer for the FAA wanting to ask some questions."

Horace jerked a pack of cigarettes out of his pocket and lit one. Sara wanted to remind him that this was a no-smoking-allowed building, but decided against it.

JR's office was flooded with calls from all over the country, people wanting to add their name to the class action lawsuit. The volume of calls required him to hire six people just to answer all of the calls. Some were legitimate; some were crazy, like the man who wanted JR to add his name to the list because a screen-door spring broke an put his eye out back in 1995. Greg stopped by JR's office.

"Anything new on the foundry suit?"

"No, but you could write a book about all of the crazy calls we are getting. Dad called and wants you and me to come by his place this evening. Can you make it?"

Greg asked, "What time?"

"He didn't say. You pick a time, and I'll tell him that is when we can be there."

"Does he have something new?"

"I don't know, but he did sound like it was important."

At seven, Greg roared up the drive and bounded up the steps, carrying a brown paper bag. Without knocking, he pushed open the door and yelled, "This is the Avon lady. Anybody home?"

"Kitchen."

When Greg rounded the corner into the kitchen, Jim looked up and said, "That has to be the ugliest Avon lady I have ever seen. What's in the sack?"

"A bottle of single malt scotch. If you are going to continue having these clandestine late-night meetings, I am going to at least have a drink. Where do you keep your glasses?"

Jim pointed to one of the cabinets and said, "Does your momma know you are drinking that stuff?"

JR popped through the door. "Drinking what stuff?"

"I brought a bottle of single malt scotch. I told the old geezer if he was going to keep dragging me to these clandestine late-night meetings I was at least going to have a drink."

"Well, I don't want to see you trying to drink it all—by yourself. So pour two."

"What about you, Mr. Colburn?"

Jim just shook his head. He was looking at copies if the depositions that he had spread out on the table.

When both of the other men were seated, he said, "Look at this girl's depositions. She has given us a lot of information, but I get the feeling she would like to give us even more. We just didn't ask the right questions."

"Why do you say that?"

"Read her answers. She obviously hates the guy she works for, and we know why. He is a scumbag."

Looking down at the questions and answers, Jim said, "Look at line one ninety-seven, 'Do you keep logs on the times that each smelting is run?' She simply answered, 'Yes.'

Then the young lawyer that Kelly loaned to you asked, 'Are any logs missing?'

She answered, 'No.'

Then he asked, 'Are all logs complete?'

She answered, 'They are all filled out accurately.'"

"Do you think this girl is trying to tell us something?"

"I will subpoena all production logs. Then we can call her back in to verify that they gave us all of the logs."

51

SELLING EVERYTHING

The next day, Jim called his broker. "I want you to liquidate all of my stock."

"Jim, you can't do that. You have been seeing the news lately? The market is in the tank right now. I'll admit that you were pretty wise in choosing where to put your money when you sold the company, but now is not a good time to sell. Where could you possible put your money that would be safer?"

"I want to convert it all to cash."

"Jim, this is crazy. Do you know what CDs are paying now?"

"Listen, I want you to convert everything to cash within the next thirty days."

"Thirty days? Jim, you are crazy."

The next day, the ACE stock closed at \$3.94. Jim bought one hundred thousand shares. The next day, it blipped up to \$4.4. Then it slipped down to \$3.87 when CNN ran a story on the foundry. Jim quietly bought another hundred thousand shares. Then he called Kelly and had him open a new LLC by the name of the Allie Group Limited.

JR called and said, "Dad, the lawyers for the foundry have filed a motion for summary judgment against us for lack of hard evidence. There is a hearing Thursday morning at nine in the judge's chambers."

"What does that mean?"

"They are going to try to convince the judge to throw out our suit by claiming there is not enough solid evidence to support our case."

"Can they do that?"

"The answer is, yes, they can file it. Ordinarily, I would say no. Judges rarely grant a summary judgment in cases like this. However, the foundry is a big contributor to the Democratic Party and to this judge's campaign fund in particular."

"What can we do if she grants it?"

"Not much. We can try to get the federal court to hear the case. They are really reluctant to take a case that has already had a summary judgment against it."

"Do you mean that if she grants them the summary judgment, this case is dead?"

"If we can come up with compelling evidence, we can refile it. The new evidence must be rock solid and compelling before a court will allow a case to be reopened after a summary judgment has been granted."

JR and his staff worked until almost midnight Tuesday and Wednesday night, going over the depositions and hard evidence.

JR said, "People, give me something that will get the judge to grant a delay on her ruling. We need time. If we can get those production logs and bring Carrie back in, we will find something. I just know it."

One of the other attorneys said, "They know it too. That is why they are rushing this summary judgment through."

"Yes, they have figured out that we really don't have anything that we can prove yet and that we are using this lawsuit to find evidence to prove what we suspect. That is what their motion for summary judgment says."

Weary from lack of sleep and exhausted from pushing so hard, JR walked into the judge's chambers at nine Thursday morning.

At nine o'clock on a Thursday morning Allie Group Limited bought five hundred thousand shares of stock at three dollars a share.

––––––––––––––

The judge said, "Mr. Colburn, as you know ACE Foundry Incorporated has filed a motion for summary judgment stating that your suit lacks sufficient evidence to support going to trial. I have read your pleadings carefully. Do you have any new evidence to offer this court?"

"No, your honor. We would pray that the court would delay making a judgment in this matter to allow us time to review certain documents we have requested and have not yet received from the defendant."

The judge removed her glasses and stared at JR. "Mr. Colburn, this court will not allow you to use the court in a witch hunt. You don't file a case in this court and then go looking for evidence to support your claim. Do I make myself clear?"

"Your honor, I assure you that we are not on a witch hunt. People's lives have been lost, and many more are at risk. It is the responsibility of the court to protect the lives and well-being of the citizens in this county and this state. Therefore, I respectfully request that the court delay a ruling and further request that the court compel the defendant to produce the production logs that we have requested, which we believe will no doubt support our claim of improper production practices at ACE Foundry. These improper production practices have caused the loss of human life and represent an ongoing health and safety risk. I would further request that the court compel ACE Foundry to stop shipping any products until an independent lab has had a chance to analyze each part before it is shipped."

The judge looked up and became aware that the cameras were recording all of what JR had said. She put her glasses back on and looked down at the papers on her desk. Taking them back off, she asked, "Is it true that ACE has not produced the production logs that the plaintiff asked for?"

Sara spoke up. "We are still working on them, your honor. It is a lot of work copying all of the logs."

"That is not true, your honor. We will be glad to send a clerk to do the copying if it will help the defendant."

The judge sat for a moment, thinking. "I am going to postpone this hearing until Monday." Looking at her calendar, she said, "Monday morning at ten." Looking at Sara, she said, "Counselor, I would advise you to produce those logs before Monday morning." Turning to JR, she said, "Mr. Colburn, don't even think of trying to drag this on. With or without those logs, I will make a decision Monday morning. Good day, ladies and gentlemen."

JR walked over to Sara and said, "Ms. Delgado, I will send a courier at one to pick up those production logs. Have them ready."

Sara glared at JR as they left the courtroom and said, "I'll call you when they are ready to be picked up."

52

GUNSHOT

Jim returned to the airport. As he rounded the curve in the road just north of the airport, he thought, *Even after all of the pain and heartache associated with airplanes, this really is a pretty sight.* The long black runway flanked on each side by a long green area of grass that resembled a well-kept golf fairway, then twin long ribbons of white concrete that made up the taxiways. Then his eyes took in long rows of white hangars, punctuated in the center on the east side of the airport by ten pastel-colored condo/hangars.

Two airplanes with magnificent paint jobs were sitting at the north end of the runway, getting ready to take off. Jim thought, *How could such sorrow be rained down on this peaceful little airport?* As he watched the second airplane race down the runway and lift into the air, it suddenly occurred to him that he had not flown one of the airplanes in several weeks. At that moment, he missed flying. The intensity of the longing surprises him. He had gotten so busy he wasn't doing the thing that attracted him to invest in the airport to begin with.

Jim walked into the hangar, looked on the schedule, and saw that the Piper Cherokee was not scheduled at all this morning. So he checked it out to Jim Colburn, grabbed the flight log and the keys, and headed out to the ramp. His walk-around inspection might have been just a little bit more thorough than in the past.

As the spirited little Piper sprinted down the runway, Jim could feel the familiar thrill was back. Jim allowed his eyes to sweep the instrument dials one last time to make sure that every needle was pointing into the green area of the dial, and then he gently tugged on the yoke. She was off and climbing. He adjusted his power, raised the flaps, and adjusted the trim.

Jim announced on the radios, "Cherokee four two two niner is turning right and would depart the traffic pattern to the northwest."

Now the fun really began. Still climbing, he gently pressed on the right rudder while rolling the control wheel to the right, sending the Cherokee into a climbing right turn.

Now the Cherokee was climbing higher and faster; the rush was on for Jim. Leveling out on a northwesterly heading, Jim allowed the little airplane to continue climbing up to 4,500 feet. At that time, he dropped the nose down level with the horizon. Then he picked out a red barn on a farm far below. Pointing his left wingtip directly at the barn, he began a 360-degree turn. What made this maneuver challenging was the wind. If you were downwind of the barn, the airplane would have to bank at a steeper angle to keep the wind from pushing the wingtip off the barn.

If you were upwind, you would have to make the turn shallower to keep the wind from pushing the wingtip over the barn. It was like a well-choreographed ballet in the sky. The pilot was always compensating for the direction and velocity of the wind to keep the airplane turning around that exact point on the ground. It was fun! Jim kept up this little dance until he had completed four 360-degree turns.

Then he flew to the Northwest Airport and did three touch-and-gos. He then reminded himself it was time to take her back home. He had work to do. For one whole hour, he had not thought of the foundry or the lawsuit. Lining up on final for runway 17, the flight path took the airplane over a small hill just north of Millport Airport. On the hill stood a few acres of trees not large enough to be called a forest, so people in Texas just refer to a few acres of trees as the woods. At this point in the landing sequence, Jim was totally concentrating on his airspeed, altitude, and lineup with the runway. You could have a bull elephant standing at the edge of those trees and no pilot would ever see it.

It had been a perfect flight. The weather was absolutely perfect. Jim was in his element; the airplane had performed perfectly. Jim had done all of the maneuvers well. Jim reminded himself that he really enjoyed flying on days like these (he always liked flying), but it was days like these when he loved flying.

Jim had the airplane at the exact right airspeed, his descent rate was right on the numbers, and he was lined up with the centerline. He never saw a man step out of the trees, and in slow motion, the person in the trees, lifted a long, shiny object and pointed it toward the Cherokee.

All at once, the windshield shattered. The noise was deafening, and the windblast was blinding. It was the longest thirty seconds in history before the plane flew over the large numbers at the end of the runway and touched down. The touchdown was rather abrupt, but who could blame him?

When he had slowed the Cherokee enough to turn off runway on to the taxi way the wind noise level had reduced enough for him to hear the engine. What a relief that was, but when he advanced the throttle to taxi forward, the blast from the prop almost ripped his headset off and almost took his head off with it.

When he slowly taxied to the hangar, he went right up to the open door into the shop.

Ralph came out when he shut down. All he could say was, "I have never seen a windshield blow out like that. What did you hit a large bird?"

"I don't know. I was on short final and concentrating on maintaining airspeed and altitude when all at once the windshield exploded. Then I was really concentrating on getting on the runway."

Ralph was looking at the airplane when all at once he said, "Jim, look at this. Someone shot out your windshield."

Jim was startled. "What do you mean?"

"There is a large-caliber bullet lodged in the back wall of the airplane."

By then, several instructors and customers were gathered around. John pulled out his cell phone and dialed 911.

"Why do you think someone would shoot out the windshield on a little Piper Cherokee?"

Fifteen minutes later, a sheriff's deputy arrived. He took down all of the information and then called for detectives. While they were waiting for the detectives, Jim called the FAA, who immediately called the FBI. Soon they had police officers all over the hillside scouring the ground.

Then they looked up, and a news helicopter was overhead.

Jim said, "Oh boy, they are listening to the police radio and know something is going down."

A dark green Dodge Sedan with government license plates pulled into the parking area, and two men in business suits came into the lobby. Twenty people were all trying to see what was happening on the hill just north of the airport when the two men walked in.

One of the instructors asked if he could help them.

The first man in asked if the owner was in. Several people pointed at Jim, who then turned around and said, "I am the owner."

The two men produced ID cards identifying themselves as FBI agents.

Jim invited them into the conference room. The agents started asking questions as to what had happened and what he had observed. Then the agents said, "We would like to see the airplane."

The agents wanted to know. "Has anybody been in the plane since they parked it here?"

"No, the sheriff's deputies specifically instructed us to keep everybody out of the plane until investigators were through with it. In fact the sheriff's deputies wrapped crime scene tape around the airplane and told us to make sure nobody opened one of the doors and broke that tape."

The senior sheriff's deputy walked back into the hangar. The two FBI agents introduced themselves and then asked, "What have your men found on the hillside?" A lengthy conversation was all cop talk, so those listening in understood only half of it.

Jim understood that the detectives from the sheriff's department had found some footprints and were making a cast of the footprint. They had found where a car had been parked off the road on the other side of the trees and were making cast of the tire tracks. All of this would be turned over to the FBI if they were going to take over the investigation.

The FBI people said, "Since this involves shooting at an airplane in flight, it was definitely going to be ratcheted up to a Homeland Security case. In fact, FBI lab technicians are on the way. We would appreciate any assistance the local cops could give us."

The agents then asked, "Can the deputies canvas the airport and see if anyone on the ground saw the shooter or anything unusual happening at the time the airplane was struck by the bullet?"

Once they knew the airplane was secure and not being tampered with, they asked, "Mr. Colburn, can you come back in the office and make a formal statement?"

"Sure." He answered all of their questions, but he knew very little. He said, "All I know is the windshield blew out and I had my hands full trying to land the airplane." As they talked, Jim kept thinking these people are good at what they do.

The two agents, with the help of Ralph's crew, pushed the airplane back to the back corner of the hangar and asked Ralph to close the door. The door had no more than closed when a news reporter and cameraman arrived, but they were not allowed into the hangar and could not photograph the plane.

Of course, the entire café crowd was out front on the ramp primed and ready to deliver all kinds of gossip about the terrorist who had invaded Tildell County and were shooting down every plane that flew, and this was just target practice before they started shooting down the airliners at DFW.

While all this was going on, several more of the dark green Sedans had arrived and a lot more men in suits were fanning out and talking with everybody; starting with the deputies, they did appreciate all of the assistance the local cops could give them.

One of the deputies said, "I talked to a rancher over on the county road beyond the hill, and he reported seeing a medium-size white man dressed in light-colored pants and a white shirt carrying a deer rifle get into a dark-colored foreign car like a Honda or something. The reason he noticed was he thought with all that white on, that hunter wouldn't get within a half mile of a deer. No, he didn't bother getting the license plate number. He just thought it was some dumb hunter trying to poach one out of season."

The FBI agent asked Jim, "Has anything unusual happened out here within the past year? Have you fired an employee?"

At first Jim said, "No." Then he thought of Timothy and told them about the crash.

The agent wanted all of the details, especially when he learned that the lawsuit had been dismissed.

They then asked, "Do you know who would try to kill you?"

Up until that moment, Jim had not thought about that. He had only been thinking about the damage to the airplane. Jim said, "I am involved in an investigation into corruption out at the ACE Foundry, but it probably has nothing to do with this."

The FBI agents want to know everything about that. They took copious notes as Jim started with his crash and worked his way forward until the court hearing this morning.

There was some discussion as to whether or not it was safe to fly anymore today. After a few moments, they all agreed that the shooter was seen leaving the area, so why not?

The question everyone kept asking was why that airplane? Why now? If it was terrorist, why shoot at a Cherokee with only one person on board. When the technical people finished with the airplane, they removed a thirty-caliber bullet embedded in the back of the cabin. The forensic people determined that the bullet missed the pilot by less than an inch. The next day, the cafe crowd was going nuts—there were terrorists. Bull Tucker came up to the café on his John Deere tractor, and he had a double-barreled twelve-gauge shotgun strapped on the back of the seat. He only had bird shot in it, but he was armed and ready if the terrorist should attack while he was drinking his coffee.

Of course, the entire café crowd was out front on the ramp primed and ready to deliver all kinds of gossip about the terrorist who had invaded Tildale County.

Rumors were flying with no rhyme or reason about them. Someone told about someone else seeing three Middle Eastern men trying to sneak into Northwest Airport, and that was just twelve miles away. Jim pointed out that whoever shot his plane was seen, and he was a white man. Nobody listened to him. It was a bunch of Middle Eastern terrorists, and that was that.

For the rest of the weekend, every pilot looked hard at those trees when they took off or landed over them. No one was seen on the hill or around the trees, so people started to relax.

53

JUDGE'S RULING

JR and his crew received the production logs at 4:00 p.m. Saturday. They immediately called Carrie in to verify that all of the logs were in fact there. Carrie took one look and said, "They are not all here."

JR was furious. He called Sara Delgado immediately and screamed into the phone, "You heard the judge say that you were supposed to deliver the production logs to me before Monday! Why are they not all here!"

Sara answered in the sweetest female voice, "Councilor, I don't know what you mean. I will have our people get on it first thing Monday and double-check."

"Delgado, you know good and well we have a hearing at ten Monday morning. I want those missing logs, and I want them now!"

"I don't think I can help you before the office opens Monday morning, but I will see what I can do and get back to you."

JR hung up and threw the phone as hard as he could into the back of the sofa in his office. He kept saying, "Of all the rotten low-down dirty tricks."

JR and his staff worked all day Sunday, but by Monday morning, they still didn't have anything new to present to the court. When he walked into the courtroom, it was all JR could do to keep from walking over and slapping that smug look off Horace's face.

When the hearing was called to order, the judge looked at JR and asked, "Do you have anything new to show the court?"

"Your honor, the court ordered the defendant to produce the production logs. We didn't receive anything until 4:00 p.m. Saturday. What we did get was incomplete."

"Your honor, we, in good faith, delivered to the plaintiff over seven hundred pages of logs. We regret that it took so long, but that was laborious task to find and copy over seven hundred pages of logs. Surely in that many pages the plaintiff has seen all he needs to present his case to the court."

The judge turned to JR. "Did you receive over seven hundred copies of log pages?"

"Yes. Your honor, we did, but we did not receive the pages we needed."

The judge looked at JR and said, "Mr. Colburn, you were told that this court was not going to allow you to go on a witch hunt. Surely, if there was any evidence to support your claim, you would have found such evidence in seven hundred pages of documents. The court was lenient with you by allowing you an extension last Friday. Since you are here in my court with no new evidence to support your claim, I will find in the favor of the defendant and grant a summary judgment that not sufficient evidence exists to allow this case to proceed to trial. This hearing is adjourned."

JR felt lower than he had felt since the crash. Now he had the unpleasant task of telling his father and all of the other victims' families that he had signed up to represent.

When he told his dad about the judge's ruling, he was surprised at the lack of reaction from his dad. JR said, "Dad, do you understand that the case has been thrown out of court. We can't appeal or anything. The lawsuit is over?"

"I have been expecting it. You did your best son. That is all a man can do. By the way, I am going to be out of town for a couple of days."

JR was surprised, "Where are you going?"

"Oh, I have some friends I want to go see. I'll be back Thursday. I want to attend that stockholders' meeting Friday, and I want you to go with me. Can you do that?"

"Sure, Dad, I can go."

54

THE MEETING

The foundry had called a stockholders' meeting for Friday at 10:00 a.m. at the Desert Room at the Hilton. When Jim and JR arrived, the room was filled. Everybody was all a buzz about the lawsuit being dropped and wondering what the stock market was going to do now that the suit was over.

Horace stepped up to the mic at exactly ten and said, "Ladies and gentlemen, we the management here at ACE Foundry are proud to report that we have won the frivolous lawsuit filed against your company." The room broke out in applause.

He droned on about how the profits were up and the fact that he was working with the senator for this district to get legislation passed that would curtail the filing of frivolous lawsuits in the future.

Finally, it was announced the floor was open for any new business. Jim stood up and said, "I am Jim Colburn and a stockholder, and I make a motion that all of the people currently on the board be replaced with the list of people whose names are on this piece of paper. He walked over and handed a typed piece of paper to the secretary."

Horace was stunned. "You can't do that."

Sara Delgado said, "Any stockholder can make a motion, but it takes a majority vote of the outstanding shareholders to replace a board member. There is not a majority of the shareholders present. It takes a majority of all outstanding shares."

JR stood up and said, "I am JR Colburn, and I am a stockholder, and I second the motion and call for a vote."

After a few minutes of hurried consultation at the head of the room, the secretary stated, "We have a motion on the floor that all members of the present board be replaced by the following persons." Then she read off the names on the paper Jim had submitted.

You could see Horace's cocky attitude from the back of the room as one by one the votes were cast against Jim's motion. When it came JR's time to vote, he said, "I vote one hundred thousand shares for the proposal." You could see heads turn when he said, "one hundred thousand shares."

Jim stood and said, "I vote one million six hundred thousand shares for the proposal, and, ladies and gentlemen, that represents fifty-one percent of the outstanding shares."

There was total confusion until Sara Delgado said, "Madam Secretary, how many outstanding shares of stock do we have issued?"

"Six hundred thousand shares of preferred nonvoting stock. Three million three hundred and fifty thousand shares of voting stock."

Sara Delgado said, "Gentlemen, may I see your papers to prove ownership of the stock you claim to be voting."

JR walked up to the dais and handed her a stock certificate for one hundred thousand shares.

She examined them closely and compared it to the official stock records. Then she said, "These are in order."

Jim handed her his stock certificate for seven hundred thousand shares and proxy votes for nine hundred thousand more shares held in the name of the family members of the original founders. All signed before a notary.

Jim walked up to the mic. "Ladies and gentlemen, let me introduce you to the new board." He read off six names, and six men stood up. Then he turned to the six men sitting up on the dais. "If you, gentlemen, will step down, and if you, gentlemen, will please take your seats."

At that moment, six armed deputy sheriff's officers stepped into the room.

Jim said, "I have one more motion, Madam Secretary, I make a motion that this meeting be adjourned and a new meeting date shall be set for one month from today after the new directors have formulated a business plan."

JR said, "I second the motion."

Someone yelled, "There ain't no use in votin'. They got all the votes."

Horace left the Hilton and hurried back to his office. Five minutes later, Jim accompanied by two deputy sheriff's officers walked in to the building and walked straight past Horace's secretary.

When Jim stepped into the office, he said, "Horace Thorn, you have five minutes to clear out your personal belongings and get out of this building. If you are not gone in five minutes, you will be arrested for trespassing. Do you understand what I just said? You will leave your keys and company pass card on the desk when you leave. The security people are being notified right now that you will no longer be allowed on the premises."

Horace stared at Jim with a look that was between that of a frightened rabbit cornered by a lion and a look of pure hatred. Jim went on to say, "Furthermore, Horace, I am going to devote my time to finding proof that you were responsible for killing my wife and all of those other people, and when I find it, and I will find it, these gentlemen"—he pointed to the police officers—"will be back to find you."

55

HAROLD GETS A NEW JOB

Harold was sitting at home filling out online applications when the phone rang. A voice on the phone said, "Mr. Johnson, this is Hazelwood from the HR department at ACE Foundry. You are requested to come to the executive office immediately to meet with the new CEO."

"Do we have a new CEO?"

Ms. Hazelwood said, "Yes, and the new CEO wants to talk with you about reinstating you."

When Harold hung up, he turned around in his swivel chair and looked at Juanita and said, "That was Ms. Hazelwood from the HR department at the foundry. Horace is gone, and the new CEO wants me to come immediately to see him."

"Oh, sweetie, I have been praying so hard maybe God has answered my prayers. What are you waiting for? Go."

Forty-five minutes later, Harold walked into the offices at ACE and was sent directly to the top floor. When he walked into the chief executive's office, Mary Ann said, "Go right on in. The new boss is expecting you."

Harold walked toward the polished oak door. He stopped and thought, *I didn't ask who the new boss is. Is it someone I know?* When he opened the door, Harold stopped and stared. Blinking, he thought his mind was playing tricks on him—the guy behind the massive mahogany desk looked just like Jim Colburn; then he noticed two other people in the room, JR and Greg.

Jim said, "Come on in, Harold. I wish I had a camera to record the look on your face when that door opened."

Jim stood up and walked around the desk. Holding out his hand for Harold to shake his hand, he said, "Welcome home, Mr. President."

"Excuse me, I am totally confused. What is going on?"

"It is real simple. Jim bought controlling interest in the company and fired Horace. I am here to write a story about the new president, and that is you."

"Sit down in your new chair, Mr. President," JR said. "I have an employment contract for you to sign. Your starting salary I think you will find adequate, and the first order of business is you will receive a twenty-thousand-dollar signing bonus. That equals the loan you received from the bank."

The FBI lab called the agent in charge of the shooting of the airplane at Millport. "I have the DNA off the cigarette butt found on the hill north of the Millport airport."

"Okay, what have you got?"

"The DNA matches one Rufus Arnold. A white male, aged forty-seven, whose address is listed as forty-three seventeen Pond Road in Millport."

Late Friday afternoon, two dark green Sedans with government license plates pulled to the curb in front of 4317 Pond Road in Millport. When Doris opened the door, four men dressed in black suits stood on the porch.

"Yes, can I help you?"

One of the men in the suits said, "Ma'am, we are federal agents." He produced a shiny silver badge in a dark brown leather holder. Each of the other three produced a similar badge. "We have a search warrant for the residence. Is Rufus Arnold home?"

"No, he hasn't come home yet from work."

"If you will please step aside, we have some specific things we are looking for. Does your husband own a hunting rifle?"

"Yes."

"If you will show it to me, it will be easier than if we have to go through house looking of it."

Doris nodded and pointed to one of the bedrooms.

"Do you have a key to the gun case?"

"There is a key on top."

The agent took Luther's deer rifle out of the case and filled out a receipt for it.

"What has he done?"

"We have reason to suspect that this rifle was used in a crime. It will be tested, and if it doesn't match the bullet we have, it will be returned."

Doris stood watching the four agents walking back to their cars. She reached over and picked up Timothy's picture and said, "Son, we got him. I know that rifle will match. Because that is the one I used. I'm just glad my aim was good and nobody else got hurt."

Saturday morning, Jim ran twelve miles and told Allie all of the things that had transpired. He felt her telling him she knew he still loved her, but it was time for him to move on. After the run, he showered and dressed for work, then rode his Harley to the airport. As he pulled onto the ramp, he had to wait for a new Diamond DA50 airplane piloted by a very attractive lady pilot from California to shut down her engine before he could park the Harley. Jim looked to the west and saw a beautiful rainbow that reached from horizon to horizon. He felt like Allie smiling down on him.